JANTZI'S

JOKERS

The Sabblonti Series

Jantzi's Jokers

A Stormy Year

Love, the Tie that Binds

BOOKS BY SHEILA EISMANN

A STORMY YEAR

A WOMAN OF SUBSTANCE

HEART TO HEART FROM GOD'S WORD

LOVE, THE TIE THAT BINDS

JANTZI'S JOKERS

POETRY TIME – VOLUME ONE

RECOGNIZE YOUR CIRCLES

STIRRINGS OF THE SPIRIT

STRAIGHT FROM THE HORSE'S TROUGH

THE CHRISTMAS TIN

JANTZI'S

JOKERS

Book One of The Sabblonti Series

S

Sheila Eismann

Desert Sage Press

WWW.DESERTSAGEPRESS.COM
WWW.SHEILAEISMANN.COM

This book is a work of fiction. Names, characters, places, cattle ranches or brands, and incidents are the product of the author's imagination or are used fictitiously. Any resemblance to actual events, locales, persons, living or dead, is coincidental.

Published by Desert Sage Press
www.desertsagepress.com

Printed and bound in the United States of America.

Cover: Sharon Breshears Photography. All rights reserved.

Illustrated by Cathie Richardson. All rights reserved.
www.meadowblooms.com

ISBN: 978-0-9897133-4-4
Library of Congress Control Number: 2015912548

DEDICATION

This book is dedicated posthumously to my parents, Fred and Rita. During their sixty-eight years of marriage, they endured major setbacks and experienced many victories as well. After more than three decades of farming, they "retired" and spent two decades trapping in two adjoining states to protect cattle and sheep on high desert ranches.

INTRODUCTION

As the author of this three-book series, I would like to extend a hearty welcome to you as you enter into a fictional world of a high desert mountain region comprised of six counties in the northwest.

The majority of the cattle ranches were homesteaded in the 1800's after the land was cleared of sagebrush and rocks. Some of the meadows containing native grasses have been in place since then, but new pastures and feeding areas were seeded in the decades after the turn of the century.

The cattle were driven into the high country during the summer months and brought back down to the lower elevations late in the fall. The ranchers sometimes sold and shipped cows to other parts of the country. Breeding bulls were a crucial aspect to the ongoing development of herds. There were bull pastures on some of the ranches. Beavers built their dams on the streams that flowed through these pastures which created ponds.

Bobcats, cougars, coyotes, and wolves were always lurking in the high country seeking to devour the cattle, horses, and cow dogs. There's an emergence of wolves in Book Three, *Love the Tie that Binds*.

More than ample snowfall in the mountains most years kept the rivers, streams and reservoirs full. Prior to the homesteaders arriving, there was a flood one spring which changed the course of the river as it cascaded down the mountain sides. When all this water came rushing down, it brought trees, brush, and debris with it. This made a new channel in the river in the northeastern portion of Chrebine County which flowed into the lower, southeastern part of

Shadow Butte County.

With water being so vital, there's been only one major dispute in this regard when one of the characters forged a land deed to pirate the coveted Alder Creek and reservoir which is owned by the Merrill Ranch. This matter finally gets rectified in Book Three, *Love, the Tie that Binds*.

The Sabblonti Cattle Ranch is by far the largest spread. *Jantzi's Jokers*, Book One of the series, includes the details of the passing of the second generation of the family, Ace Sabblonti, and his wife, Jantzi Belle Siddonz Sabblonti. Pursuant to the specifications contained in Jantzi Belle's will, Stormy Castins, the oldest daughter, inherits everything. Sarita Sabblonti, her younger sister, is cut out of the will.

As the reader will discover in the second book titled *A Stormy Year,* it doesn't take long before Stormy lets the vast domain fall into shambles. As anyone in real life can attest, there's a drastic difference in working for an honest living versus inheriting a large fortune. She's created to be an enigmatic character. If you can figure her out, you'd be well on your way to becoming a psychologist or psychiatrist.

Just in case you might think that a somewhat sparsely populated region is void of any mystery, drama, intrigue or excitement, read on! The census of an area has no bearing upon whether or not there are characters who stay on the straight and narrow path or those who traverse the wide, dangerous, swaths of land. Mirroring real life, there are triumphs and tragedies along with victories and defeats.

Before starting to read this book, I would encourage you to take a few minutes to familiarize yourself with the family tree, map, and legend in the front of the book. Also, there's a cast of characters in the back.

After penning this first book, *Jantzi's Jokers,* I received emails, telephone calls, and written letters with reader's sentiments. They had definite opinions as to whether or not one character should marry another one; who should be punished for his or her actions; who they trusted and did not; and what made them happy or sad. I commented to someone, "Oh my goodness, some readers think these are real people!"

Obviously, none of the characters mentioned on any of the pages are real. Perhaps there are those with whom you can identify or relate.

Thanks for reading, and enjoy!

§ *Siddonz* &

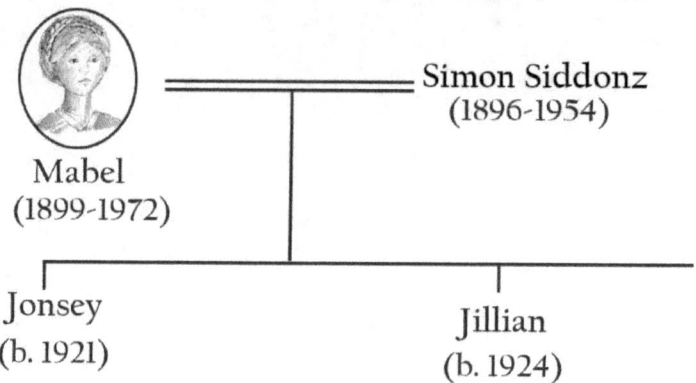

Mabel
(1899-1972)

Simon Siddonz
(1896-1954)

Jonsey
(b. 1921)

Jillian
(b. 1924)

Sabblonti Family Trees

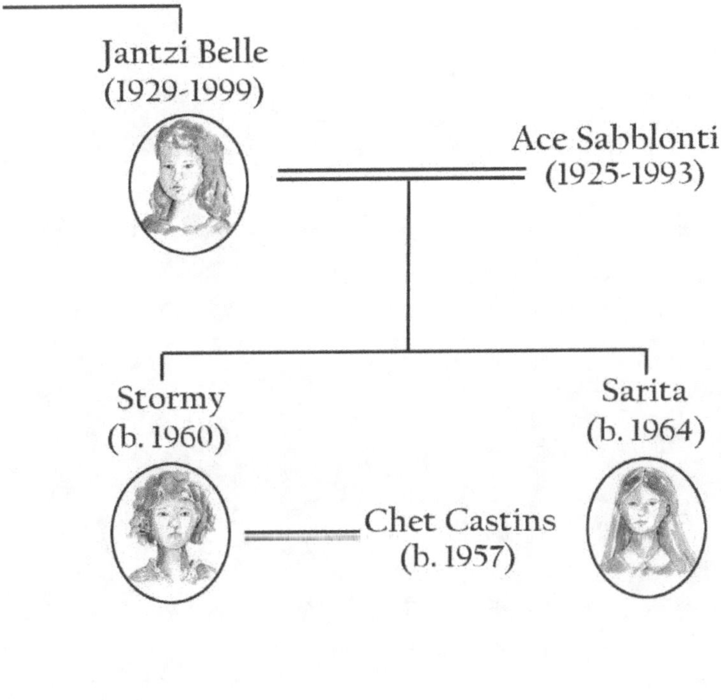

Legend

	Ace Sabblonti Ranch
	Nelson Merrill Ranch
	Tom Toppens Ranch
	Rees Broomfield Ranch
	Wilbur Drebner Ranch
	Main Highway
	Ranch Road
	Meadows/Pastures
	Creek/River
	Reservoir

County	* County Seat
Blunte County	Blademere
Chrebine County	Limnosa
Clarey County	Horsewood
Ignee County	Cinder Valley
Shadow Butte County	Ridgemonte
Tranquility Falls County	Fantone

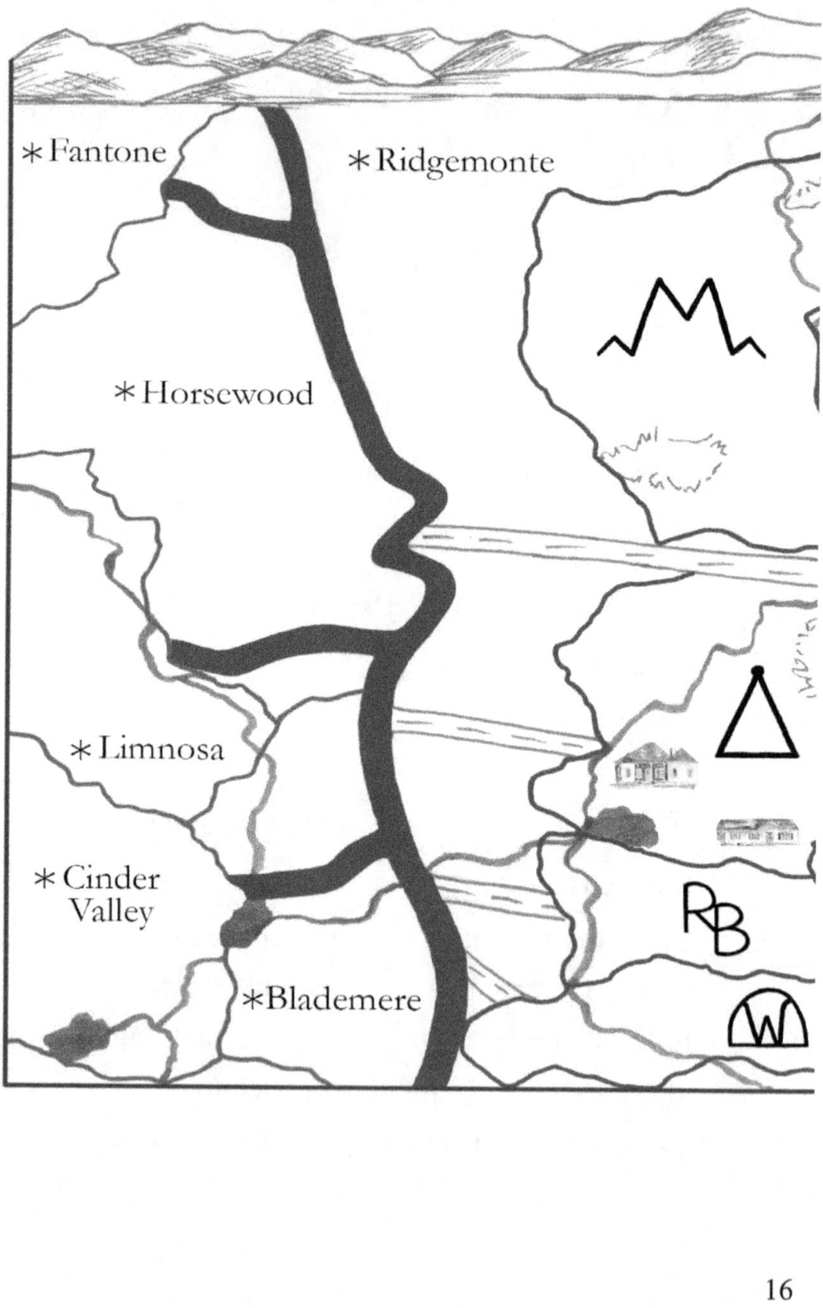
*Fantone
*Ridgemonte
*Horsewood
*Limnosa
*Cinder Valley
*Blademere
RB
W

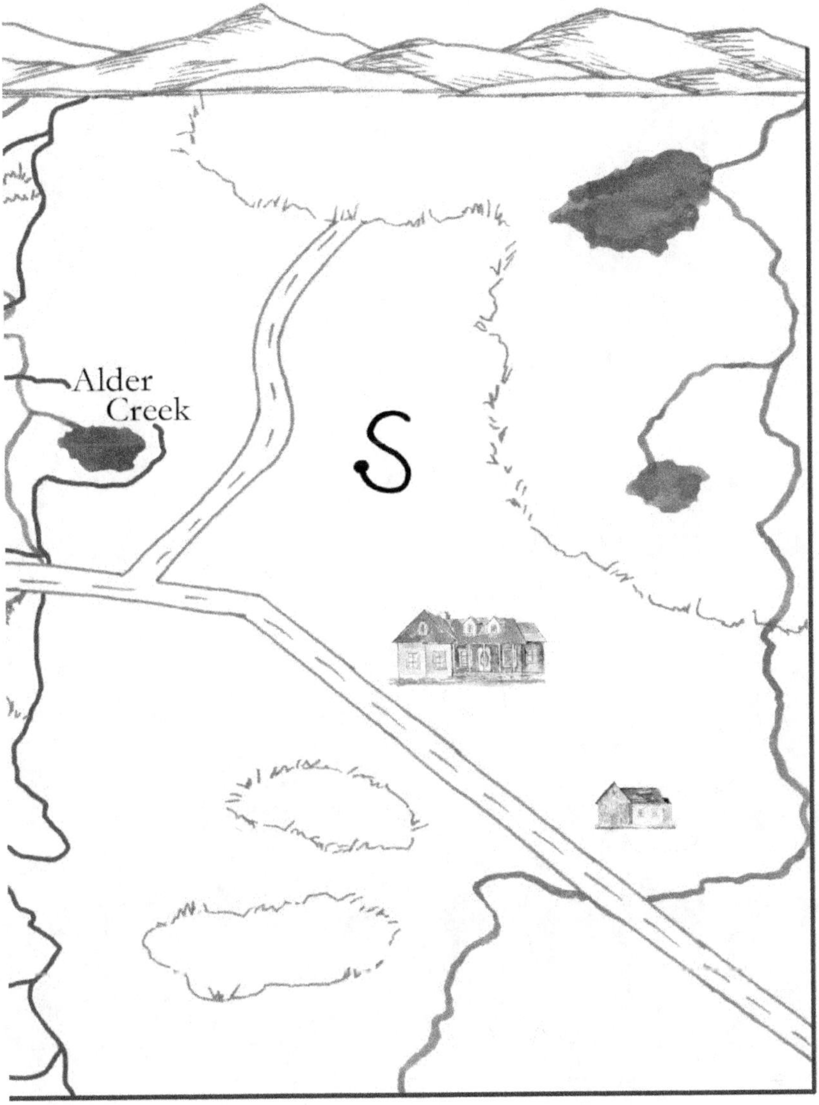
Alder
Creek
S

Merrill Ranch Cattle Brand

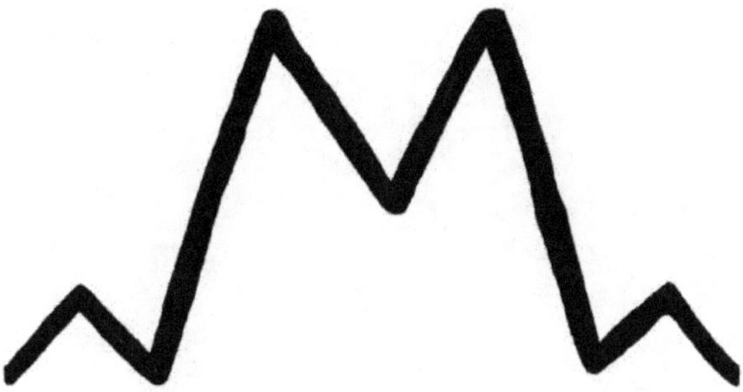

Sabblonti Ranch Cattle Brand

Siddonz Ranch Cattle Brand

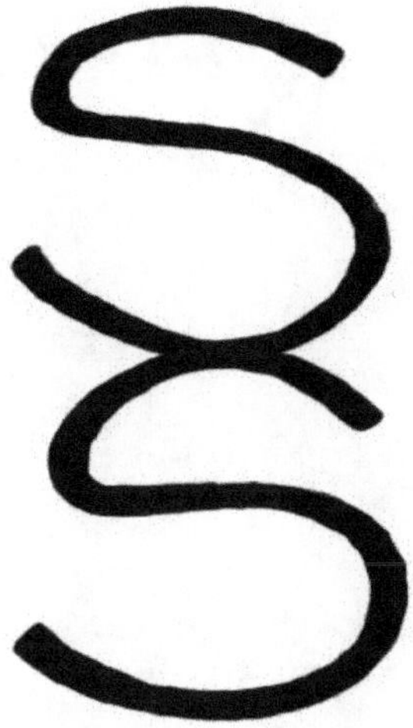

Toppens Ranch Cattle Brand

CHAPTER ONE

Widowhood was wearing Jantzi's last nerve quite thin when she turned in for the evening. Her dearly departed husband, Ace, never did cotton to satin sheets so now that he was gone, she had adorned her sleigh bed with bright purple ones in a feeble attempt to try to convince herself that she was forever royalty. Just because she was not crowned queen of the Shadow Butte Stampede did not mean she was not the best horsewoman in the entire region. The Rodeo Board Chairman's daughter prevailed in everything except the barrel racing event, but never mind all that nonsense from all those years ago.

Laney Burnett may have worn the crown for that one short season, but the last time Jantzi Belle surveyed her vast domain, Laney was still working at the local beauty shop dubbed *The Roll Up & Dye.* As far as she was concerned it was sort of a play on words, "Laney could just roll up and die." And rest assured, Jantzi drove to the hair dresser in the next town to have her long locks colored jet black. No way was she going to empty her pocketbook to give Laney one thin dime for her monthly dye job.

Diamonds were not dripping from Laney's pudgy fingers, and she had not gotten her teeth straightened either. Jantzi had always had a penchant for people's dentition. It was the first thing she noticed about anyone. When Jantzi admired herself in the multitude of mirrors hanging throughout her palatial abode, it was as if her overly large teeth consumed half of her face. The larger the teeth, the easier to devour something or someone. Surely it's all relative since beauty lies in the eye of the beholder.

Having worked from the crack of dawn until 11:00 o'clock each night for three straight weeks, Jantzi reasoned that she would treat herself and not set the alarm on this particular Friday evening. She spread the new western wear catalog across her bed, and memorized a portion of the merchandise as she sipped her peppermint tea.

A spattering of late fall evenings seemed warmer this year. Jantzi had not yet consulted the *Farmer's Almanac* to see what the projected winter weather was supposed to be. If the warming trend continued, surely all of the cattle and horses would be happy about that. Gathering up her empty tea cup and catalog, Jantzi placed them on the mahogany hexagonal nightstand. Walking toward the wall to close the bedroom window, she took one last look outside. Since her early childhood days, she had never liked the dark of the moon. Too bad the earth was not designed so that every night was a full moon. Turning off the oil lamp, she crawled into bed and fell into a deep sleep.

The spirit entered the old ranch house without opening a door or window, and ascended silently up the thirty steep stairs into Jantzi's bedroom. It stopped four feet from the side of her bed and drew in a deep breath. Exhaling with all its might, the spirit blew across Jantzi's face which sent her long black locks flying.

Jantzi awakened suddenly and saw the sixty-eight inch tall piñata standing a few feet from her bed. Her mind reeled as she clutched her satin sheets with both hands and looked into the eyes of dancing fires. As the piñata turned around to leave the room, it let out the eeriest laugh imaginable straight from the bowels of hell. Even though it never spoke, Jantzi seemingly knew the meaning of the spirit's visit. Her games were over and her days were numbered.

During their childhood years, Jantzi's daughters, Stormy and Sarita, had attended birthday parties for their friends featuring piñatas filled with candy. This piñata was nothing of the sort. As it stalked toward the bedroom door to depart, Jantzi took note of its colorful brown, red, and white stripes.

Why did this spirit appear in the form of a piñata with those specific colors in that striped pattern? Who sent that thing and how did it get inside the ranch house? Was it something from the Sabblonti ancestry lineage or perhaps the silent chapters tucked away in the branches of the Siddonz family trees? All of these questions and many more consumed Jantzi's mental and physical energy. She was totally out of sorts and could not concentrate or perform even the most basic of daily tasks.

Was Jantzi reading too much into the visit? Was her life coming to an end, and did she really need to get her household affairs in order? She was only seventy years old, her kingdom was just beginning to take shape, and there was so much more that she planned to do. Stormy had not yet given her any grandchildren as a result of three miscarriages, and it looked as if Sarita, unstable as the waters of the river, could never manage to make a prudent decision about anything. It had taken Jantzi thirty-five years of marriage and six years of widowhood just to get to this point. Surely it could not end this way!

Peace alluded Jantzi in every way, shape, and form. With only three weeks remaining until Christmas, nervous took on a whole new meaning.

For as long as she could remember, Jantzi had always been in control of her own life and made her own decisions. This was no time to change that paradigm. Her mother Mabel's sweet voice flitted through her mind, "Jantzi Belle, always error on the side of caution. You must not throw caution to the wind, not even once, daughter dear."

Caution and control. Maybe that combination had worked far better for Jantzi for decades than she had ever realized. It was probably time to add another "c" to the mix so it would now read, "calculation, caution, and control." Jantzi knew exactly what she must do. She would plan her work and work her plan. She could tell no one of the stranger than fiction very late Friday night visitor as she had been accused repeatedly of being mentally deranged.

CHAPTER TWO

Swiveling in her black leather office chair in front of her antique roll top desk, Jantzi stopped to stare at the handwriting on the yellowing paper. Where had the time gone? The last time she looked at this document was 1993, the year her husband had expired. Since he had never trusted lawyers, Ace wrote out his will by hand, which is what any seasoned cattle rancher did. Who needed to shell out any cold hard cash to those weasely attorneys anyway? Thankfully, the state laws still permitted a holographic will and considered it valid, whether or not witnessed, if the signature and the material provisions were in the handwriting of the person making the will. Truth be known, Jantzi had written out exactly how she wanted Ace's Last Will and Testament to read and instructed him to copy it verbatim in his own handwriting and sign it. Jantzi was appointed Ace's personal representative, and his entire estate was left to her. How handy.

Fearing the worst following the piñata incident, Jantzi determined it was now time to pen a holographic will of her own. It needn't be lengthy at all. There was no need to reinvent the ranch on this one. She could simply mirror the will she crafted for Ace all those decades ago. A lengthy list of various items of tangible personal property to be left to other people was unnecessary as Jantzi wasn't favorably disposed to sharing much of anything. Controlling and sharing did not seem to co-exist in her mind.

Dusting off the top sheet of college ruled paper stacked in the right-hand desk drawer, Jantzi laid it down in the center of her oak desk, dipped the writing nib of her Lapis Lazuli quill pen in the black ink well, and began writing. Ace would stand bolt upright in his grave if he knew she was using one of his Christmas gifts for such a time as this.

"Last Will and Testament
Of
Jantzi Belle Siddonz Sabblonti

. . ."

This all seemed so final and morbid. Perhaps Jantzi was just imagining things. After all, had she really seen that colorful piñata in her room or was it a figment of her imagination? She reasoned that fear would not be her initial reaction had she not really seen something. And those stripes! Jantzi knew her eyes were not playing tricks on her when she saw the brown, white, and red figure cut loose with that macabre cackle. The recent memory made her blood run cold as she continued to write.

"I, Jantzi Belle Siddonz Sabblonti, being of sound mind, do hereby make my last will and testament."

Surely here was another confirmation that she could not tell anyone else of the recent happenings at the ranch house.

If she did, others could opine that Jantzi was not of sound mind. Granted, she had been accused of being many things in her lifetime, but no one had better question her thinking or rationale.

Ginger tea steadied Jantzi's nerves and digestive system during trying times. This morning was no exception. Some brain food might help advance her mental gymnastics. Days like today were when Jantzi longed for a maid or housekeeper. But, then again, those types of women tended to be really snoopy and gossipers to boot. Keeping calculated moves close to the vest was always sage advice.

As she made her way down the stairs, Jantzi remembered that she had some leftover lentil and kale soup in her upright freezer on the porch. Setting a pan of water on her kitchen stove, she placed the bowl of frozen soup inside, and slowly let it warm to eating temperature. Cooking had always been such a pain in the clavicle anyway. As far back in her family lineage as she could remember, Jantzi could not recall even one female who liked to cook or who could boil water without burning it. In their minds, the only reason a kitchen existed was because it came with the house. The men folk could just eat in the barn along with the rest of the farm animals as far as these women were concerned.

During their marriage, Ace ate whatever Jantzi placed in front of him. She had trained him to not complain about one single thing, especially her cooking. At least, she reasoned, she had let him die a natural death and not helped him along such as Camdie, one of the local rancher's wives, had done when she ground up the fine pieces of glass and placed them inside her husband's hamburger before serving it to him. How Camdie ever cleared that one with the local coroner was beyond Jantzi, but, alas, she had far more important things to concentrate on now. Camdie never did tumble as to why Jantzi repeatedly declined her annual ranch barbeque invitations.

Ace's canine, Blue, barked his warning from the front yard. Jantzi wondered who could possibly be paying her a visit this early on a weekend morning so close to the holidays. Merna Toppens from the adjoining ranch down the road was working the horseshoe door knocker quite hard when Jantzi finally decided to venture from the kitchen to the stone entryway.

Removing her worry mask and donning her good neighbor one, Jantzi slowly opened the large wooden door, feigning a pleasant surprise.

"Why, Merna, what brings you to my front door this morning? I have not seen you in forever. I'm sure you are busy getting ready for Christmas and preparing all of the guest bedrooms for your visitors."

"Actually, Jantzi, we aren't having anyone visit this year. It's going to be a very quiet Christmas around our house. Since I have so much time on my hands, I thought I would pay you a long overdue visit on my way to town today. To tell you the absolute truth, I sensed a real urgency to stop by and check on you. I can't explain why I felt this way. It was the oddest thing."

"Uh, well, that's so neighborly of you, Merna, but, um, I am feeling a bit under the weather today and am not very talkative. It's nothing personal and thanks for understanding. Normally I would be in my denims and ropers by this time of the day, but that's why I am still wearing my housecoat. It's so frustrating as I am far too busy to be bothered with any ailments. Have a very Merry

Christmas and Happy New Year."

"I could lend you a helping hand if you need something," offered Merna as she inhaled the savory aroma of the lentil soup wafting through the doorway.

"I don't need a single solitary thing, Merna, but thank you anyway. Have a nice day in town."

As Merna got into her one-ton dually, short bed truck and turned around in the driveway, she pondered her verbal exchange with Jantzi. Driving down the lane toward the main road and passing under the large black metal ranch sign showcasing the Sabblonti family cattle brand, she had the distinct feeling all was not well in ranching land. But what did she know? Jantzi Belle ran her own spread on her own terms. Most people, men and women included, usually gave her a very broad berth. Merna knew all too well there were several shades of truth to all that mystique surrounding the life of Jantzi Belle Sabblonti.

Completing her lunch tray with soup, toast, dried apricots, and a second cup of tea, Jantzi made her way up the staircase once again to her office on the third floor of the house. Savoring each bite, she surveyed the recesses of her mind to determine if there were any stones left unturned or any issues yet to be resolved.

A manufactured peace settled over Jantzi as she finished authoring her will. After dating and signing it, she folded the paper as one would a business letter and placed it inside a number 10 white envelope. She made no reference on the outside of the envelope as to the contents therein and placed it inside the small metal box that contained her most important documents. Jantzi's instinct was to lock the box, but for some unknown reason, she decided to leave it unlocked and sitting in plain sight on the top of her desk.

CHAPTER THREE

Monday morning's fog rolled in like an unwelcome visitor. Having called at 9:00 on the nose, Jantzi's appointment with the bank manager was scheduled for one o'clock. It's a good thing she had made it later in the day since she would have to follow the fog lines along the main highway into Ridgemonte. Admittedly, there were a few days such as this one, where she would not mind if Ace was still around to help.

Preferring a man's world to a woman's any day of the week, Jantzi had no trouble speaking to, negotiating with, or gaining the upper hand with the men folk. She had determined that today would be no exception.

Parallel parking was not one of Jantzi's strengths so she opted to bring her extended-cab pickup truck to a complete stop in the back lot adjacent to Cattlemen's Central. Pulling down the visor on the driver's side and peering into the lighted mirror, she surmised another layer of bright red lipstick was in order. Ugh! Jantzi discovered she had left her new tube of lip color at home on her vanity. Oh, well, it's all vanity anyway, isn't it? She would just have to flash those big chompers of hers, and hope they would make up for the deficit in red.

Grasping the handle of her leather tooled briefcase and slinging her red holiday purse over her shoulder, Jantzi stepped from her vehicle onto the pavement. Her feet nearly flew out from under her as they failed to gain traction on the thin layer of ice deposited by the early morning fog. Steadying herself, Jantzi stepped gingerly across the parking lot toward the front door. Once inside, she was greeted with a warm welcome by Chara Tankton, the friendliest teller any bank would ever want to hire.

"Good Monday afternoon to you, Jantzi. Mr. Sanders is just winding down his telephone conference call and will be with you shortly. Would you like a cup of coffee while you wait or the county newspaper to catch up on all of the goings on?"

"No thanks. I had such a hair-raising drive into town on that curvy county highway that I think I will rest my nerves a bit."

Stewart Sanders emerged from his office, extending his right hand enthusiastically toward Jantzi.

"So nice to see you, Jantzi Belle! You don't mind if I call you by your full name, do you? My, you look absolutely marvelous this early afternoon. What brings you to my domain so close to the holidays? Normally you don't pay me a personal visit until closer to income tax day each spring. Rest assured, we always have enough capital on hand to take care of all your needs."

Jantzi tried to remain calm as she reminded herself that she had never really liked this bank manager. The one before Stewart had been far easier to look at, and it did not seem as though he was wound as tightly. Maybe Stewart's mother had aptly named him because he always seemed to be stewing about something. Ace was as laid back as a rug compared to this guy. Was it Jantzi's imagination or did Stewart's skin seem to crawl as he spoke? No time for comparisons now.

"Oh, I am just trying to do something extra special for my relatives for Christmas this year," Jantzi explained. "I got kind of a late start with my gift planning. There's no time to order monogrammed or leather tooled goods this late in the game so I plan to just gift some cash. I checked with my accountant, and he told me that I could give each one $10,000.00, which includes our extended family members, too. I feel like I am finally pulling out of the slump from when Ace passed away unexpectedly six years ago. It's like I have been in a cave since then. I plan on selling off some of our large herd next year and downsizing some. I will just have to wait and see how it all plays out."

Peering intently into Jantzi's pale blue eyes, Stewart pressed her for more specific details.

"Just exactly how much cash were you thinking of withdrawing today, Jantzi?"

Having done her manual calculations independently over the weekend, Jantzi explained, "I will need a quarter of a million in $100 bills, please."

"Oh, no problem, Jantzi, and that's probably a good way to gift wrap it for the holidays to dole it out just the way you want it. For a minute there, I thought you were going to break the bank today via your cash withdrawal. I know Sabblonti's holdings are worth far more than a quarter of a million dollars. Why, that's just a drop in the old milk bucket compared to what you are really worth! Excuse me for a few minutes, please, while I round up Chara to get the cash counted out and bagged up for you. Is there anything else I can help you with as long as you are in here today? I would be more than happy to do anything I can for you. I have a real heart for widows in our ranching community."

Jantzi wanted to say, but caught herself just in the nick of time, "I'll bet you do have a real heart for widows, and for their large bank accounts, too, Buster!" She did not dare express what she was really feeling at the moment. The sooner she could rid herself of this fish bait the better. After all, Jantzi had bigger fish to fry, even though fishing season did not technically open until next spring.

Chara gently knocked on Mr. Stewart's office door and waited patiently for him to answer.

"Please come in Chara, and thank you for getting Jantzi's Christmas cash counted out so quickly."

As Chara approached Jantzi sitting in one of Stewart's high-backed chairs reserved for high dollar customers, she continued to pour on the charm, "Jantzi, I counted these bills four times just to make sure that I had done it correctly. Since some of them are new bills, they have a real tendency to stick together so you will want to keep that in mind when you gift wrap them. How large is your briefcase as this stack measures almost a foot high? I could separate this large bundle of bills into smaller ones and secure it inside your leather briefcase if you like. Is there anything else that I can do for you while you are here this afternoon? You know our motto, 'Cattlemen's Cares the Most!'"

Jantzi was tempted to ask what kind of syrup Chara drank for lunch because no one in real life was that syrupy sweet, but she refrained from doing so. "Thank you, Chara, that would be most helpful, and I fully trust that you have counted the money accurately. With Christmas on the horizon, I will scarcely have time to make another trip to town."

Jantzi surveyed the long green bills inside her briefcase and zipped it securely shut. As she rose from her chair, she thanked Stewart profusely for his assistance and wished him a very happy holiday season. Chara's curtsy in her long denim skirt and blue cowboy boots was a bit dramatic prior to leaving the manager's office, but Cattlemen's stressed customer service above everything else. Exiting the bank building, Jantzi walked slowly to her vehicle. Footing was still quite marginal, and she certainly could not afford a slip and fall injury at this stage of her game.

Safely inside the cab of her pickup truck, Jantzi unzipped her purse, removed her Smith & Wesson Centennial 38 Special, and carefully set it on the front seat. She laid her black thermal outdoor gloves over the hand gun and turned the key in the ignition. Jantzi's prized son-in-law, Chet Castins, had programmed her pickup so that when the ignition was turned on all of the doors automatically locked from the inside.

A light glaze of frost had formed on the front windshield in just the short amount of time Jantzi had met with Stewart. Turning the defrost dial to *high* afforded her nervous system some much needed cooling down. Granted, she could get out and scrape the windshield, but that was man's work, and since there was no man around, his invention would just have to do the work for her.

Keeping a sharp eye on the road and any unwanted visitors en route home, Jantzi drove ten miles below the speed limit. Mondays were typically not very busy on the county road from Ridgemonte to the Sabblonti Ranch.

Arriving home without incident, Jantzi parked her pickup inside the horse barn. The less anyone knew of her comings and goings over the next few weeks the better.

CHAPTER FOUR

Ace had kept the 105-year-old barn in excellent shape, but it was already starting to go downhill quite fast. When he was alive, it seemed that on certain days you had to drive stakes to see if he was moving. There were some projects, like preservation of family holdings, which were right up his alley. Chet, on the other hand, wasn't remotely interested in maintenance of any sort, and Jantzi reasoned it was not a high priority item right now anyway.

It did seem much quieter in the barn since Snipper, Ace's grey gelding, had died along with him. What a freak day that had been! At least Chet was kind enough to prepare a special burial spot under the old juniper tree for Snipper. He even fashioned a head stone of sorts for him.

Securing the barn door with her double lock system, Jantzi walked to the mail box, tucked the mail inside her briefcase, and made her way into the house.

Lounging next to the fireplace, Blue was such great company on days like today. The best part about him was that he did not complain, question Jantzi's judgment, or talk back. She made a mental note to herself that next year she would have to round up some firewood that did not leave so much ash after it was burned. Cleaning out the fireplace and hauling the ashes outside might have kept her in decent physical shape, but those sorts of chores belonged to the hired help. The Queen of Diamonds needed to keep her gems polished for display, and did not have time to bother with such messy chores as disposing of ashes.

After laying her purse and briefcase on the entry table, Jantzi removed her fur lined jacket and hung it in the closet. Using the horseshoe-shaped boot jack, she removed her boots.

Looking around the lower level of the ranch house, Jantzi determined that she needed to have more curtains designed and hung for the windows. She would put that on her to-do list for right after the first of the year. The old ranch house was quite secluded in the large draw between the hillsides, and all the years that Jantzi and Ace had lived in the house, she had never really paid much attention to window coverings. Most of their company, very few and far between, visited during daytime hours while riding the ranges.

A fresh memory jolt from last Friday evening reinforced the idea of drapes, especially at night. Who and or what was lurking outside after dark at the onset of winter?

Collecting her briefcase along with her belongings, Jantzi headed up the stairs into her master bedroom. After changing from her business attire into lounge wear, she sauntered down the hall into her office where she opened the mail and sorted it into her various piles for answering correspondence, paying bills, and so forth.

Peering inside the small metal box containing her most valuable documents to take one last look at her newly penned will, Jantzi could have sworn that she placed that plain white envelope inside the box before she left the house to go see Mr. Sanders. As she searched frantically for it, the envelope was nowhere to be found! Now her mind was really playing tricks on her. First the spooky visitor, and now the missing envelope. It was as if it had grown wings and flown away. The next three hours were spent virtually turning every room on every level of the ranch house upside down looking for the will, but Jantzi came up empty handed. Maybe, just maybe, that colorful piñata had some other striped friends.

Slumping down in her office chair, Jantzi studied the wall calendar. Time was slipping through her fingers. She had a lot of ground to cover, and did not want to enlist any help from either one of her daughters. She only hoped that she had enough of everything she needed so that she would not have to make another trip into town. She could remember her mother saying, "Haste makes waste." Yes, it surely does!

Jantzi lamented the fact that she had not done more long-range thinking and planning so that she could have picked up any last-minute supplies in Ridgemonte allowing her to just hole up for the next few days. Well, she would just have to make do with what she had on hand. Keeping her freezers on the porch well stocked was never a chore since Sabblonti Ranches raised prime cattle.

Some of the neighboring ranching wives grew gardens and preserved lots of food for winter consumption, but Jantzi had never taken the time to learn to do those sorts of things. Only women with a poverty mindset would waste their valuable days and resources with those types of chores. Any activity that stole time and energy from Jantzi's command control center was not even entertained. In her mind, that's why they designed grocery stores, cupboards, pantries, freezers, and basements. And making anything from scratch was to be scratched from her list. All a woman needed was a crock pot, cast iron skillet, and a saucepan. Those three pieces of cookware could handle most anything that she ever served Ace or anyone else. For their entire childhoods, Jantzi had drilled it into her daughters' heads to eat like a bird so they could stay razor thin.

As her day wound down, Jantzi reminded herself, "Early to bed, early to rise, makes one healthy, wealthy, and wise." Considering herself plenty healthy and wealthy, she reasoned she could use a bit more wisdom right about now.

CHAPTER FIVE

Never keen on raising chickens, Jantzi grew to rely upon the calling of coyotes for her alarm clock. This morning was no exception. Breaking her usual morning routine and drawing on her deep reservoir of carefully catalogued schemes, Jantzi stiffened her back, and sat up straight in her office chair. Opening the right-hand drawer of her antique solid oak roll top desk, she plucked a fresh sheet of plain paper from its stack. She was not in the mood for lined paper, and by using something more spacious, perhaps it would expand her creativity when she needed it the most.

Elegant dinners did require some advance planning, and this one must be no exception. In fact, it must be her best effort in all her born days. Okay, first of all, a short guest list must be prepared. Her two older sisters, Jonsey and Jillian, flitted through her head. Should she invite them? No, too much trouble right now. There was no need to concern herself with those lashups. Oh my, Jantzi remembered that she had better get their Christmas cards addressed and in the mail! Pulling out one of the little drawers in her desk, she let out a sigh of relief when she saw that a book of first-class postage stamps was nestled in the bottom.

Jantzi attempted to write a few lines inside the holiday cards to her sisters, but was unable to concentrate. Her normal meticulous penmanship was barely legible, and closely resembled advanced hieroglyphics. She definitely did not want Jonsey or Jillian to view her handwriting as anything less than perfect. Pausing her Christmas card ritual for the moment, she resumed her search for her will throughout every room of the main ranch house. Where, oh where, was her written will?

∞∞∞∞∞∞∞∞∞∞∞∞∞∞

Mabel would be honored to know that her youngest daughter's dining room table would be graced with the family's heirloom dishes, especially the large shallow soup bowls, for Jantzi's annual Christmas Eve dinner.

Actually, Jantzi reasoned, she should not put the wagon before the horse, so she hoped Stormy would be available to talk on the phone for a few minutes on a mid-Tuesday afternoon. She glanced down at her right index finger as she dialed the numbers on her antique phone sitting atop her desk. Sure, she could have purchased a more modern one, but it made her feel large and in charge when she could watch herself go through the dialing motions. My, how thin her skin had become on her hands. Was this the first time she had paid any attention to this? Perhaps one of her Christmas gifts from her darlings could be a tube of that fancy emollient tea tree oil stuff made with mint. Then again, maybe The Shadowy Merc did not even carry such items. It had been quite a while since she had stopped in or even walked past their window displays. Some years it seemed as though it needed to start preparing for the next century, and get with the program with respect to the merchandise it sold.

Stormy answered on the third ring with a groggy, "Hello."

"Is that you Stormy?"

"Mother, you never call me this time of day! Is everything all right?"

Not wanting to upset her most beloved possession, Jantzi purred, "Oh, sure, darling, everything is just ranches and rosebuds. I thought I better take a break from my usual rambunctious ranching routine and give you a call since Christmas is nearly upon us. The time has really crept up on me this year. Most years, I am way ahead of the game. I am sure you can relate."

"Yes, mother dear, it does seem like this year has been another whirlwind. Not to mention that with suffering the loss of another baby, I am not my normal self quite yet. Chet has been such a love through it all, and I don't know how I would manage if he was unkind and did not jump each time I called his name."

"Stormy, I am so sorry you have had to endure yet another loss. It saddens my heart as well because I desire grandchildren more than anything to carry on my legacy and carry out my plans."

"Oh, Mother, let's move to another subject, shall we? I am finding that if I don't dwell on loss, I can get through my days far better. What did you have in mind when you called? Oh, just a minute, I think I will get my lap quilt and sit in the recliner while we visit. Okay, all settled now, so go ahead."

Jantzi exhaled slowly, "I thought that since you and

Chet had been so sad the past couple of months, I would plan something stupendous for our Christmas Eve gathering. And I know how much you love the smell of juniper, so I was contemplating using that as my overall theme this year. How does that sound?"

"Fabulous, just super duper, and yes, juniper would give me a real lift. Do your trees have lots of berries this year? Maybe I should let you in on a little secret that Chet and I have held close to our hearts for years now. We have planned to name our first child *Juniper*! And never mind if we have a boy or a girl, that's still our number one choice. Oh, silly me, I don't know what ever prompted me to tell you that."

Jantzi refrained from giving her number one daughter a tongue lashing when she heard the name they had selected for her grandchild. No one in her right mind named her offspring after a tree, river, mountain or some such. Juniper Castins sounded like something that would grow in the mountains. Well, come to think of it, Juniper would sort of grow up in the mountains providing Chet and Stormy never relocated. Jantzi was sure that Chet had dreamed up that name. Then again, she could not really criticize her daughter in this regard. Jantzi had determined her oldest daughter would be named 'Stormy.' She had wanted to name her second daughter 'Sable.' Ace pitched a fit because he thought it sounded too much like *stable,* so Jantzi relented and allowed him to assign her the name, 'Sarita.'

"Oh, that reminds me," continued Jantzi, "before we move on from the subject of trees, I thought that I would pass on putting up a Christmas tree this year. Chet has been so faithful to take care of that for me the last few years, but I think I will just forget about it for the time being. I don't think we really need a tree with all of that tinsel, horse bells, and falterah. Plus, that will save Chet a trip of driving up to the far end of the ranch, cutting down a fresh pine tree, hauling it, and getting it set up in my living room. You can tell him that's one of my early presents to him this year. I can only imagine how relieved he will be."

Stormy stayed in lockstep agreement with her mother, "What would we ever do if you were not continually twenty steps ahead of all of us? It's so comforting to know that you monitor every detail so the rest of us can just relax and go along for the ride. Every daughter should be as blessed as I am in having their mother take care of the heavy mental lifting for them. And, come to think of it, you won't even have to wrap that early gift for Chet! I am not really in the mood for a tree this year either. I think I will put up a few small decorations and call it good. Chet just scored the double win on that one."

Jantzi smiled from ear to ear as she listened to Stormy who was far more talkative than her mother thought she might be.

"Daughter dear, how does this menu sound for our gathering? Soup in Grammy Mabel's heirloom bowls, ready-to-bake bread with butter and chokecherry jam, condiments, and that chocolate cake made with tomato sauce that Chet likes so much. Can you think of anything to add?"

"Oh, do you mean that sort of upside down real moist cake that you bake in your cast iron skillet in the oven? Chet will be so thrilled that you are doing something special for him. Three losses in a row now have been quite hard for him to handle. Before the weather turned off much cooler, he would get on his horse and ride for hours at a time. I think he was just trying to make sense of it all."

"Well, bless his heart," mused Jantzi. "I had never given it much thought, but I guess passing time on horseback would be therapeutic. For some reason that I never did really comprehend, your father used to spend days in the saddle. Yes, the cake with tomato sauce is the one thing I seldom bake, and the real boon to it is that it does not require frosting. You just throw together a few ingredients, pour them into a greased skillet, and slap it in the oven. Sort of one of those fix it and forget it type of things. You know all too well how we women love cooking. When I hear of all of these ranch wives and their domestic endeavors, I want to scream!"

"The rest of the menu sounds fine as I have not really had much of an appetite lately anyway," lamented Stormy. "I would imagine that the temperature would be pretty cool on Christmas Eve, so hot soup would hit the spot. Who will be attending?"

"I am glad you asked. There will be you, Chet, of course, and then I will have to invite Sarita, too. I wish there was some way around having to include Wyn Moreland, the drifter that has Sarita bowled over. I had entertained the thought of asking the new vet in the area, Dr. Ben Shaw. While I certainly have disagreed with his methods of how to treat our cattle from time to time, I wondered if he might not be a good long-term match for Sarita. He does not seem to be nearly as strange as Wyn."

"What don't you like about Wyn? While he might not be my first choice or yours of a man to marry, we must let Sarita choose her own mate. After all, you and Daddy did not balk one bit when Chet came on the scene and we got married in our mountain meadow. Why, we even let you pick that Preacher Len guy to perform the ceremony. I guess there really is something to that saying, 'Love is blind.' It's as if I have worn a blindfold of sorts every day since then. It has been pure bliss except I still don't have a little bundle in my arms while rocking in my recliner." Secretly, Stormy was becoming more worried by the day as she had heard that if a woman did not have her first child by the time she was forty years old, there was a slim chance that she would be able to deliver one full term after that.

Jantzi stiffened when she realized that she had better rein this conversation in immediately. "Now Stormy dear, I did not mean to stir the waters during our pleasant time of conversing, and cause tears to tumble from your pretty face. Now, now, honey, just calm down. I can't bear to see you sad or hear you crying. Ever since you were born, I have tried to move heaven and earth to make you happy. That's still my grandiose plan."

"Please forgive me, Mother," whispered Stormy. Clearing her throat, she continued, "I don't want for there to be any strife between us, so I will listen as you continue to lay out your plans. Go ahead."

Relaxing somewhat, Jantzi jumped right back into her dialogue, "Okay, so there will be you, your beloved Chet, Sarita, Wyn, and let's see . . . Oh, Merna Toppens stopped by the other day to visit, but I had a busy morning so the timing was not good for me. She said they were not having any out-of-town company for the holidays, and I had entertained the idea of perhaps inviting them just to be neighborly. But, then again, I think it's more prudent to just have an intimate dinner with the five of us, don't you?"

"That's perfectly fine with me, Mother. I want this to be our most meaningful Christmas ever, especially since Daddy is no longer with us. I miss him so much, and I am sure you do, too. I couldn't bear it if something happened to my Chetter. I like to call him 'Chetter.' I can tell he sort of likes it! So what time are you planning for Christmas Eve? Will we be starting at our usual time of six o'clock so that we can eat, exchange gifts, and get home before it gets late? One good thing, though, I was just noticing on our kitchen calendar this morning that there will be a full moon for Christmas. That will make it much easier for our drive home."

"Yes, I was thinking that six would be good. The weather has been all over the place the past few days. The fog was a bit unexpected yesterday morning. I am hoping that any major storms don't roll in until after New Year's Day."

As Stormy got ready to hang up she recapped her phone conversation, "Mother, I appreciate you so much. You are so loving and supportive. What would I ever do without you? Christmas Eve Chet and I will be there with bells on. Is there anything that you would like for us to bring besides our gifts to exchange with the family members?"

Jantzi's shoulders fully relaxed as she replied, "I love you too, darling. You are my firstborn and my best work. I can't think of a single thing that I would like for you to bring as I will have everything under control and operating in high gear as usual. Please give Chet my love, and I will see both of you real soon."

As Jantzi placed the receiver back in its cradle, her spirits soared once again. Oh, everything was really cooking on the front burner with gas now! Never mind that she did not have a gas stove, but she had always liked that analogy.

Without further delay, Jantzi dipped her writing quill in

the ink well inside her roll top desk and began making her lists. She was bound and determined to stay as close to the house as possible until the New Year dawned. Christmas Eve and her guests would arrive soon enough.

CHAPTER SIX

Every task has its unpleasant aspects and Jantzi's upcoming family celebration was no exception. As much as she abhorred cooking, she would still prefer doing that to contacting Sarita and talking with her. Until the time she had met Wyn and started seeing more of him, Sarita seemed to be not quite as contrary and uncooperative.

Suffice it to say, the last few years had been rather turbulent anytime mother and daughter were near each other. Jantzi blamed this, in part, on the fact that Sarita had always been Ace's little princess, and since he was no longer alive, Sarita was continuing in a downward spiral. After Ace passed away, she moved into an apartment in Ridgemonte, and had been working for the local dentist, Dr. Diller, ever since. Jantzi could not imagine anything more demeaning than having to look inside someone else's mouth all day long. To each her own, she reminded herself.

Wyn, a drifter and cow hand, was rarely forthcoming about any of his family history, background, relatives, or anything of the sort. Jantzi reasoned that one of her ranching neighbors, Tom Toppens, hired him to get even with her following their various ranch debacles over the years. Tom's wife, Merna, had fixed a place in their bunkhouse for Wyn to stay. Jantzi would describe Wyn as being weirder than a wooden watch. He had no possessions, and what did he do with the money he earned? He had no vehicle, and did not even have a way to get into town. This was not the horse and buggy days of the 1800's.

Tom Toppens had gifted Wyn one of his best horses for branding, roundups, and essential cattle ranch work. How on earth could she have raised a daughter who set her sights so low on someone who had so few belongings? Perhaps his poor mother should have named him Lose instead of Wyn. Jantzi surmised she was not the outstanding lifelong teacher she had hoped she would be. She learned a long time ago that if you trust in your land, herds of cattle, and riches, you would never be taken captive.

Determining that periods of reflection were good for the body, mind, soul, and spirit, Jantzi carefully placed her prized pen back inside its holder. Sliding her chair back on its castors, she stood and stretched her back for several minutes. Walking to the window and looking into her back yard nestled inside the tall evergreens, she decided the weather was warm enough and there was still enough daylight to enjoy a horseback ride before nightfall.

With a fresh wind in her spirit, Jantzi glided effortlessly down the flights of stairs. Opening the pantry and grabbing an apple from the fruit bin, she removed the barn key from its place on the wall hanger, pulled on her riding boots, and headed for the tack room. After collecting her riding gear and donning her western range clothing, she walked to the horse barn. Blue was not far behind as he liked the range just as much as the other critters that inhabited the Sabblonti Ranch.

Jantzi had a special whistle that she mastered a few months after she purchased her mare, Diamantae. In fact,

Jantzi could swear that this mare was part human as she seemed to understand her owner far better than real people did most of the time. When Diamantae heard Jantzi's personal greeting, she stuck her head outside the window of the barn and began to nicker.

Jantzi unlocked the barn and laid her saddle and accessories just inside the door. Grabbing a brush from where it hung on the wall, she approached her mare like a long-lost friend. Brushing Diamantae's coat with one hand and offering her an apple in the other, both animal and owner seemed to be in horse heaven for a brief moment in time.

"Your mane is getting so long, my dear friend! I need to give you a trim before Christmas. That will be one of my gifts to you. How would you like that?"

Slipping Diamantae's bridle over her head and getting her saddle blanket, saddle, and breast tie down adjusted, Jantzi placed her foot in the stirrup and swung her right leg up to get situated in the saddle.

Thankfully, Diamantae was only fifteen hands high and had such a good walk, canter, and gallop. Jantzi had really lucked out with this horse as she seemed to be the all-in-one package. It was worth every penny to pay for registered stock even though Jantzi had never bothered to send in the papers for Diamantae. To arrive at her name, she used a combination of her dam and sire's officially registered names. Jantzi was confident that with her mare's excellent confirmation, white diamond shape on her forehead against her black hide, and four white stockings, she could have surely been a beautiful show horse. But there wasn't time for all that chasing hither and yon during these days. Besides, most western women her age were not still showing their horses. They had retired from the circuit decades ago.

Jantzi studied Diamante's coat for a few minutes wondering if it was going to be a hard winter or a mild one. Thus far, her hair was not super thick or lengthy.

"Oh, I almost forgot," muttered Jantzi. "I need to grab those pruners to cut the junipers! Hold on a minute, Diamantae and Blue, while I get myself together."

Dismantling from her mare, Jantzi went into the next room of the barn and opened the drawer where some of the odds and ends of tools were kept. She located the small pruners that she would need and ventured into the tack room to grab an extra rope. She did not want to use her good lariat to tie down the bundle of juniper swags. "Better get the small saddle bags and tie them on too," Jantzi reminded herself as she placed the pruners inside one of the bags and closed the tarnished buckle.

"Okay, critters, let's try this again," coaxed Jantzi. She had forgotten how long it had been since she had ridden the range into the higher elevation. She secretly hoped that the juniper trees would be heavily laden with berries as it seemed to differ from one year to the next.

"Pick up your pace, Diamantae!" chided Jantzi. "We have got a lot of ground to cover between now and nightfall."

It seemed as though the beautiful mare understood every word that her master had said. As she looked down at the ground, Jantzi realized that she needed to contact the farrier and get Diamantae's feet trimmed right away. Ugh, that was another thing that would just have to wait until January! Hopefully some of the juniper trees would not be near the rock outcroppings so Jantzi could ride in areas to help protect Diamantae's feet. She would also need to keep a sharp eye out for those pesky badger holes. That's all she would need right now is for her dependable mare to drop her front leg in one of those.

Jantzi realized that she had forgotten to put on her turquoise and silver wrist watch before she left the house. Glancing toward the western horizon, she guesstimated that she had about three hours of daylight remaining.

It was a good thing that Diamantae had a great sense of direction as Jantzi's mind began to drift to its farthest recesses and ravines. Life did not always seem to go as planned, she reflected, even when one tried her very best to exercise control over everyone and everything in it.

Taking stock of the past forty-one years and since it was the holiday season, Jantzi decided to be kind to herself. After it was all said and done, had she not done quite well for herself? She owned the Sabblonti Ranch which was a real show piece on anyone's scale. Also, had she not managed to acquire a portion of the Merrill Ranch with that vital stream running right through it? Now, that was a real fait accompli in anyone's book, hands down. Not many people, men or women, could have managed to pull that one off and still maintained the upper hand. Concentrate on the positives and never mind the negatives. Yes, that was tried and true advice. There was no way to go through seven decades of one's life and not pick up a few snags, losers, and losses along the way. As long as one ended up with more assets than liabilities at the end of it all, that's what really mattered. Most people did not bother to think long term, but Jantzi did.

"Great work, Blue, 'Ol Buddy, you are keeping up just fine! Do your feet hurt yet?"

Diamantae was making her way up the side of the hill

just like an old pro. Suddenly, four mule deer jumped out in front of them. "Great job flushing those mulies out of there, Diamantae!"

In the distance, Jantzi spotted a nice cluster of trees. The lone juniper that served as the landmark for the northern point of the ranch looked so elegant today. "I'll bet that old tree could tell some interesting tales if it could talk," opined Jantzi. As she drew closer to the tree grouping, a pair of red-tailed hawks circled overhead.

Jantzi dismounted from Diamantae and led her closer to the grove. Looking up, Jantzi was pleasantly surprised at the abundance of berries. "Goodness, gracious, I must be living right today! Look at all those nice blue colored goodies on those trees. This is exactly what I was hoping I would find."

Blue lay down close to Diamantae as she bent her left hind foot to give it a rest. Jantzi wished she would have brought a second apple along to give to her beloved mare right now just to let her know how much she appreciated her. "You two take a short rest while I cut these branches and get them tied onto the back of my saddle," instructed Jantzi as she glanced up at the sky one more time trying to determine how long it would take to get back to the barn.

Jantzi threw herself into overdrive as she snipped the branches from the trees. "Curiosity killed the cat," Jantzi commented as Blue trudged over to where she was working and sniffed the branches. "Blue, get out from under my feet! Can't you see that I am busy and don't have time to be bothered with you nosing into what I am doing? Get back over there and lay down by Diamantae right now."

Blue, a very sensitive creature, bent his head down as he slinked back near Diamantae. He let out a big sigh, crossed his front paws, and laid his head in the middle of them. His blue eyes darted back and forth as he watched Jantzi in her snipping and bundling frenzy. She had forgotten to take her riding gloves when she left the ranch, and after tying the branches together, she looked down and let out a shriek as she surveyed her scratched and bleeding hands. Jantzi had recently noticed that her skin was getting very thin and this sure proved it. She tied the bundles of juniper branches on the back of her saddle and sincerely hoped that she would still have the berries intact when she arrived home. Granted, this was not the smoothest operation she had ever launched. One could only hope for the best.

Jantzi got herself in the saddle one more time and headed down the hillside toward the barn. If Diamante had set a pace faster than a walk, she wondered if she would have anything beyond stripped branches and a mare with a blue rump when they arrived. "Get a move on, girl, we are burning daylight fast," ordered Jantzi. She could have sworn it was taking twice as long to get home as it did to ride to the juniper trees.

Arriving at the horse barn with just enough light to unsaddle Diamantae and get everything put back in its proper place, Jantzi offered praise, "Good girl, Diamantae, you got us home safe and sound. I am so proud of you! And, come here, Blue. I am sorry I snapped at you. You are a good doggie, too, even if you were Ace's dog and he could not think of anything more original than the name 'Blue' to name a Blue Heeler."

Jantzi fed Diamantae some oats and hay after brushing her. She filled her small inside water trough and spread three more bales of straw in her stall for a nice bed for the night. "Good night, Darling, sleep tight. I will try to get your mane trimmed before Christmas, but no promises. I have a lot to do between now and then."

Jantzi made one more trip through the barn, tack room, and side room. Everything seemed to be safe as she secured the locks. Picking up the bundles of juniper branches, sporting a large toothy smile of satisfaction, she turned the lights off and walked through the yard.

Laying the branches down on the porch and feeling inside her jean pockets for her ranch house key, Jantzi's heart began to race when she could not find it anywhere. "How will I get inside the house without my key? How could I have been so foolish as to leave without taking it with me? What if something would have happened while I was riding alone?"

Instinctively Jantzi reached down to turn the door handle which readily opened. In her haste to get to the barn and saddle Diamantae, she had forgotten to lock her front door and take her key with her. She had been telling herself that she needed to keep an extra ranch house key in the barn, but never got around to doing it.

Safely inside, Jantzi slumped down in her kitchen chair with Blue settling on the floor by her right foot. She looked into his face and contemplated what he might be thinking. "Did dogs have cognitive abilities?" she wondered.

CHAPTER SEVEN

Jantzi removed her riding socks and massaged her tired feet. Foot cream sounded better by the minute. During the winter months, she pampered Blue by adding some warm beef broth to his dry food. Thank goodness that stuff came in a package and all you had to do was add water. After all, he had been a real gem to troop all the way into the hills with her and Diamantae in search of juniper branches and berries. Every dog needed his treats, just like some people, but not everyone was entitled to them. She secured the front door and turned the porch light off. Wow, was it ever comforting to be back inside her headquarters! The euphoria of satisfaction swept over Jantzi like a tidal wave.

First opening the refrigerator door, then the pantry door, and finally the cupboards, and then closing all three, Jantzi decided she was too tired to cook tonight. She did not even feel like warming up a can of soup for herself. Her critters were cared for and she would not concern herself with food for the time being. She would get a good night's sleep, rise early, fix a bowl of instant oatmeal with prunes, and shift into high gear tomorrow. Great minds manufactured perfect plans!

Never tiring of walking up the steep staircase, Jantzi made her way into her master bathroom. She drew some extra hot water in the antique bathtub that Ace had installed for her and added some Epsom salts, which she hoped would soothe her aging muscles. Soaking and relaxing in the warm tub afforded her the opportunity to recap her day, and look long into the next few ones on the horizon. She fell asleep for about ten minutes and awakened suddenly when the water turned tepid.

After Jantzi finished with her nighttime routine and was readying herself for bed, she headed down the hallway to her office to sit down for a brief moment at her desk to look at the calendar one more time. Lifting her right hand, she placed her index finger on each of the two-inch calendar squares and counted out loud, "One, two, three, four, five, six, seven, eight . . . Great, I have more time than I had originally thought until my guests will be here for our annual dinner. Whew, that takes a load off my mind!"

Suddenly, Jantzi's eyes rested upon a folded sheet of paper. "What on earth could this be?" she asked herself. Picking it up with her right hand and unfolding it, she was stunned when she saw that it was her Last Will and Testament! But she had placed it inside a white business envelope and secured it inside her metal box. How did it get out of the box and the envelope? She was the only one who knew this piece of paper even existed.

Jantzi broke out in a cold sweat. She felt her hands starting to tremble as her narrowing eyes darted frantically around the room. Then she remembered that she had left earlier in the afternoon without locking the front door. When she had returned right before dark, she did not notice anything unusual in the front yard, and there were no noticeable tire tracks left by any of the vehicles normally driven in the area.

Jantzi looked around the room for the envelope. Since it was white, she should be able to spot it right away. She reminded herself that she must remain calm. Having been in very tight situations before, she had always managed to land on her feet. This was no time to lose her cool, control, or footing.

Jantzi would call Stormy in the morning under the pretense of asking about a Christmas gift for Chet and try to determine if she had made a trip to the ranch in her absence. She would need to exercise finesse without tipping her hand.

Surely no one else would enter her ranch house uninvited and make his or her way to the office on the third floor. In all the time she had lived on the Sabblonti Ranch, nothing like that had ever transpired. She seriously doubted that Sarita had driven out during the daytime when she would have been working at Dr. Diller's office. It seemed of late that she almost had to offer to pay her to come out to the ranch for a visit. Jantzi's head was spinning like a washing machine rinse cycle.

Lots of luck getting any sleep on this night. Jantzi spent the next hour looking around and under virtually everything in her bedroom, master bathroom, office, and extra bedrooms. She came up empty handed. It was as if the white envelope had vanished into thin air. She determined she would sleep on the matter and rise and shine early thirty to resume her search.

Sleep eluded Jantzi throughout the night. She tossed, turned, and lay awake for hours, or so it seemed. She fell into a deep sleep right before dawn. Blue's bark awakened her with a start. "Blue, what on earth are you doing in my room? I hardly ever find you in this part of the house. You don't even like those stairs."

Jantzi rolled over and looked at the clock which read half past nine. She flipped the covers back and set her feet on the floor. As she motioned for her canine friend to come near her, she said, "Blue, you are such a good caretaker. I guess you knew I needed some extra sleep. I'll get you outside so you can get some fresh air and watch the front yard for me, okay?"

Changing into some jeans and a holiday-themed sweatshirt, Jantzi brushed her long jet-black hair and secured it with a plastic butterfly clasp. There was no time for the plastic princess routine this morning. She would need to get downstairs, fix a cup of strong coffee, and start spinning the phone dial. She hoped it was not too early to call Stormy. She looked at the kitchen clock, and it was straight up ten, so surely Stormy would be up by this time.

Jantzi situated herself comfortably in her favorite living room chair and propped her feet onto the ottoman. Setting her coffee cup on the end table, she picked up the phone and dialed the number. After six rings, Stormy finally answered. Jantzi could tell from her voice that she was quite fatigued and may not want to talk for very long.

"Good morning, my Mountain Bluebelle," cooed Jantzi. "I hope I did not wake you. Did you sleep well last evening? I sure hope you did because I have been so worried about you and just don't know how to help you. I sincerely wish I could be of more assistance and just don't feel like I have been a good mother to you, and I don't want you to be disappointed in me, and would feel terrible if I let you and Chet down when you needed me the most."

"Wind down, Mother. You are wound up tighter than an eight day clock the way you are carrying on. Have you been up since the crack of dawn and downed four cups of strong caffeine already this morning? What is wrong with you?"

"Oh, please forgive me, daughter dear. I have had so much on my mind and so many little details to tend to that I must have forgotten my manners. It's nothing personal. Actually, I just remembered late last night that I wanted to have something very special made for Chet this year for Christmas and did not get around to it. He has wanted that silver belt buckle with the Sabblonti cattle brand on it for several years now, but I did not get it ordered from the silver smith. Some days I feel like I need a secretary, office manager, or personal attendant. So, I am hoping you can give me some other gift ideas. Is there something at The Shadowy Merc that he might like?"

"Oh, for pity sake, don't worry about a gift for Chet. What we really want we can't seem to obtain. The tangible things in life are just stuff. People and our relationships with them are what are important. All of those other things are just lures that seem to trap people. Who needs that? I certainly don't, and I know Chet doesn't either."

Jantzi felt herself getting riled up inside so she determined she needed to end this conversation post haste. "Stormy, you are so correct. I guess I just lost my perspective momentarily. Please forgive me. I hope you can get some rest this afternoon. Give Chet my love and I will talk with you later. Oh, before I hang up, did you happen to stop by the main ranch house late yesterday afternoon? I took Diamantae and Blue on a little high mountain adventure. I thought I might have missed seeing you."

"No, I have not driven anywhere for a couple of weeks now. I don't feel like going anywhere so I have been staying at home trying to heal my body. Thanks, and yes, I plan on getting a good long nap this afternoon," Stormy said as she let out a big yawn. "I have not been sleeping well at night, and have been keeping Chet from getting a good night's sleep, too. I am thankful you have a lot to keep you busy with all that energy you seem to have. Goodbye for now."

Jantzi slammed the phone receiver onto its base. There were times when she wondered if it was even worthwhile having children. Stormy had worked herself into an absolute frenzy over this miscarriage business. Jantzi was confident if Stormy could just rid herself of her obsession of having children that she would be able to carry a baby to a full-term pregnancy. The things people wasted their time on were beyond amazing.

With Jantzi's and Stormy's biological clocks ticking, mother was becoming acutely aware that there were several lifelong goals that still needed to be reinforced to daughter. Jantzi could only hope that despite Stormy's losses, she had at least been able to absorb her mother's modeling methods, one of which was the principle that people needed to be controlled every single day of their miserable lives. Stormy also needed to be reminded that the reason her mother had assigned her that name at birth was so she could learn to create storms in peoples' lives in order to control them. During her lifetime, Jantzi labored to collect as many Jokers as she could. If she did not have a full deck by the time she passed, Stormy would need to continue in her mother's footsteps so the Sabblonti's would have one in the end.

CHAPTER EIGHT

Toast and choke cherry jam would have to suffice for Jantzi's late breakfast this morning. Hot instant cereal could wait for another day. On second thought, maybe she would fix that for supper. Breakfast food always tasted good later in the day.

Opening the door and stepping onto the porch, Jantzi gazed around the front yard. Blue was nowhere in sight so she let out a whistle for him, and he dutifully came around the corner. "How can you be watching my front yard if you are in the back yard?" scolded Jantzi as she carried the juniper bundles inside and laid them on the dining room table.

Making her way into the kitchen, Jantzi collected the trash can from inside the pantry and the kitchen shears from the wooden knife block on the counter. She was trying to design the dining room decorations in her mind, but was having trouble concentrating. Pulling out the second drawer of the buffet, she selected a roll of inch-wide silver velvet ribbon with which to tie the bundles as she formed them into swags. She experimented with positioning the decorations in various places on the table and in the dining room itself. Truth be known, her heart was not really into all of these holiday traditions, but she must honor her commitment to her daughters, especially since she had already spoken with Stormy about it on the phone.

Jantzi reasoned that if she could get all of the trivial things taken care of first, such as minimally decorating the house, setting out the canned goods for Christmas Eve dinner, and so forth, that would free up her time for the most important preparations later. Then she would have plenty of time to rest before the main event.

One year for Christmas Ace had surprised Jantzi and given her an antique buffet with many drawers to hold her tablecloths, napkins, silverware, candles, candle holders, rolls of ribbon, and ad infinitum. Even though she did not like to entertain, it made her feel rich and valuable just to be surrounded by such aesthetic fineries. People were such a nuisance and so difficult to have around unless they could be of great use to accomplish one's overall schemes and themes in life. Otherwise, Jantzi considered them the equivalent of plastic silverware that someone used once and then discarded.

It seemed like overkill to drape the oak dining room table that seated twelve with the cream-colored linen tablecloth. The holly berries appeared to smile at Jantzi when she looked at them. She surmised that someone had made a small fortune designing all of these Christmas themed things that folks used for a few days each year.

Even though there would only be five of them seated for the dinner this year, Jantzi liked the overall dramatic effect of the large table. Granted, she could take out a leaf or two, but her motto was "large and in charge at all times." Well, that was just one of her enduring mottos. Truth be known, she had many of them that had served her well for decades.

The Shadowy Merc had sold the matching green, white,

and holly berry set of dishes a few years ago. Jantzi purchased them on a day when her least favorite clerk was working. There was no need to think of such unpleasant things to detract from her decorating energy. She completed setting the table and placing the twelve-inch silver tapers inside the candle holders. Stepping back from the dining room and pausing inside the threshold, a large grin of satisfaction graced Jantzi's face. Now there were two things that she could check off her list — collecting the juniper branches complete with berries and preparing the dining room table.

"What was the menu that she and Stormy put together?" queried Jantzi. "Oh, that's right. Soup in Grammy Mabel's heirloom bowls, baked bread with butter and chokecherry jam, condiments, and that chocolate cake made with tomato sauce that Chet likes so much. Grammy Mabel's soup bowls? Forget about those!" Yes, she had told Stormy they would be using the bowls, but too bad, Jantzi was only going to set this table once.

Opening the pantry door, Jantzi looked around on the shelves and located the ingredients she would need to bake the cake, a jar of pickles and olives, and several cans of different kinds of soups. When Ace was still alive, Jantzi would mix two or three kinds of soups together and serve them to him. He must have liked them because he ate and never said a word. Too bad if the various kinds of soups did not go together. Hunger makes a good cook every time!

CHAPTER NINE

Memories of prior Christmases raced through Jantzi's mind as she walked from the dining area into the family room. She reminded herself once again how thankful she was that she had dismissed the idea of a pine tree complete with trimmings for this year. Glancing around the room, an idea suddenly came to her of where to set up her Christmas display.

The mantle clock bonged twice as Jantzi walked toward the front door and grabbed the barn keys to go check on Diamantae. She started apologizing to her mare as she unlocked the door, "I totally lost track of time! I should have been out here much earlier with your oats and hay. Can you please forgive me?"

After completing her outside chores and making sure everything was in its proper place, Jantzi walked to the tack room and removed Snipper's horse blanket from its peg on the wall. She also grabbed a pair of Ace's spurs and his bridle with the roller ball bit. Jantzi set the items down on the ground and went back in one more time to hug Diamante, tell her that she loved her, and explain to her that she would try to be more punctual about her feedings, waterings, and combings in the future. Diamante did need to understand that this was the holiday season, however.

Hearing the key turn in the lock with the final click was always a comfort to Jantzi. She shoved the keys in her right front jeans pocket and headed toward the house with her horse items in hand. Lugging all of this stuff around was a bit of a bother, but then again, there were definite advantages to the solo route.

Jantzi flashed a big toothy grin as she strolled past the large oval mirror hanging on the wall. Entering the family room, she dumped the tack in the middle of the floor, grabbed the horse blanket, and spread it out on one corner of the fireplace. In front of the blanket, she placed Snipper's bridle and Ace's spurs. Jantzi wondered why she had never thought to do something like this when Ace was still alive. My, how he would have loved her decorating idea!

Stepping back a few feet, Jantzi's eyes shifted back and forth as she drank in the total overall effect thus far. Yes, she reasoned, this would be just perfect. Hopefully, there would be adequate paper left over from prior years to wrap this year's gifts. Boxes? Yes, that could present a problem. Well, she only needed a few of them and hopefully they would be different sizes.

Scouring the pantry and bedroom closets yielded a half dozen boxes of assorted sizes. Jantzi decided that Stormy's childhood bedroom on the second floor could be pressed into service for wrapping this year's holiday gifts. She hardly ever stepped foot into Sarita's old bedroom.

Speaking softly to herself, Jantzi rounded up scissors, a red marker, and tape from her office. The green rubberized tub stored the colorful wrapping paper, ribbons, and gift stickers. This project would not take too long; however, she must be as meticulous as possible and concentrate on what she was doing.

Placing a twig of juniper complete with its bluish colored berries on each gift, Jantzi was just as pleased as punch when she surveyed the stack of colorful packages. She had almost forgotten to label each one, which could have proved disastrous later on. How embarrassing it would be to have the wrong person open the incorrect gift. A stitch in time does save nine!

Jantzi was beyond confident that she still maintained sufficient balance in her body, even at seventy years of age, to carry the complete stack of gifts down the stairs in one load. Midway down the steps, the top package started to wobble, but she managed to make it all the way to the bottom without dropping one.

Timing of this day must be carefully monitored, Jantzi reminded herself, as she needed to call Sarita when she got off work this afternoon. Jantzi was thankful that there was a dentist in the next county and Dr. Diller was not the only game in town. No way was she going to spend a minute sitting in a dental chair where Sarita worked and people in the same county would have access to personal medical records.

Sarita's phone was ringing as she unlocked the door to her apartment. She doubted it would be Wyn calling this early as he probably had not finished his evening chores. He called at varying times on differing nights, depending upon when the phone in the bunkhouse was not in use. But, then again, it just might be him.

"Hello," Sarita said as she caught her breath after climbing the stairs to the second floor of the building.

"Oh, Sarita, you sound completely winded! Are you alright?"

"I am fine, Mother," Sarita replied in an even tone. "I

was just getting home from work and walking into my apartment. Had you tried to call earlier?"

"No. I have been so busy that the day nearly got away from me. I wanted to visit with you for a few minutes about our Christmas gathering."

"Go ahead," Sarita responded cautiously.

"Well, it does not seem like it should be time for our annual family gathering once again. My, how time flies! Not that I am having that much fun anymore, but you know how that old saying goes. Anyway, I wanted to invite you and Wyn to Christmas Eve dinner. I think we will start at our usual time about six so we can have ample time for our main meal, rose hip tea with dessert, opening of our gifts, and all that rig-a-ma-roll. So, if you can extend the invitation to Wyn that would be great. I realize that you will have to drive to Toppens' bunkhouse and pick him up since he doesn't even own a vehicle."

There was silence on both ends of the telephone line.

Jantzi continued, "Sarita, are you still there? I can't hear anything coming from your end of the phone."

"Yes, Mother, I am still here," seethed Sarita. "I will plan to contact Wyn and extend your invitation to him. Is there anything that you would like for us to bring to your dinner?"

"Not that I can think of right now, but I will let you know if I come up with anything. I have had such fun and am taking great pains to make this gathering the most memorable one that we have ever had in the history of our family. I think that you and Wyn will be pleasantly surprised. Okay, I will plan to see you Christmas Eve. 'Bye for now."

Sarita hung up her phone without even saying a word.

She would really have to muster up the courage to take Wyn to this family dinner. She had not heard much from Stormy the past few weeks, and hoped she was recovering physically and emotionally. One of the women with whom Sarita worked with in Dr. Diller's office had also suffered a miscarriage, so she was able to explain some aspects of it to Sarita. Chet never said more than a few words in Sarita's presence, and there was a part of her that had never really understood him. It seemed as though he was just along for the ride and was biding his time until he and Stormy could oversee the Sabblonti Ranch.

CHAPTER TEN

Tears tumbled from Sarita's eyes onto her blue wool coat. She missed her dad more than she could bear. Each Christmas season was becoming increasingly more difficult since his death, and it seemed as though she was truly the odd man out in this whole family scheme of things. She sensed that her mother genuinely despised her. But was that even possible for a parent to hate a child? Sarita was convinced that every parent loved his or her child just like her father had loved her. Just because her mother had worn the pants of the family did not mean that her dad was any less of a man. Sarita knew in her heart of hearts that true love and adoration could never be feigned. She purposed in her heart that if she ever did get married and had children, she would treat them the way her father had adored her when he was alive.

Sarita's apartment seemed colder than normal. She checked the thermostat on the wall; it read 72 degrees. When she became sad or stressed, it seemed that her body temperature dropped several degrees. Rather than shell out hard-earned cash to the Parsons Power Company, she opted to don a warm cardigan sweater, thermal-lined sweat pants, and wool socks. A cup of hot chocolate with miniature marshmallows sounded good before fixing a light dinner.

Sarita sipped her winter beverage as she reflected upon the phone conversation with her mother. After scooping out the last little bit of marshmallow residue from the bottom, she set the cup on her coffee table and lay down on the couch. She pulled the dark grey wool blanket over herself and drifted off to sleep. She awakened with a start as she had the sensation of someone shoving her repeatedly.

The phone rang. Sarita jumped off the couch and ran to answer it.

"Hi, Wyn, is this you?" Sarita answered expectantly.

"Yes, my sweet Sarita, 'tis me," soothed Wyn. "You sound a bit on edge tonight. Is everything okay?"

"I guess so. My mother called as soon as I got home from work this afternoon. She invited us to Christmas Eve dinner at the ranch. I am hoping that you will go with me."

"Sarita, as much as I love and adore you, I am not up to spending an evening where everything is all show and no go. You know that your mother despises me and thinks that I am a real loser because I was orphaned and grew up in a boy's home, don't even possess a truck, and barely own the shirt on my back. But I do have a secure plan in place for our future. It started when I was in about the fourth grade and going to the school connected with the boy's home. My favorite books and movies featured horses, cattle, ranches, and the west. It's beyond a miracle that I even made it to this geographic area. You just need to fully trust me in this regard."

"But I just can't go to the ranch alone for the family dinner, Wyn," Sarita eked the words out as she started to cry.

"Sarita, sweetheart, don't cry. Can you please listen to my heart for a few minutes?"

"Yes, I can listen for as long as it takes."

Wyn continued, "In my estimation, your mother drags you, Stormy, and Chet around like rag dolls. I have nothing against rag dolls for kids to play with, but all of you are adults. Chet is a total lackey and a yes man. He is void of masculinity. He is just holding out until Jantzi dies so he can take over the reins of the Sabblonti Ranch."

"Stop right there, Wyn. My sister and brother-in-law have been through a lot with three miscarriages. You need to have some compassion."

"I have compassion. That's not the issue here. Control is the crux of the matter. Since moving to the Toppens' bunkhouse on their ranch, I have been informed that it was actually Jantzi who paid the local jeweler to have Stormy's three carat diamond engagement and wedding ring designed in the shape of a horseshoe. She also bought Chet's pickup along with his five-horse trailer complete with personal sleeping quarters. Your mother also pays them a hefty monthly allowance for who knows what besides Chet driving around in that fancy rig of his? I may not have all of those material things, but I plan to pay my own way, thank you very much."

"Wyn, please don't get so overheated by all of this family business. "

"Jantzi Belle Sabblonti is as phony as a $3 bill and an average fifth grader can figure that out for himself. I am not going to attend a fancy meal and eat the bread of insincerity and suffer through an evening of pretense. I have far more respect for myself than that. For those of us who grew up in the boy's home, we can tell the people who actually care about us and those who are just going through the motions to make themselves look good. Their motives are as glaring as the noon day sun."

It was as if Wyn's words were permeating Sarita's very being for the first time in years. She opined, "I have been trying to develop several degrees of separation from my mother since Daddy died, but it's like she has this invisible hold over me that I cannot break. I had thought by moving to town and starting to work for Dr. Diller that my situation would improve. Since I was old enough to look at myself in the mirror, I knew that because I was born with one blue eye and one brown eye, my mother couldn't stand to look at me. My Grammy Mabel and Daddy were the only two people who accepted me for who I was until you came along."

Wyn, rising up in his defensive posture, stated emphatically, "I was struck by your unique beauty the first time I laid eyes on you. I have never considered you as having an unusual appearance. True beauty comes from within, and you are gorgeous inside and out. Quit belittling yourself and allow me the privilege of having you be my beauty to rescue."

"Oh, Wyn, you always know just the right thing to say to calm my heart and help my spirit soar! I will muster the courage to put in an appearance at the annual gathering. I am realizing that I need to start taking control of my own life and destiny. Thanks for being a listening ear and faithful friend."

Sarita placed the phone back in its receiver, walked slowly into her bedroom, and opened the lid to her cedar hope chest. Ace had made this for her as a high school graduation gift. He secured the lumber from The Shadowy Merc, and had burned the Sabblonti cattle brand onto the top of the chest.

Kneeling in front of the hope chest, Sarita fingered the

hand stitched double wedding ring pattern quilt so lovingly made by Grammy Mabel. At that moment, she pondered if she would ever get married. Time was marching on, and she did not know if Wyn was the one for her. How does any woman ever know who is right for her? The old adage of, "Pay your money, take your chances" surely would not apply now since she had no extra money in which to take a big chance. Money did not control her life anyway. Sure, it was nice to have, but it was not the end all. Sarita dug way down to the bottom of the chest and felt the familiar yarn. Placing a firm hold on the head, she retrieved her favorite childhood toy from its secure storage spot. She slowly lifted Pansie up and pressed her hard against her face. Tears freely flowed as Sarita clutched her rag doll.

As she stood to her feet and headed toward her rocking chair, Sarita sat down to contemplate and reflect. She lifted Pansie by her flaming red yarn hair and began to move her from one side to the other. Pansie's stuffed appendages began to sway back and forth and spun out of control soon enough. Sarita whispered, "Pansie, I would never drag you around by your hair."

At that definitive moment, a sudden revelation came to Sarita as she jumped to her slippered feet and screamed, "Yes, Wyn, yes! My mother, Jantzi Belle Sabblonti, has indeed been dragging me around like a rag doll for thirty-five years! How could I not have realized this? What a terrible loss of probably half of my life already!"

A calm eventually settled over Sarita as she sat down in her rocking chair once again. This heirloom piece of furniture, hand crafted by her maternal grandfather, Simon Siddonz, had been passed down through the family to her. She wondered why it had not been hauled to the designated dumping area on the Sabblonti Ranch and burned along with so many other items Jantzi Belle decided were worthless.

Drawing Pansie close to her heart, Sarita began to sing,

"Pansie, I will always love you, always love you, always love you, yes I will.

"Pansie, I will never leave you, never leave you, never leave you, no I will not.

"Pansie, you are my special treasure, special treasure, yes you are. You may be just a rag doll, but you are like a sister and forever friend to me.

"Pansie, when I have real little girls all my own, I will always love them, always love them, always love them, yes I will."

A peace descended upon Sarita as she placed Pansie inside her hope chest. Hope, yes, genuine hope, that's what would give Sarita the courage to stand against opposing forces and place her feet securely on her path to freedom.

CHAPTER ELEVEN

With Christmas shopping days slipping away, Sarita came to the sudden conclusion that since she had been in such a mental fog, she had not even purchased one gift, card, or the like. She had helped to decorate the small fresh pine tree in Dr. Diller's office and hang the holiday banner across the top of her wall work area, but that was the extent of it thus far. Hopefully, The Shadowy Merc would not have sold most of their decent gift items. Clinker's Feed Store carried a few odds and ends, but nothing Jantzi would deem worthy of a holiday gift. There really wasn't time to drive to one of the nearby towns to see what those stores might have on hand.

During her lunch hour, Sarita window shopped as she walked past the local stores and businesses. Some of them really got into the holiday spirit whereas others must have thought that Christmas was just like any other day, and there was no need to make any fuss or go the extra mile. Thankfully, Dr. Diller had given his employees their bonus checks early this year. Sarita made a mental calculation of how much she could spend on each person which wasn't an extravagant amount. She reasoned that there's more to life than just acquiring stuff, especially this time of the year. In addition, she was wary of presents that came with underlying motives. Who needs those, anyway?

Stormy and Chet seemed to enjoy anything with a horseshoe theme. In the main storefront window of The Shadowy Merc, Sarita spotted a large red and black polar fleece blanket with the picture of a silver horseshoe smack dab in the center of it. Now there was a great gift idea for those two! Sarita hurried inside the store and checked the price tag for the blanket which came to $49.95. This was just perfect since she had mentally budgeted $50.00, give or take, for Chet and Stormy. She had originally thought of getting a little something for a baby, but decided against it since Stormy's miscarriage had occurred so recently. Sarita secretly hoped that she would never have to endure anything so sad, but realized that there were never any guarantees in life.

Scooping up the red and black blanket and draping it over her left arm, Sarita fingered some other blankets lying in the same stack. Since Wyn was living in the bunkhouse, courtesy of the Toppens, perhaps this would make a great gift for him as well. His favorite color was green and her eyes settled on one that featured a blue border, and a bay mare with her foal standing in a meadow. The corners of Sarita's mouth began to move upward as she smiled to herself, and knew this would be so helpful for Wyn.

"Three down but the most difficult one to go," Sarita reminded herself.

To accommodate their holiday customers, the employees of The Shadowy Merc had designated one section of their store for holiday gifts. Sarita could have sworn that she saw some of the same merchandise this year as last year, but in cattle country, some people's desires, needs, and tastes really did not vary much from year to year. Most of the people tended to be very practical as life demanded it.

Sarita glanced down at her watch and realized she had only twenty minutes of her lunch hour remaining. Dr. Diller was a fantastic boss, but he counseled his employees to be courteous and timely as some of their patients who drove into Ridgemonte were from remote areas so they typically carved out the whole day in which to get all of their supplies and tend to their personal needs.

Brenda, one of the girls in Stormy's graduating class and a store employee, spotted Sarita standing in the holiday section of the store with the two blankets draped over her arm. "Sarita, can I take those blankets from you and place them at the counter so you don't have to hold them while you finish your shopping? It's great to see you! Are you still working for Dr. Diller? And how is Stormy these days?

Sarita drew in a deep breath, "Hi Brenda, it's nice to see you, and yes, thank you for taking these blankets to the counter for me. I am completing my Christmas shopping on my lunch hour. I did not know if you had heard that Stormy just lost another baby. It's been very hard for all of us."

"Oh, no!" gasped Brenda. "I am so sorry. I had not heard that, and I hope that I did not upset you by inquiring about Stormy. That's so sad. I don't know what I would have done if I would have lost one of my babies. I hope that doesn't sound cruel in any way."

"I did not take it that way. It seems like it's harder to deal with since it's the holiday time of the year when families gather for special occasions. I have purchased all the gifts I need except one for my mother. Do you have any ideas?"

Brenda leaned back, raised her eyebrows, and answered, "Gift ideas for your mother? Well, let's see. Not off hand, I don't. She strikes me as being quite a difficult person to buy gifts for, and we sure don't see her in town much. Before your dad died it seemed she sent him in here quite often to get what she wanted. Then after that, the duties must have been assigned to Chet because that's who we see in here every now and then. It's interesting how the men folk in your family seem to do most everything. Does Jantzi just whip out a *Honey Do List* for everyone everyday or what gives? Oh, please forgive me. Our boss coaches us that we must be very friendly to our customers, but that was probably borderline rude and nasty. Those kinds of comments need to be kept to myself. Does your mother like jewelry?"

"Yes, she likes silver jewelry, but I probably can't afford anything that suits her. "

"Speaking of silver," Brenda continued, "I heard that there's a real likelihood that the Sabblonti Ranch is loaded with silver deposits. Is that true?"

"Silver deposits? I have never heard of such a thing. Where on earth would there be silver buried on the family ranch?"

"Well, Sarita, surely you took Earth Science in high school, same as I did," Brenda snapped with a real edge to her voice. "Did you have Mr. Whatchacallie, you know, that science teacher, I can't remember his last name right now? Your sister and I were in the same class, and neither one of us paid any attention as we liked the history classes the best. Who needs science anyway? Talk about a total waste of time!"

"Yes, I did have Mr. Felume for Earth Science and I learned a lot in that class. Come to think of it, parts of the Sabblonti spread are littered with igneous rocks. I can remember seeing them when I would ride during the summer time among the junipers, pines, and quaking aspens in the higher elevations. Now that I have moved to town and am working for Dr. Diller, I don't get out to the ranch very often. The rumor mill around town never takes a holiday or stops running so I don't pay any attention to any of that baloney. I have better things to do with my time."

"Speaking of your time, are you and Wyn Moreland still an item? Somebody told me the reason we don't see him in town is that he doesn't even own a pickup! Can you imagine living in this country and only having a horse? Now that does take one back to the days of the wild, wild west."

"I think my mother would like a lipstick holder for either her bathroom vanity or her leather purse. Do you happen to have anything like that in the store?"

"We do have a few small accessories on Aisle #7 if you would like to join me over there. A couple of days ago when I was rearranging that section, I saw a little metal lipstick holder with fake looking jewels that would hold about three to four tubes. Do you think that's fancy enough for Jantzi Sabblonti?"

Sarita joined Brenda in the area of the small gifts and accessories.

"This is the one I had in mind," Brenda offered. "It's only $29.95 which I think is really steep for something this cheap looking. But then, what do I know? I am only a store clerk. I sure do wish I would have taken some time after I graduated from high school to look around and marry into one of the rich cattle company families in these parts. That would have been so easy to do. But, I was in too big of a hurry, I guess. I have four adorable kids that I wouldn't trade for anything so that's my real prize of the whole deal."

Realizing that nothing she ever purchased or gifted her mother would ever be good enough, Sarita decided the metal lipstick container was as good a gift as any. "Brenda, this holder will be just fine for my mother. Thank you so much for your help."

"You are welcome," Brenda said as she walked toward the cash register. "Would you like any of these gift wrapped? We charge $2.00 per gift for that special service which I think is very reasonable. It's just a little country touch that we try to offer each year."

"Sure, that would be so helpful, and thank you. That will save me a lot of time and energy. How late is the store open so I can plan to pick the gifts up after I get off work this afternoon?"

"The store is open until seven in the evening until Christmas Eve, and after that we will be closing at our normal time of six o'clock. Thank goodness for that since it's already dark by then, and I have to drive home most evenings with my headlights on bright."

Exiting the store and still having some cash reserve from her yearend bonus, Sarita pondered the idea of silver being present in the rock formations on the ranch. She wondered if her mother had filed any mining claims and how would a person go about finding out if there was any truth to the mineral deposits? She supposed she could check with the Shadow Butte County Recorder's office regarding the mining claims, but she really had no interest or energy to start down that road, whether it proved to be crooked or straight, narrow or wide. Speaking of rumors, Sarita could only imagine what had been said in the past about her family, the ranch, and everything that went with that whole enterprise.

The next several days flew by with the flurry of activity in Dr. Diller's office. Many ranching folks were coming into town for their dental appointments this time of year as it tended to be not quite as busy as the spring and summer months. The Shadowy Merc was doing a land office business as well.

It was Dr. Diller's custom to work one half day on Christmas Eve to give his employees time to drive home in the daylight in preparation for time spent with their families in the evening. He had not quite gotten over the fact that as soon as Sarita started working in his office, her mother called and requested her dental records be sent to the local dentist in the next county. After working on Jantzi's teeth for years, Dr. Diller was unable to arrive at a plausible explanation for this, but he had so many patients that it did not really matter. He had made note of Sarita's unusual quiet preoccupation of late, but had said nothing to her since she was a very loyal, competent, and trustworthy employee. Dr. Diller reminded himself that there's oftentimes more than meets the eye to certain situations. Assumption and presumption were precarious plus, to say the least.

CHAPTER TWELVE

"How could this day be here already?" Jantzi demanded as she stomped around the ranch house, and up and down the stairs. "That dread mahawk flu almost put me out of commission and I had no time to lose!" When she glanced at the clock on the kitchen wall, her heart skipped a couple of beats when she realized it was already two in the afternoon.

In her haste to make the dessert for Chet in her iron skillet the night before, she had removed it from the pan too quickly so it resembled an earthquake cake. To that end, Jantzi scoured around and found a bottle of wild red berry syrup that Stormy had given her last year for Christmas. Arranging the chunks of cake on a high rimmed oval serving platter, she dumped the whole bottle on top of the cake. She would just set a large serving spoon at Chet's place setting so he could spoon and slurp the excess syrup. Somehow, he sort of earned this little bit of extra since he took care of so many things for Jantzi, including the pleasant along with the unpleasant.

Jantzi walked from room to room checking to see if everything met with her final approval,

"One, two, three, four, five, yes, all place settings and

dining room are good to go.

"Cake and syrup are secure on serving platter.

"Blue, let's get you fed an early supper before our guests arrive. Since it's a special day, you get an extra can of your favorite beef flavored food. I will mix it with your dry kibbles and stir it up. Do you want me to heat it for you in the microwave? Oh, Blue, my Blue, Jantzi Belle loves you!

"I will take care of Diamantae after everyone leaves tonight. I fed her mid-morning, gave her extra oats and two apples, so she will be fine until later.

"Oh, Ace's silly silver spurs keep falling down from my Christmas fireplace display. I am not going to keep trying to prop them up so they can just fall any old way they want to. I don't have any extra time today to train those spurs to obey me."

Jantzi surveyed the stack of gifts on the corner of the fireplace and realized she had placed Sarita's and Wyn's boxes in the wrong place. She rearranged them so that Stormy's and Chet's were in front. She would plan to stack all other gifts behind theirs or on the floor next to her display, depending upon how many were brought by her dinner guests.

Continuing with her walk through, Jantzi's voiced her mental planning,

"I am going to dump these five cans of soup in this

saucepan. Who cares if the mixture sits on top of the stove for awhile? I will heat it before I serve it so there should be no problem. Food poisoning can't set in that early. Speaking of such, I wonder if that's what happened to me the last few days?

"Oh, I better go and sweep off the front porch. It seems as though the light windstorm that we had blew some pine needles and other sticks right where everyone will be entering the house. I just don't want anything to look messy. Everything has got to look especially inviting tonight. I want Sarita to realize what she is missing by moving to town and living in that dingy apartment. There's no way she can be happy on the second floor residing in a two-bedroom unit. Why, she does not even have access to a washer and dryer and has to lug her well worn clothing to the local Wash 'N Dry. Surely by now she would have realized that when you don't play by the family's rules you lose big time.

"Good grief, I almost forgot that I need to check how much room is on the coat rack to hang everyone's winter jackets when they get here. I don't want to get distracted with little details. Stormy will be in no shape to help me hostess at all tonight. Chet is flat out worthless in that regard.

"I need to get myself ready. I feel like devoting any extra time that I have to that today. Yes, that can be my gift to myself. I must create the overall effect."

When Jantzi reached the thirtieth step of her staircase,

she stopped, looked down, and surveyed her efforts of the past few weeks. "Well done, Jantzi Belle, if I say so myself!"

Flipping through the clothes in her closet, Jantzi located her bright red sequined long-sleeved blouse, red ankle length skirt, red boot socks, and red boots to wear for the evening. She selected a silver necklace and red and white beaded earrings that Chet and Stormy had gifted her four years ago for Christmas.

Dressed to the nines for the occasion, Jantzi sat down in her chair in front of her vanity and carefully laid out her cosmetics. She spent an hour meticulously applying her makeup complete with a medium shade of red lipstick. Three layers of liquid foundation were needed to add a little extra color to her depleted skin tones due to her recent unexpected, unexplained sickness. She had entertained the thought of gathering her long black hair in a ponytail and tying a bright red and green ribbon around it, but opted to just let it hang down for the evening.

Posing in front of her full-length oval mirror, Jantzi smiled from ear to ear as she admired herself. Too bad Ace was not still here to take a picture of his beautiful bride. She was beyond confident that she could lasso any rancher within the entire state to marry her at this point in time. But, then again, it would take far too long to break him to lead, so why even entertain the thought?

CHAPTER THIRTEEN

The last few rays of sunlight streamed through the western windows as Jantzi readied herself for her big event. She was sure that her guests would not stay long so she could dash out and tend to Diamantae once they were gone. Those oversized floodlights Chet had installed on the outside of the barn and shop would really come in handy on nights like tonight.

Chet's pickup could be heard a half mile away before he drove into the driveway and parked under his favorite tree. Actually, it did not become his special spot until Jantzi told him that was the only space in the yard and surrounding area where he was permitted to park. One thing was for sure about Jantzi's number one son-in-law; he only had to be told something once. She reasoned that he must have been raised by a fantastic mother, same as Stormy had been.

Even the weather was cooperating for Jantzi this evening. It was cool and dry, and the road surfaces were still in pretty good shape for this time of year.

Turning off the ignition, getting out his side of the pickup, Chet walked around to the passenger side and opened the door for Stormy. As Jantzi watched from her kitchen window, Chet stood by the pickup door for a few minutes, and it seemed as though he and Stormy were having a rather labored discussion over something. Jantzi secretly hoped that whatever was going on between her daughter and son-in-law would not derail the evening. Nothing had better go south as too much time and effort had been expended on this entire project.

Eventually, Chet extended his right hand to Stormy to help her out of the pickup. She began walking toward the house as Chet opened the door to the back seat and began piling packages onto his left forearm.

When Jantzi answered the front door, she could tell that Stormy had been crying. Extending her arms for a hug, Jantzi comforted her daughter, "Stormy, have you been crying? What on earth is the matter? I want everyone to be oh, so happy tonight. Why, after all, it's Christmas Eve when we all get to be together."

"Oh, it's nothing really, Mother. I tried to take a nap this afternoon, but could not really sleep. When I am sleep deprived, I get really weepy. Don't concern yourself with me tonight. Devote your time and energies to your other guests. I know how nervous it makes you when Wyn is around, so never mind me. I will be fine."

"Stormy, you are the most important thing in the world to me. I just can't bear to see you unhappy. I don't know what I can do to help speed your recovery, and deliver you from this blue slump that you have been in of late. Perhaps after our gift exchange this evening your spirit will be enriched!"

Jantzi held the front door open for Chet as he made three trips to his vehicle to carry in large loads of beautifully adorned gifts.

"My goodness!" exclaimed Jantzi. "Who are all of these gifts for, and who wrapped all of them with the different colored papers complete with special ribbons?"

"None other than your faithful servant," quipped Chet. "Nothing but the best for you, Jantzi Belle. Of course, my lovely wife had to direct me as to which paper and bows to use for which gift since I am red-green color blind. Some of this wrapping paper looks brown to me, and I don't think most people use that color for Christmas gifts. Do you think I get an A+ for my efforts? I even picked out a couple of these gifts myself!"

"Chet, dear, please just lay the gifts here by the front door. I will place them exactly where I want them in the family room," ordered Jantzi. "There is a definite flow and order to this evening. I need to make sure that I am paying attention and don't get distracted."

"No problemo," agreed Chet. "That makes it a whole lot easier for me."

Jantzi busied herself by looking through each package that Chet and Stormy had brought over and stacking them in her order of preference by the corner of the fireplace in the family room.

Chet sauntered into the kitchen and lifted the lid from the saucepan as he inhaled the soup mixture sitting on top of the stove. "Smells good, Jantzi. What kind of concoction, or I mean, what's in the pot for supper?" inquired Chet.

Jantzi answered from the living room, "Oh, it's just a little holiday surprise that I blended together, which I am sure you will enjoy. With Stormy still being quite fatigued and it turning dark so early, I thought we would have sort of a light meal and then retire to the family room to open our gifts. You know, I don't want anything to run too late into the night. The holiday time of the year just puts too many pressures and demands on folks."

"It's half past six, Mother, and Wyn and Sarita are not here yet," Stormy commented with concern in her voice.

"Oh, you know your sister and how uncooperative she can be," chafed Jantzi. "She had to stop at the Toppens to pick up Wyn, and as belligerent as he can be, there's no telling when they will be here. On second thought, that's another reason I am glad that I did not pull out all the stops and plan to fix a big prime rib feast or some such. When you're dealing with unreliable people, it's best to go with a simpler menu. Simple menu for simple people I guess you could say."

Chet was famished and started to walk from the family room into the kitchen once more to open the refrigerator to see if there was something to snack on, but then realized that was probably not a very good idea. Jantzi was not the warm and welcoming type of woman who you could stop by unannounced to visit or help yourself to a snack sitting on her kitchen counter. Everything was by invitation only and on her terms. Chet reminded himself, "Good manners help to keep one in the number one spot."

"I see headlights coming down the lane," reported Chet. "Better late than never as they say." As he glanced at his mother-in-law, he could see that her overly large teeth were clenched and she was not smiling. "Oh, boy, this was going to be a wonderful evening . . ."

Sitting in the living room to remain calm, Jantzi asked, "Chet, can you please answer the front door, let Wyn and Sarita in, and hang up their coats? I need to rest a few more minutes. I don't have my full strength back after being ill the past few days."

Sarita collected her large box of Christmas gifts and purse. After locking her vehicle, she walked slowly toward the front door.

"Good evening, Sarita," greeted Chet. "Where's Wyn? Is someone else bringing him or is he not coming to dinner? I was really looking forward to visiting with him tonight. I have been wondering how things have been going at the Toppens' Ranch lately. Could I take your coat and hang it up for you?"

Jantzi bolted from her chair, rushed to the front door, feigning surprise and regret that Wyn was absent. "Sarita, darling, so good to see you. Why, where's Wyn? I thought for sure that he would be here. Is he not feeling well? I sincerely hope that he has not come down with bronchitis or something worse living in that drafty old bunkhouse this winter. Oh, and as a gag gift, I meant to get some mouse traps at Clinker's Feed Store for Wyn so that he could fend off those rodents as they are really bad in the dead of winter. Can you imagine those creepy things crawling over your face when you are trying to sleep at night? What if they get down inside your covers? Does Wyn even own bed covers or does he sleep in a sleeping bag?"

Bracing herself, Sarita calmly replied, "Good evening everyone. It's nice to see you. Wyn is unable to join us. He wanted me to tell you hello and wish you a Merry Christmas and Happy New Year. Mother, where would you like me to put the gifts?"

"Let me take them from you, Sarita. I have just the perfect spot for them. Please come in and make yourself comfortable."

After a few awkward minutes, Jantzi directed her guests to the dining room. "Okay, everyone, please make note of where your place cards are and get yourselves seated. I am confident that you will enjoy all my special expressions and decorations at the table. Supper will be served shortly."

The atmosphere throughout the house was as thick and suffocating as a giant tub of lard. Stormy seemed preoccupied and was not very talkative, despite Sarita's repeated efforts to reach out to her and spread a bit of holiday cheer.

Jantzi dished the soup into bowls which she placed on a serving tray. She nearly tripped as she was carrying them from the kitchen into the dining room. Since she had filled them to the brim, the mixture sloshed onto the outsides of the bowls and onto the tray. "Oh, mercy me, how could I be such a klutz, anyway? You will just have to wipe the excess from your bowls with your napkins. Sorry about the drip effect. If this is my only mishap of the entire day, I will be doing just fine."

"Mother, I could have helped you if you would have asked," offered Stormy. "I know that you like to be fiercely independent, but everyone needs a little help now and then. That's what family is all about."

"I just wanted to be the All-Time, Happy, Holiday Hostess tonight," charmed Jantzi. "One of my little gifts to all of you this evening is to let you sit while I serve you. After all, I really am quite capable."

"Sounds like a great plan to me!" boomed Chet. "Now, I will have to admit, it's not every day that I get to have the Queen of Diamonds wait on me."

Chet and Jantzi continued to banter off and on throughout the meal while Stormy and Sarita sat in virtual silence, sipping their soup. Sarita was so thankful that Wyn had declined Jantzi's invitation. She knew that he would not tolerate the hypocrisy and spoke his mind when pretense was on parade.

Stormy spoke from her silence, "Mother, everything looks so elegant this evening. I especially enjoy seeing all of the juniper branches, twigs, and berries. They have been my favorites since I was young girl on the ranch. You have given me a great idea for holiday decorating when I have a child of my own. You are the best mother and mother-in-law anyone could ever ask for."

"Agreed," said Chet. "You have been so generous to me since I married into the Sabblonti family. I only wish Ace was here with us tonight. I miss him so much."

At the mention of her father's name, Sarita burst into tears, pushed her chair back from the table, ran into the bathroom, and closed the door. Grabbing the hand towel, Sarita placed it over her face to help muffle her crying sounds. She felt like regurgitating into the bathroom sink.

Jantzi glanced down at Sarita's soup bowl. It looked like only a few spoonfuls had been consumed. Everyone else had eaten every drop of their soup mixture.

"Stormy, will you please go in and see if you can comfort your sister for a few minutes?" requested Jantzi. "With the darkness rolling in, I would like to retire to the family room so we can open gifts and have our dessert and tea before we call it a night."

Without saying a word, Stormy pushed her chair back from the dining room table, stood to her feet, walked down the hall, and tapped lightly on the bathroom door.

"Sarita, it's Stormy. Can I come in for a minute, please?"

Responding to her softness, Sarita slowly opened the door. "Yes, please come in. I am sorry that I started crying. I miss Daddy so much, especially at Christmas. He always called me his *Little Princess*. It seems like it gets more difficult with each passing year."

As Stormy extended her arms to hug her sister, Sarita draped the hand towel over the wall hanger and embraced her sister. Time seemed to fly backwards several decades to when Stormy and Sarita were young girls and used to hug quite often.

"I miss Daddy, too," Stormy said softly. "And I long for the babies that I have lost along with him. Sometimes life seems so unfair. I wonder if the sadness will ever end. I just don't know what I have done to deserve all of this heartache. I am not an unkind or vindictive person."

"I know you're not. As I have told you so many times before, I am so sorry for your miscarriages. If there was anything I could do to change things, I would. I hope you have a dozen kids someday! Well, maybe not a dozen . . . how about a half dozen?"

Stormy laughed out loud, "A dozen kids? Are you for real? Would you help Chet and me raise some of them? Since I like girls better than boys, how about I ship my boys, if I ever have any, to your place so that you can raise them?"

"It's wonderful to hear you laugh out loud, Stormy. "

"Agreed. It's a far more extravagant gift than whatever you wrapped up for me in the package you brought over this evening. The best things in life are not things. The invaluable things are people and the memories you make with them. You can't put a price tag on those."

Stormy gave her sister one more hug, "I will love you forever."

The sisters walked down the long hallway with their arms around each other's waist. As they rounded the corner into the dining room, Sarita heard the ever-familiar sound of her mother's long, curved, talon-shaped fingernails drumming on the table. She reminded herself that yes, it was indeed a very good idea that she had moved into town and secured an apartment of her own. It may not be fancy in some people's estimation, but peace had its own price tag and redeeming features.

CHAPTER FOURTEEN

"Shall we transition into the family room so we can open some gifts?" encouraged Jantzi. "More time has elapsed than what I had allotted for our meal this evening. I need to train time to obey me."

"Nice juniper log on the fire, Jantzi," commented Chet. "There's just nothing better than sitting around the fire and chatting for a spell. Good gravy, look at all those presents! I guess Santa Claus found the Sabblonti Ranch a little early on his reindeer ride from the North Pole this year. We will be another three hours just opening them. I could imagine seeing a passel of gifts that big if there were little kids running all around. But we're all big kids. I'll bet somebody shelled out a chunk of change for all that merch."

"Yes, it does seem like we ended up with a lot more gifts than normal this year," agreed Jantzi. "Now, I am going to play Mrs. Santa Claus, and I will pass out this big stack of gifts, but you must wait to open them until I give you permission. If some of you end up with more gifts than others, I don't want to hear any complaining. That's really in poor taste for adults to do any grumbling at Christmas."

Jantzi picked up the gift closest to the ledge of the fireplace, walked over to where Stormy was sitting, and placed it in her lap.

Instinctively, Stormy lifted the ornately wrapped box and shook it. "Wow, this is as light as a feather! Is there a gift certificate in here?"

"Now remember what I said," snapped Jantzi. "Do not even think of opening any of your gifts until I have distributed every single one of them. Children, you must obey."

Plucking a package from the large stack, Jantzi approached Chet and set it on his lap. He fingered the silver ribbon, and commented on the meticulous wrapping job of metallic red paper and blue juniper berries on top. Jantzi was amazed that Chet even knew what the word *meticulous* meant.

Stormy continued to compliment her mother, "Yes, Chetter, everything Mommie does is meticulous, carefully detailed, and orchestrated. Everyone who obeys benefits by the boatloads, or should I say, the horse trailer loads!"

"So true, Stormy darling, so true," cooed Chet. "There are many advantages of marrying into the Sabblonti family. In fact, that was one of the things I was going to talk to Wyn about during our evening together. If he played his cards right, he just might be able to end up being Jantzi's other prized son-in-law. Too bad he chose to stay home in that old, cold, bunkhouse. That's no way to spend the holidays. Of course, when you grow up in a boy's home, there's really not much hope for you, and your horizons are not very broad. I guess it's no surprise that he's such a loser, I mean loner, and drifter."

"I think we should change the course of our conversation," Sarita reminded those in attendance. "If there is ever a time during the year to be genuinely kind and generous, even in our speech, it should be now. Is this how all of you express yourselves when Wyn and I are not around? If so, I am thankful that I have spent my time elsewhere in more hospitable company."

"This is the perfect time to present your gift to you, Sarita," sniped Jantzi. "Yours comes with a clue that I will demonstrate to everyone."

Stomping toward the corner of the room where the gifts were stacked, Jantzi selected Sarita's package, returned, and held it in front of her. Sarita did not move a muscle. Walking dramatically back to the front of the fireplace while viciously ripping the wrapping paper off, Jantzi reached inside the box and grabbed a handful of $100 bills. She whirled around and began to drop the bills, one at a time, into the fireplace. Raring back on her heels, Jantzi let out an eerie cackle from her innermost being.

"Sarita, anything that you ever hoped to get from me is going up in smoke tonight. Your inheritance burns brightly. Do you understand me? Ever since you were old enough to walk and talk, you have been insubordinate to me, and I will tolerate it no longer! You will have no portion, right, or privilege as long as I am the head of the Sabblonti family."

Jumping to her feet, Sarita replied in an even tone, "You can have your money, and the trappings that go with it. May your money perish with you if you do not repent of your wicked ways. You are blinded by pride and evil ambition, but you have never been able to recognize it. You have given me something far more valuable than money. You have brought me to the realization that I can choose freedom or bondage. I choose freedom from your control, and Stormy, you can make the same choice. I hope you follow suit. Mother, I am dealing myself out of your calculated card game. I am no longer a joker in your hand!"

Bolting for the front door, Sarita swung it open and ran into the front yard. Blue raced after her.

CHAPTER FIFTEEN

Jantzi rushed up the flights of stairs into her master bedroom, grabbed Ace's 30-30 rifle from the corner of the wall nearest her bed, and pushed the western window wide open. Shoving the rifle barrel through the screen, she fired one shot into the dark. Blue let out a loud yelp, and Jantzi feared that she had killed him.

Stormy crossed the threshold of her mother's bedroom screaming, "Mother, Mother, have you gone completely mad? Why are you trying to shoot my sister?" She ran to the window and grabbed for the gun to wrest it from her mother. Jantzi fired off another round which went through the bedroom ceiling. In an adrenaline rush providing extra strength to Stormy, she shoved her mother backwards into the bedroom window. Jantzi lost her balance, and fell thirty feet to the ground. Stormy's heart sank as she looked out the window and heard a loud thud.

Stormy raced back down the stairs pleading for help from her husband, "Chet, Chet, where are you? Why didn't you come upstairs and help me try to rescue my mother from herself? Chet, I need you. Please answer me."

Once she got outside, Stormy ran to find her mother's limp broken body lying on the ground. The blunt force trauma from the impact of hitting the ground so violently had killed Jantzi instantly. Blood oozed from her mouth. Stormy had to shoo Blue away from the pool which was starting to form on the ground.

Falling upon her mother's chest, Stormy began to sob uncontrollably. Suddenly she leaned back and screamed at the top of her lungs, "Somebody help me! My mother died because of me. How will I ever be able to forgive myself?"

Nothing seemed to move in the darkness. Blue was lying by Jantzi's body. As Stormy looked down the lane, she saw Sarita's tail lights. It was obvious that she had driven off before her mother plummeted to her demise. But where was Chet?

Once again Stormy summoned her husband, "Chet, please come and help me. I cannot take care of this situation by myself!"

Stormy sat down on the cold ground in the center of the front yard. She was uncertain as to how much time had passed when she became chilled and her body began to shake. As she narrowed her focus and looked toward Chet's pickup, she thought she saw his silhouette in the front seat.

Jumping to her feet, Stormy ran to the driver's side of the pickup and opened the door. Chet was slumped over the steering wheel. Fearing that he had suffered a heart attack, Stormy began shaking her husband. He sat upright in the driver's seat.

"Chet, are you alright? What is the matter with you? Have you not witnessed what just transpired at the Sabblonti Ranch? How could you not step up to the plate and intervene since you are the only man on the scene?"

"Stormy, the last thing on earth I was going to do was run up those wicked steep stairs and follow your mother into her bedroom. That's the height of indecency! How was

I supposed to know what a tragic turn of events this would all turn out to be and that this would be the last day of your mother's life? You cannot lay that blame at my feet. I will not accept it. My grandfather worked in the lumber mills, and he told me when I was eight years old, 'Never run into a buzz saw.' When all of this commotion started tonight, it was as if I literally heard the sound of a buzz saw in my head. That's why I retreated to my pickup so that I could stay out of the fray."

"The worst of it is," lamented Stormy, "I don't think Sarita even knows that our mother is gone."

"You better get inside the house, Stormy, call the sheriff's office, the ambulance, and get things moving in the right direction," ordered Chet.

After placing the calls to the proper authorities, Stormy retreated outside to the front yard. Chet was still sitting in his pickup with the window rolled down. Stormy leaned against the vehicle. It was as if she was paralyzed in time and could not think, reason, or speak. The blaring siren and flashing lights of the first responders could be heard in the stillness of the night.

CHAPTER SIXTEEN

"Well, if it isn't the one and only Shadow Butte emergency crew," snarled Chet as he emerged from the front seat of his pickup. "I'm sure glad there was nothing needing immediate attention here tonight. It took you guys forever to get out here. I guess you will know who it will be filing the complaint at the next County Commissioner's meeting."

"Watch your words," warned the paramedic. "Shadow Butte seems to be having a very bad night all the way around. Every one of our crew members have been called to other emergencies. Some of the locals started their Christmas Eve celebrations at high noon, and there have been injuries from bar fights and all kinds of craziness. There's a big fire at the J. T. Robbin's Ranch on the other end of the county which is a long way from here. Alright, tell us what happened."

Stormy led the paramedics to the side of the house and gestured to the ground where Jantzi was lying. She briefly explained how the evening had evolved with the tragic demise of her mother. Chet stood behind Stormy to lend support to her small physical frame when she talked to the first responders.

"We've heard all we need to hear," stated the captain of the crew. "You better save some of your strength to talk to the sheriff when he arrives."

Jantzi's lifeless body was loaded onto a gurney, draped with a blanket, and loaded into the EMS vehicle. Chet, Stormy, and Blue followed closely behind.

Chet spotted a set of headlights turning from the main road onto the lane leading into the Sabblonti Ranch. "I would imagine this is the county mounty heading our way right now. I just hope it's one of the deputies, and not Sheriff Jensen. I've heard that he can be a real project, and our night has been difficult enough already."

The driver of the EMS vehicle waited in the front yard until the Shadow Butte County sheriff's pickup pulled into the driveway. Chet could see that it was a deputy that had been dispatched for which he was grateful. The officer walked over to the driver's side of the EMS vehicle and motioned for the driver to roll the window down. The two men exchanged a few words, and the EMS vehicle headed down the lane toward town.

The deputy returned to his pickup to gather a tape recorder, clipboard, and various other items before entering the front yard. Extending his right hand to Chet, he stated, "Hi folks, I'm Deputy Dennis Whillson from the Shadow Butte County sheriff's office. It sounds like you have had a pretty tough night out here at the Sabblonti Ranch. I apologize it took me so long to respond, but we have had some head spinners happening in these parts. I've worked for the county for fifteen years now, and have never seen anything bunched up quite like this. Shall we go inside so I can sit down, please?"

"Sounds like a good plan, Deputy Whillson," agreed Chet. "Can I get you a cup of coffee? Never mind, I plum took leave of my senses. This isn't even my kitchen, yet . . . I meant to say, this isn't even my kitchen. Stormy and I live down at the lower ranch house."

"No need to stand on formalities or manners tonight, Chet. I appreciate the offer, but let's wade into the duties at hand here, shall we? Now, I am going to turn on this recorder, and I will ask each of you to give your account of the happenings. Please don't talk over one tother 'cause if you do, the clerk will be really chapped with me. She likes it when one person talks at a time, and not a bunch trying to talk over the top of one another, even if they aren't wearing big tall cowboy hats. I can't see what difference it makes, but she can be kind of persnickety. I think it's just 'cause she's older and has worked for the county too long. You know how that goes. Well, on second thought, maybe you don't. Some of us folks have to work for a living. We don't have everything handed to us on a silver platter with a silver "S" engraved in the middle with silver spurs dangling from the sides."

Stormy felt Chet stiffen at the deputy's snide remarks, and reached down to pat his left hand to signal the importance of remaining calm.

"Are you two comfortable here at this kitchen table or shall we go into the family room?" asked Deputy Whillson.

"We can go into the family room if you like," replied Stormy. "The chairs are far more comfortable, and since we don't know how long this is going to take, it might be better."

Deputy Whillson walked into the family room and stopped abruptly. He blinked hard, and stepped back as he drank in the charred scraps of $100 bills that littered the hearth in front of the fireplace. "What in the name of glory is this on the floor? Now this truly is a first in all of my law enforcement career. I have heard that saying, 'If I had your money, I would burn mine,' but I always thought it was just a joke. Was the Sabblonti Family having a money burning contest tonight or what? Yep, sometimes truth is stranger than fiction. Stormy, I sense that I need to commence with your account of the evening. Now, start from the very beginning of when you first arrived out here tonight and don't leave any details out of the story as everything little thing is important. Take as long as you need to as I can only imagine how traumatic all of this has been for you. Come to think of it, let's just pull some chairs around this coffee table. Would that be alright with you?"

"Thank you, Deputy Whillson, and I will try to remember as much as I can. Never in my lifetime did I ever imagine anything as horrific as these past few hours have been."

As the deputy set his recorder on the coffee table, Stormy began to recount the details of the evening. There were times that her emotions overcame her and she needed to stop, get up, walk around for a few minutes to regain her composure, and start speaking again.

The old family clock bonged eleven times. "I am completely exhausted, Deputy Whillson," Stormy said as she slumped down in her chair. "Do you think I have given you a sufficient statement? I am completely drained and cannot recall another thing. It's too late and I'm too spent."

"I think you've painted a pretty complete picture, Stormy," reassured Deputy Whillson. "Chet, do you have anything else of importance that you can add or has Stormy pretty much summed up what happened? I am not standing in judgment of you, but it does strike me quite odd that you just skeedaddled out to your pickup truck and holed up there while there was shooting going on and your mother-in-law fell to her death. I am not intending to be unkind here, but that is something folks would see in a western movie. Sad to say, there was no movie filming going on here tonight."

Chet arched his back as he mounted his defense, "No, Deputy, I really don't have much else to add to Stormy's account. I did not run up the stairs and enter Jantzi's bedroom for obvious reasons. How was I supposed to know that she kept a loaded gun up there? The only time I ever heard from Jantzi Belle Sabblonti was when she had prepared my to-do list, called me up, and reeled it off. In real life, I was scared to death of her. She took intimidation to a whole new level. I figured out a long time ago to just do as she ordered and keep my mouth shut. She did an awful lot of nice things for me. I never once questioned her motives for why she did what she did. You have no right to come in here tonight and drop any kind of insinuations as to how you think this family might have operated. That's completely out of your boundaries and jurisdiction. I cannot stand confrontation, so I headed to a safe quiet place which was the cab of my pickup. A lot of family gatherings get out of control around the holidays as that's when people let their hair down and are really themselves. That's when things can turn ugly, just like they did here tonight. I seriously thought Sarita would just tear out of here and head home, and Jantzi would boil up the stairs, stay up there a few minutes until she cooled off, come back down the stairs, and we would finish opening gifts and call it a night. That's what I have to say about all of this business. You can't pull something out of me that I don't have in me, so don't even try."

"Chet, don't get riled up," cautioned Deputy Whillson. "I can only imagine how trying and tragic this whole episode has been. I am truly sorry for your loss." He reached down, turned his recorder off, and placed it inside its holster on his belt.

"Well, sad as it all is, everything sounds pretty straightforward and innocent to me," surmised Deputy Whillson. "I am going to walk around inside and outside the house and yard and take some pictures, and then I will be on my way. I'll give my report and pictures to Sheriff Jensen so he can take it from there. I don't know how long it will take to process all of this. As I said, the county officials have been real busy tonight. One thing about Sheriff Jensen, though, is that he is really thorough and fair. After the last election and Sheriff Koslen was voted out of office due to his lackadaisical practices, the powers to be tightened the reins, and we are riding herd a whole lot better these days."

"How do we proceed with mother's arrangements, Deputy Whillson?" inquired Stormy. "Her end came much sooner than I ever thought it would. I don't even know where to start."

"Since tomorrow is Christmas Day, you can go to Lambent's Funeral Home on Monday, and they can help you with whatever you need. They have some real nice folks working there and they have oodles of mercy to pour out to the whole community. I have seen them do it time after time after time. I would imagine that Donna Bosticker, the county coroner, would determine the cause of death as being accidental, so there should be no issues there. But, again, I want to emphasize that's only my opinion. You can't take that one to the bank. As far as the ranch goes, do you know if your parents had a will made out ahead of time?"

At the mention of a will, Stormy and Chet squared their shoulders and lifted their chins simultaneously. "Will?" they questioned in unison.

"As big of an operation as this ranch has been for decades, I would hope someone had the foresight to have some paperwork in place," remarked Chet. "It will be a real cattle corral mess if all of that gnarly business has not been spelled out somewhere. Leave it to you law enforcement people to think of everything, even when the timing does not seem the best. The last thing on my mind tonight is a piece of paper reading, 'Last Will and Testament of Thus and Such.'"

"Mine, too," lamented Stormy.

While Deputy Whillson walked around taking pictures of whatever he deemed important, Chet and Stormy sat in stone silence in the living room of the Sabblonti ranch house. When they heard the deputy depart in his vehicle, the two of them rose from their seats, walked out the front door, got in their vehicle, and prepared to drive home.

Blue, Diamantae, and the other critters belonging to the Sabblonti enterprise would just have to fend for themselves until someone remembered them.

More importantly, who was going to call Sarita and give her the bad news?

CHAPTER SEVENTEEN

"What time is it now?" Chet asked, as he drove from the main ranch house down to the lower ranch house where he and Stormy lived.

Stormy looked down at the silver analog watch complete with pearl insets that her mother had given her five years ago for her birthday. Pressing the side feature which allowed her to see the time in the darkness, she replied, "It's half past one. Why do you want to know?"

"Well, I am just trying to decide when we should visit Sarita to let her know your mother is no longer with us. I mean, if it was my mother that had died, I would certainly want to know as soon as possible."

"Yes, I have been wondering if we should wait until Christmas morning to go see her."

"It's already Christmas in case you had forgotten."

"Give me a break, Chet. I have just lost the most important thing in the whole wide world," sobbed Stormy. "How could you be so insensitive and uncaring? Why, you ran to the pickup like a coward when all badness broke loose. What kind of a man are you anyway? Even a child would have tried to help. But not you. I can't even think of a way to describe you right now. Maybe it's a good thing we have never been able to have any kids. Even a newborn would probably be more of an adult than you are."

"Do you want to walk home tonight, Stormy? If not, I would advise you to think before you speak. It's times like these that you remind me a whole lot of your mother. You have no clue the amount of sweat equity I have invested in your whole Sabblonti charade. I am not about to toss nine years of my life out the window. Don't forget that this is a community property state."

"You're right, Chet. I am sorry that I spoke to you the way that I did. Please cut me some slack as I don't know if I am a foot or horseback at this point in time. Can you please turn around, drive to town, and let's swing by Sarita's apartment to see if she is asleep?"

There was not another word spoken between Chet and Stormy for the remainder of the drive into Ridgemonte and the final stop in the parking area adjacent to the building where Sarita lived. It was the old Greystone Motel that had been converted into apartments.

Stormy looked at the metal stairs rising along the side of the building to the balcony that led around the corner to Sarita's apartment. "What a shabby dwelling for Daddy's little princess," she thought.

"Let me walk up the stairs first to see if there are any lights on in her apartment," Stormy directed. "If so, I will go to the end of the balcony and motion for you to come up so that we can break the news to her together."

Stormy slowly climbed the stairs to the balcony. When she rounded the corner, she saw that there was a dim light shining in the kitchen window of the apartment. Walking back to the corner of the balcony, Stormy gave Chet the thumbs-up signal.

Stormy waited for Chet to climb the stairs. When they

stopped in front of Sarita's apartment, she gripped his right hand and tapped lightly on the door. They waited in silence for what seemed an eternity, and walked a few feet to head back down the stairs when the door opened slightly.

Running softly back to the door, Stormy spoke through the crack, "Sarita, are you still up? Can we come in and talk with you?"

Stormy and Chet waited at the door for a few more minutes.

"Sarita, I have something very important to tell you," Stormy pleaded. "I know that you are upset about what happened at the ranch tonight, but please let us come inside."

Sarita cautiously opened the door to her apartment. Her disheveled appearance revealed that she had been crying since leaving the family dinner and driving home alone. Without saying a word, she gestured for Chet and Stormy to come in and sit down.

"Wow, this is one small apartment! Maybe it's just because it's so dark in here. Don't you have any lights you can turn on so we can see one another? Or do you live in darkness so you can save money on your monthly power bill? No wonder you seem so down and out all of the time."

"I will turn on the light in the hallway," Sarita conceded. "That should shed enough light on what needs to be said right now."

"Sarita," Stormy proceeded cautiously, "There's no easy way to tell you this, but after Mother fired off that one shot at you when you ran through the front yard, I bolted upstairs to see what was going on. I tried to grab Daddy's 30-30 away from her, but she was standing too close to the open window, lost her balance, and fell to the ground. She did not make it. She died suddenly when she hit the ground so hard. I am still in shock."

Upon hearing the news of her mother's demise, Sarita buried her face in her hands and began to whimper. Time seemed to pass ever so slowly as Chet, Stormy, and Sarita sat in the eerie quiet of her humble abode. No one seemed to be in a hurry to go anywhere.

Sarita rested her head on the back of her rocking chair. Looking at the living room ceiling, she spoke ever so softly, "Stormy, you cannot blame me for Mother's death. I will not allow you or anyone else to do so. I did not kill her. She has despised me since I was a young child. I looked different and there was no way I could ever measure up to her standards. I gave up trying a long time ago. I made a definite decision to no longer be a joker in her game."

"Sarita, I am not blaming you or accusing you of anything to do with Mother's passing. I think that your whole perception of your childhood is skewed, and that you are not looking at it in a proper perspective. Mother loved you just as much as she loved me. You were Daddy's favorite and everybody knew that. I did not take up an offense against Daddy because of that. Granted, Mother always wore the pants and ruled the roost, but Daddy was a good person, none the less. Chet and I love you, and we want to keep our family together. I even stood up for you when Mother would attack Wyn. You need to realize that she was my mother, too."

Chet interjected, "It's been a very long night, and it's Christmas Day already. Stormy, I suggest we go home and get some sleep, if that's even possible. Sarita, I hope you can rest for a few hours. Come to think of it, somebody needs to go back to the ranch and check on the animals. Stormy and I will plan to do that later today. Sarita, do you want to join us at the main ranch house around four thirty this afternoon so we can start talking about making a few important decisions?"

"Nothing personal, but I am not going to commit to any certain time frame for anything right now. The two of you can take care of Mother's arrangements. Just give me a call and let me know when the funeral services will be. This is the best time to be making a clean break. Deal me out of anything to do with the Sabblonti card game from this point forward. Compromise and control always come with a price I am not willing to pay nor can I afford long term."

"I am sorry that you feel this way, Sarita," Chet commented. "Somehow along the path of your life, you seemed to venture in the wrong direction to your own detriment. After you give it some thought, you can always get back on the right track. It's been perfectly blazed for you and your sister."

"It may have been prepared for my sister, but I am not so sure about that for myself. My road seemed pretty bumpy and full of boulders and potholes."

Reaching down and gathering her purse next to the love seat where she was sitting, Stormy rose and started toward the front door. "Sarita, I echo Chet's sentiments, and remember, we are here if you need us. We will be in touch."

Closing the apartment door behind her early morning visitors, Sarita turned the light off and retired to her small bedroom to rest her weary soul.

CHAPTER EIGHTEEN

Sunlight danced softly through the ivory lace curtains in Sarita's bedroom. She rolled onto her left side to look at the clock on her nightstand. She blinked twice to determine if she had read it correctly. "Three in the afternoon!" she exclaimed as she completed a log roll and placed her feet on the warm oval rug. "Am I living a nightmare or am I back in real life?" she questioned herself out loud.

Securing her heirloom brush from the drawer of her nightstand, Sarita began brushing her long straight chocolate brown hair. "World, can you just go away today? That would be the best Christmas gift you could give me."

After she showered and dressed in something that would lend cheer, Sarita collected Wyn's gift, stepped outside, and locked the door to her apartment. Glancing down at the light brown mat showcasing a large black capital letter "S", she caught the glimpse of the corner of a red envelope. She retrieved it, tore it open, and removed the folded piece of paper.

"Sarita, when you did not show up at the bunkhouse earlier today, I asked Merna Toppens to give me a ride into town so I could check on you. We heard some sirens blaring last night that sounded like they were in the direction of the

Sabblonti Ranch. I knocked on your apartment door as loudly as I could but nobody answered. Since I did not want to keep Merna waiting very long, and she had a brunch planned at the Toppens' Ranch, I figured I better head back with her. Merna wanted me to tell you that you are welcome to come to Christmas Dinner at their house tonight if you like. Somehow, I sense that something is terribly wrong. I am concerned about you. Can you at least call me at the bunkhouse so that I will know you are alright? I love you, Wyn."

Sarita stuffed the paper inside her purse and headed down the stairs. Driving to the Toppens Ranch afforded her some time to collect her thoughts. Entering the ranch property, she drove past the house and down to the bunkhouse. She knocked on the door three times, but there was no answer. She called out Wyn's name. He emerged from inside the barn where he had been doing his chores earlier than normal since the Toppens family guests were gathering for dinner in a short while.

Brushing the hay leaves from his jacket and removing his gloves, Wyn approached Sarita. "Ah, look at me, Sarita, all covered with hay leaves and grain dust. I wanted to get cleaned up before I saw you today. Can I give you a hug anyway?"

"Of course you can, Wyn," Sarita said as she slumped onto his chest, and began to cry. "The most terrible thing in the whole universe has happened!"

"Oh, come on now, Sarita, it can't be that bad. I am right in the middle of feeding the horses and heifers. Can you come inside the barn and sit on the bench so we can talk? Besides, it's still a bit chilly out here now that the wind has picked up a notch or two."

"Sure, Wyn, that would be great. I just want to be where you are. You are my only source of comfort right now and the only person that I can fully trust. I will sit here in the quiet of the barn while you finish your chores. Then I can explain everything to you."

"I'm sorry there's no privacy in the bunkhouse so we can talk. The Toppens family is so kind and generous to allow a few of us cow hands to live there right now. Merna Toppens has to be the sweetest, most loving older woman that I have ever met. I sort of think of her as my adopted mother since my birth mother never really wanted me and put me on the doorstep of the boy's home. This isn't very fancy inside here but then again, maybe the critters would consider it so! We could talk in here for a while if you wanted to." Grabbing a horse blanket off the wall, Wyn draped it over Sarita's shoulders as she began to recount the last few hours of her life.

Wyn sat on some sacks of grain across from Sarita as she painstakingly retold everything that had happened from the time she arrived at the Sabblonti Ranch for the Christmas Eve dinner. Tears welled up in his eyes during portions of Sarita's retelling of the events. Sarita reached into her purse and offered some tissues to Wyn to dry his eyes and blow his nose.

"I don't know what to say or what to do at a time like this," confessed Wyn. "We learned a lot of things in the boy's home, but never how to handle anything like what you have just experienced. I would be dishonest if I told you that I thought your mother liked me. It's sort of ironic, in a different sort of way, but both of us are motherless now."

"We have more in common than you might realize, Wyn

Moreland. Your mother obviously had her reasons as to why she gave you away at such a young age. Who is to know if she had the chance, and there would have been a graceful way to do it, that my mother would not have chosen to do the same thing? It was my dad who always showed me that he really cared about me. All of Mother's efforts were poured into Stormy. True love cannot be feigned, manufactured, or purchased. People instinctively know if they are loved or not. If one removes money and possessions from the picture, motive rises to the top like cream from the milk of a Jersey cow. You can't miss seeing it if you tried."

"Well, I can't say as I have ever seen cream rise to the top from the milk of a Jersey cow, but I will agree that it paints a pretty good word picture," Wyn said as he laughed for the first time that day.

Looking down at her watch, Sarita informed Wyn that the Toppens' dinner would start in one hour.

"Can you wait here just a couple more minutes, Sarita? I have something for you."

"Oh, and I have something for you as well! While you walk to the bunkhouse, I will get my things from my vehicle and be right back."

Holding the barn door open for Sarita, Wyn gestured for her to enter. "After you, my sweet. Or shall I call you my princess?"

"You are so kind, Wyn. I like how you refer to me as 'My Sweet.' Daddy always called me his little princess, so I would like to preserve that special memory of him in my heart."

"'My Sweet' it will be," Wyn said with firm approval.

Placing the blue, red, and yellow horse blanket around

her shoulders once again, Sarita handed Wyn his Christmas gift.

"I hope you like it, and I think you will find it will come in real handy during the winter."

Picking up his gift, Wyn shook it from side to side. "My, the wrapping job looks like it was done by an expert. I can remember how excited all of us would get at the boy's home as we gathered around the big tree each Christmas morning. One of the benefits of living out here in the big wide-open spaces is that we get to see a lot of real pine trees. The tree at the home was one of those fake jobs, but we just got used to it year after year and were thankful to have it. Each of us in the home received one gift a year and we had to open them in alphabetical order. Before we opened it, we would shake it and try to guess what it was. I was never really very good at those guessing games. To me, they are a complete waste of time."

"Go ahead and open it then, Wyn. I really wanted you to try to guess what it is, but now that I think about it, you really are not into games."

"No, not into games, Sarita, but I do like gifts that are given from the heart, and I am sure this one is."

"Wyn, you are correct about that."

"The male part of me just wants to rip this paper and bow off in one fell swoop," chuckled Wyn. "But I want you to know that I did learn manners growing up in the boy's home."

Gently removing the paper and opening the box, Wyn grabbed the green blanket with a blue border featuring a bay mare with her foal standing in a meadow. Pulling it to his face he commented, "This is just perfect, Sarita! Someday I hope to own a ranch with a big meadow where lots of mares with their foals can graze securely. What a serene picture. Thank you for putting so much thought into my gift."

"You are more than welcome, Wyn."

"Time is marching on so I want you to close your eyes and hold out your hands. This package is so big you might not be able to hold it with both hands. But we shall see what we shall see, shall we?"

Wyn placed the box inside Sarita's hands. "You can open your eyes now, Sarita."

"This is some kind of first-rate wrapping job if I say so myself. Did you also have exquisite wrapping lessons as part of your curriculum at the boy's home?"

"True confession time, Sarita," explained Wyn as he looked down at the ground, and pushed a bit of dirt with his work boot. "Merna Toppens helped me wrap it. She let me pick out the paper and the bow. She said I didn't need one of those stickers for the package as you would know it was from me. Turnabout is fair play. Since you were the one who pushed to try to guess the contents of the gift, give me your best one."

Smiling for the first time in hours, Sarita shook the small square package from side to side. "What's that sound that I hear? It seems like there's something floating around inside the box. You didn't put some kind of rodent or insect in here to play a practical joke on me, did you? Trust me when I tell you that I am not in the mood for any kind of pranks or jokes."

"Now don't get on your high horse, Sarita. You have really underestimated me if you thought I would do something like that, especially on the biggest gift giving day of the year. And it's not like it's April Fool's Day or some such. Cut me some slack, and have a little bit more faith in me, will you?"

"Wyn, I'm sorry for being short with you. Even though I got some sleep, you can tell that I need a whole lot more."

"Enough with the trying to guess business, and open your gift. I only wish I had a camera to take your picture when you reveal the contents."

Warily, Sarita unwrapped the box. "What is this tape anyway? Is it some sort of clue as to what's inside? Wyn Moreland, I am just about fit to be tied getting to know you!"

Sarita cautiously removed the five strips of one-half-inch wide black electrician's tape from the top of the box. Looking inside, she discovered that it was a box of long grain brown rice. "Seriously, Wyn, are you trying to give me a hint that you want me to fix dinner for you or what? And since when does rice come in unmarked brown square boxes? Somehow, I can't believe that Merna's fingerprints are all over this project. Are you sure that your bunkhouse buddies did not con you into doing something to embarrass me?"

"Hold on a minute, Sarita. I have the perfect idea." Reaching for the metal grain bowl and wiping it out with his shirt tail, Wyn took the box from Sarita's hand. "Shall I dump the contents into the bowl so that you can see you can trust me?"

"Sure, why not? That way if there is something that's alive in the box I can get outside the barn in a hurry. I mean, who gets a box of rice for Christmas?"

"Sit tight and discover your delight," Wyn waxed poetically.

With great fanfare, Wyn slowly emptied the plain square box into the metal bowl as Sarita stayed fixated on the contents. Exercising great finesse, he was able to dump just about every grain of rice into the bowl before the rectangular shaped blue velvet box tumbled onto the small pile inside the bowl.

Peering intently into Wyn's eyes, Sarita remarked, "Um, I think I know what it might be now. You know how much I love jewelry! A while back I saw you studying my ears and the length of my neck. I am guessing you were trying to decide what kind of earrings I might like. Am I correct?"

"No hints," warned Wyn as he moved closer to Sarita, picked up the velvet container, opened her right hand and gently wrapped her slender fingers around it.

One would have thought there was a miniature invisible snake inside the box given the amount of caution with which Sarita proceeded to open her Christmas gift. If she thought there was jewelry inside, there was no need to wait so long. Steadying the box in her left hand and lifting the lid with her right, she suddenly let out a squeal of delight! "Oh, Wyn Moreland, how did you?"

"How did I what?"

"It's absolutely beautiful!" Sarita exclaimed with tears flowing once again.

Bending down on both knees on the barn floor, Wyn carefully removed the white gold engagement ring from the box. Taking Sarita's left hand, he slipped the ring onto her finger.

"It fits perfectly! But how did you know what size of ring I wore? And how did you get into town to purchase it? More importantly, how did you pay for it, Wyn?"

"I knew if I chose the correct size that it would be a sure sign to me that you were the one I was supposed to marry. As for how I managed to get to town to make the purchase, don't concern your beautiful self with those details. There's no end to folks willing to help at the Toppens Ranch. As for the money to pay for the ring, a lady never asks a gentleman those sorts of personal questions."

Blushing while kneeling and looking around the horse barn, Wyn took both of her hands and asked, "Sarita, would you do me the honor of being my beloved wife for all our remaining days on earth? I love you the world full, and I promise to honor and cherish you. Life is worth living just because of you."

"Wyn, of course I will! I want you to know that I will stand with you no matter what or who attempts to come against us. Genuine love honors and protects."

Standing to their feet they embraced for what seemed not nearly long enough.

"About that rice," Wyn explained, "That was Merna's idea. She said that rice is symbolic of blessings and after the wedding ceremony, people sprinkle rice on the bride and groom to offer their blessings upon the marriage. I don't know if it's just an old wives tale or what, but it sounded good to me. I want all of the blessings life has in store for me. It seems like I have been robbed of mine until the day I met you. That's why I wanted to save every grain that I could from the box when having you open your gift. I'm going to put the rice back in the box and save it for our wedding day."

"That's interesting about the rice. I had never heard that before. When Stormy and Chet got married in the meadow, it was just a very simple country ceremony. People mostly showed up for the big barbeque afterwards. If you don't hurry up and get cleaned up for dinner, we will be late. Here, don't forget to put your new blanket in the bunkhouse."

Sarita got inside her old Light Saddle Metallic Ford Bronco, turned on the ignition, and adjusted the heat inside while she waited for Wyn. Emerging within a few minutes, Sarita was amazed at how much quicker a man could ready himself for an occasion compared to a woman.

Sarita parked in the driveway next to Merna's truck. Walking to the front door and holding Wyn's hand she expressed her concerns, "I don't want to throw a damper on the Toppens' Christmas Dinner by having to explain what happened to my mother last night. Can you please go inside and ask Merna if she can come outside so that I can talk with her for a few minutes before the meal?"

Sarita stood on the front porch while Wyn went inside to locate Merna. As soon as he opened the front door, Sarita could hear about thirty people talking simultaneously. She wondered if she should just politely excuse herself and not worry about trying to get through a big, neighborly meal and all that entailed on an evening such as this.

Merna came outside wearing a very concerned expression on her face. "Sarita, you wanted to talk to me? I thought for sure you would be spending tonight at the ranch with your family."

"Didn't Wyn tell you? Something terrible happened last night at the ranch house after I left. Mother fell from her bedroom window to her death."

"Oh, no, child! Does Wyn know about this?"

"Yes, he knows everything that led up to the tragic event, and all of the gory details starting with when I went to the house for Christmas Eve dinner. He has my permission to tell you privately. I don't want to be rude and cast a shadow over your dinner tonight. Thank you for all of your kindness extended to Wyn and the other men who live in the bunkhouse. Merry Christmas, Merna, and I think I should drive back to my apartment in town. The past twenty-four hours have seemed like ninety-six, at least."

Merna hugged Sarita, told her that she was sorry to hear of her mother's death, and offered to help in any way that she could. She was so stunned upon hearing of her neighbor's passing that she forgot to ask Sarita if she had opened her Christmas gift.

CHAPTER NINETEEN

En route from their log cabin home on the southeast corner of the Sabblonti spread to the main ranch house, Chet drove in silence for what seemed a very long time. "Stormy, what is happening to our lives? Your mother was the absolute anchor of the entire Sabblonti operation, and none of us know how to function without her. When the anchor disappears the whole outfit drifts. She would bark orders, and I would obey which served me extremely well. The best part of the deal was that I scored you in the process. How are you coping?"

It was as if Stormy had gone deaf and mute and did not speak. A few minutes later she responded, "Honestly, Chet, my brain feels like scrambled eggs. It's like two and two are adding up to be twenty-two instead of four. Mother was always the queen, in control of the castle, and everyone did her bidding or she bid them farewell. That's the way I remember it since I was old enough to remember."

"Let's go check on the horses and get Blue fed," Chet suggested. "Oh, how could I forget about him? He can fend for himself for a short while, but we had better get a plan drawn up right away so that we will know everything is taken care of properly. Jantzi Belle would not want it any other way. I hardly slept a wink last night. While I was awake, I was thinking a lot about Sarita. Her imagination has gotten the best of her after Ace died. Your mother loved her just as much as she loved you. Where she ever got those other notions in her head is beyond me. Does she read paperback books when she gets off work in the afternoons or does she watch those soap operas? Why do they call those TV shows by that name anyway?"

"Don't ask me about Sarita's thoughts and opinions. We were not particularly close growing up. She liked to be a house mouse, play with her rag doll, and have tea parties in the front yard on that little wooden table that Grand Pappy Siddonz made for her a decade before he died. It was as if he knew mother was going to have a little girl someday that would like something along the lines of a little table and four chairs. As for me, I liked to get out in the wild blue yonder on my horse and explore. Actually, you couldn't find two offspring who are more opposite than Sarita and me. And we can't forget that she has one blue eye and one brown eye. The kids in elementary school teased her unmercifully, called her *BB Freaky Eyes,* and who knows what else behind her back."

Blue ran toward Chet's pickup as he pulled into the driveway of the main Sabblonti ranch house. He barked loudly several times as if to say, "Well, it's about high time you showed up to take care of me! Have you been on vacation?" Chet reached down, stroked Blue a few times, and patted him on his head. After all, animals need comfort when their owners have passed.

"Stop, Chet! I cannot go inside that house until someone else has gone in there and cleaned it. I won't walk around the outside of the house until all of that residue is washed away."

"Well, what do you suggest then, Stormy? We drove all the way over here and now you decide you won't even go inside your mother's house? Honest to Sabblonti, Stormy, you are becoming more demanding and increasingly difficult, just like your mother. It's like you are a new and different person now than the one I married nine years ago. I have heard of the seven-year itch, but we blew past that red mark in the timetable. Make up your mind already!"

"Have you completely forgotten that it's still Christmas Day, Chet? Get over there, start your pickup, and turn on the seat heater on my side. Don't be such a dolt. You know how I like things. After all, it's me that has lost three babies and both parents so far. Then get out there and get those horses fed and lock everything up. Load Blue in the back end of the pickup. I don't want him in the cab. I will figure out our next move while you are taking care of the hired-hand work."

Chet could not remember having received a tongue lashing like this one during the entire time of his marriage. He reasoned that he should just keep quiet and extend mercy to his wife since both of her parents were now dead.

After tending to the animals and securing the outbuildings and the house, Chet opened the door to the driver's side of his pickup and got in. Removing his gloves and laying them on the seat he asked, "Is there anything else that you want done at the ranch right now?"

"I trust that you have taken care of everything to your own satisfaction. Since you will be the one doing all of the mundane chores in the future, I suggest you get it figured out sooner rather than later. Let's head home so I can devise my master plan."

Dutifully, Chet drove back to their house on the far end

of the Sabblonti land. He did not even want to give Stormy a peripheral glance until he sensed she had calmed down and could be civil to him.

Stormy broke the silence, "Chet, first thing on Monday morning let's plan to go into Ridgemonte and see someone at the Lambent's Funeral Home. I am going to ask for a referral from them for someone who can go out to the main ranch house and tidy things up. You know, someone who is not a blabber mouth, and can keep things confidential. Tongues will be wagging for a long time in the future about what the townspeople and neighboring ranchers speculate happened Christmas Eve. It's none of their business, and I intend to keep it that way. Surely Mother has enough money in her bank account to pay some flunkey a few bucks to go out there and do some back bending work. Come to think of it, I need to stop in at Cattlemen's Central and talk to the banker. I sincerely hope Mother had the presence of mind to put someone else's name on her accounts. What would happen if she didn't?"

Laughing out loud, Chet replied, "You are asking me that serious of a question? Surely you jest! If you remember when we were dating a decade ago, I told you when I went to high school, I did not even have a bank account so I did not need any kind of an accounting class. I concentrated more on sports, wood shop, FFA, and, of course, the most important class which was scoping."

"Scoping? What is Scoping? There's no class in any high school anywhere that goes by the title of Scoping. You are pulling my leg."

"Scoping is just an imaginary class that I dreamed up while I was scoping out the chickie babes in school and dreaming about them. I will bet you the Sabblonti Ranch and all its holdings that I was not the only one enrolled in that non-existent class."

Chet gave himself permission to extend Stormy a very quick peripheral glance from his right eye. He thought he saw the corners of her mouth turn upward very quickly. Then she began to laugh out loud.

"You tuna bait! I don't even want to know what you did in high school. I am so glad that you moved from another state so I don't have to contend with the history of the Castins' outfit. At least you go by the name of Chet and not Chester."

"Chet is my real name, not Chester. Whatever made you think that Chester was my actual name? Have you never looked at our framed marriage license hanging on our bedroom wall? And what's with this tuna bait bit? I've never heard that one before. Well, at least you didn't call me a horse thief. That would be the worst accusation ever."

As Chet and Stormy entered the driveway of their ranch home, Blue announced his arrival to the canine of the domain, a border collie named 'Beebee.' Chet parked the pickup, got out, walked around to the rear and opened the door of the camper shell. His introductions began, "Blue, meet your new buddy, Beebee. Let's see, Blue and Beebee, I like the sound of that. Or should I say, Beebee and Blue? It's sixes at this point, I guess. How about some grub for you two? You better buddy up straight out of the shoot because I don't have time for doggy sitting along with everything else we have going on right now. Somebody needs to pitch a tent over this circus!"

"Chet, quit clowning around with those stupid dogs, would you? It's like I lost three children, but now I really do have three children counting you and those lame-brained dogs. You could at least act your age, Chet Castins. Feed those dogs, get inside, and fix yourself some supper. I am going to lie down for a while. I need some peace and quiet so just plan to fend for yourself. If I fall asleep, you had better be extremely quiet when you enter our bedroom. On second thought, why don't you plan to sleep in the guest bedroom tonight? And don't let those fool dogs inside the house. They can sleep in the lean-to next to the barn. Blue needs to be shown who is boss around here. Beebee already knows."

Chet was having a very hard time managing the stinging words coming from Stormy's mouth the past few hours. He figured that he had just better lay low and do as he was told until she processed her grief. Surely it couldn't take that long to get over someone's death. There was far too much to do on a huge cattle ranch even in the dead of winter to get bogged down.

"Beebee and Blue," Chet called out, "Let's get you a secure place fixed down by the barn so you don't end up in a scrappin' match in the middle of the night with those coyotes. Those cats we tried to keep around here for awhile to be mousers ended up as hors d'oeuvres for those pesky howling critters. I can't let anything happen to you two. You will really need to help me come spring time on this spread. Why, each one of you can walk alongside my horse, Blitz. I am sure he will enjoy the extra company. Welcome to our place, Blue."

Darkness descended quickly as Chet completed his outside chores, locked the front door behind himself, walked around the corner, and removed his boots with the boot jack sitting on the floor of the mud room. Hanging up his winter coat and hat, he rubbed his face with his hands. Exhaling loudly, he washed his hands and face in the utility sink.

"Now to try to round up some supper," Chet mused. "I sure hope there's something in this fridge."

Sorting through the few items on the refrigerator shelves, Chet could not find anything to suit his taste buds. He had been told once that when tragedy happens, some people lose their appetites. Sporting a six-foot-four-inch frame and topping the scales at 227 pounds, a peanut butter and jelly sandwich probably was not going to cut the mustard, even in the midst of turmoil and loss. He gently closed the door and carefully opened the pantry door lest he should provoke the ire of his bride. "How long has it been since Stormy went to the grocery store?" Chet questioned under his breath. Stormy prepared most of their suppers from boxes or packages to which she added some Sabblonti beef, so it was ready in 30 minutes, and slapped on the table. Take it or leave it.

On the very top shelf of the pantry, Chet found a large can of baked beans with bacon chunks. Opening the can, he dumped the contents into a sauce pan and turned the knob on the stove three clicks to the right. There was no use turning it to the welding point. Yes, beans were better served warm than cold, but since Chet had been scalded quite a bit via Stormy's rants the past few hours, he planned to heat the beans slowly. He didn't need to burn his tongue so he could not shoot back verbally if needed.

After consuming one can of the beans, Chet was still hungry. Taking another gander inside the pantry, there were only boxed meals, and he didn't want to take the time to mix something with something else, add water, and wait for it to do its magic. It was getting late and he was dog tired. He opted to open another can of beans. Surely his stomach would be full by then as he would need all the protein he could get in the next few days.

In the nine years of their marriage, Chet had never slept in another bed, especially on Christmas night. Granted, this would be one holiday he would never forget. Memories were selective, however, so this one would be filed in the farthest recesses of his memory bank. Speaking of banks, Chet sincerely hoped that things would go smoothly on Monday at Cattlemen's Central. Jantzi had taken care of every single financial detail since he married into the family. Chet was far more comfortable doing the manual work on the cattle ranch and having someone else tend to the dollars and horse sense that went with it.

CHAPTER TWENTY

Peering into the guest room, Stormy had to purse her lips together to avoid laughing uproariously. As a result of his state of fatigue, Chet's head was located at the foot of the bed underneath the overhanging book shelf.

"Chetter, can you please forgive me for being sort of harsh to you?" purred Stormy as she gently stroked Chet's face. He awakened from a deep sleep, sat straight up in the guest bed, and bumped the top of his head on the shelf. "Ouch, double ouch!" Chet complained as he rubbed the top of his head. "Don't start another scrappy day by calling me a knot head, either! I need an alarm clock close to this bed."

"I am not going to call you a knot head. Let me feel the top of your head to see if you really did end up with any knots or bumps." Tracing the top of Chet's head with her hand, Stormy felt one bump. "Wow, you really did nail your noggin' when you reared up!"

"You startled me. I sure did not expect anything gentle and soft on my face this morning after your treatment of me lately," Chet complained as he got out of bed. "Do I have permission to use Her Highness' bathroom to take a shower or am I relegated to the guest bathroom, or better yet, do I get a pass on personal grooming today?"

"Now don't be difficult, husband. Have you lost track

of time? What have you been doing the past twenty-four hours while I have been recuperating in my bedroom? I gave you the day off so you could catch up on your sleep and get your chores done. We need to look our very best today. You know, just like we stepped out of a hat box, all dusted off, and primed for the rodeo parade. Muster up your charm, plan to be quiet, and let me do all of the talking. You are just my escort for today. Got it? You plan to accomplish all that, and it will be smooth riding all day long. Any questions?"

"No questions, Queenie Stormy. Now that Jantzi Belle is gone, since she crowned herself the Queen of Diamonds, can I call you Queenie Stormy? Would you rather I put the Stormy before the Queenie so I would say, Stormy Queenie? Your choice."

"Don't get smart-mouthed with me. Get your shower taken, your chores done, and fix your breakfast. I don't care which shower you use, just don't get in my way. Be ready at ten o'clock. Let's just hope all of the places that we need to be today are in fact open since it's still the Christmas holiday season."

Chet carried out Stormy's orders to the letter. He was grateful that he could talk to the horses, cows, calves, and dogs. Maybe there was some truth to that saying that a dog was a man's best friend. At least dogs could not sass back and their barks did not bite.

Looking at the clock in the kitchen, Chet fixed himself two more pieces of toast and gulped down another cup of coffee. He couldn't even find the butter to put some on his toast. There were no eggs to be found. Whoever heard of a refrigerator inside a ranch house that did not have eggs to cook? There was no need to focus upon the shortages as time was slipping by very quickly. He needed to cowboy up and be in the chauffer's seat of his pickup by the stroke of ten. There was no time to horse around this morning.

The last thing Stormy felt like doing was getting dressed, fixing her hair, and going through the beauty queen routine to cover her washed out appearance, but duty called. She secretly hoped there were no snafus they would need to deal with during the course of the day. Those kinds of things demanded a person be at the top of her game, and she was definitely at the bottom of hers.

"Well, you sure clean up nicely, Mr. Chet. Maybe I should order you to look your very best a little bit more often so I could remember why I married you in the first place."

"I thought you married me because you loved me. Ace told me about all of those hot shot high school wanna be cowboys and rodeo bronc riders that tried to sidle up to him because they knew you were the ticket to the Sabblonti Spread, especially since you were his first born."

"I might have been Daddy's first born, but I was definitely not his favorite. There were huge fights galore over who was the preferred daughter. It's a good thing our house was located miles from anyone else's ranch. Some of those knock down drag out fights and screaming matches lasted until the wee hours of the morning. Mother always knew how to put the patch job on anything though and just how far to push everything. The ranch came down through the family line to Daddy and Mother did not want to get the boot. It's the strangest thing though. While Sarita and I were growing up we knew a lot about Mother's family and saw our maternal grandparents on occasion. Daddy hardly ever spoke of his family. I never really thought much about it when I was a young girl. The week days were full of school stuff. I couldn't wait for the weekends so I could get outside in the wide-open spaces and revel in the peace and quiet. There's a lot of open country out here."

"I guess I never really did think much about your dad's outfit either, especially when I first married into the family. Since his parents had already passed onto the happy ranching land by the time we married up, it never really occurred to me to ask. I figured out really quickly those were not the kinds of questions one asked Jantzi Belle, no matter how long they had been in the Sabblonti lashup. Before we move on, I want your heartfelt answer as to why you married me. Honestly, I thought you loved me. You do love me, don't you?"

"Of course, I love you, Chet Castins. Doesn't everyone get married because of true love? How could you question my motive for marrying you when I could have had anyone in these parts that my little old pea pickin' heart desired? Consider yourself the luckiest rancher in all of Shadow Butte County and beyond. Are you ready to drive your beautiful bride to town to deal with the matters at hand?"

Getting Stormy situated comfortably on the passenger's side of his pickup, Chet closed her door and walked around to the driver's side. His mind drifted back to their wedding day in the beautiful meadow. His groomsmen wore black jeans, long sleeved white shirts with black pearled snaps, black bow ties, black cowboy hats, and black cowboy boots. He had remembered it as being the happiest day of his life. Had he married someone who truly loved him or deemed him an easy catch to carry out one's bidding? There was no time to delve into such a deep subject right now. Duty and performance called, and Chet knew that he must answer or else. Besides, he had decided a long time ago that if he played his cards right, he would end up owning the whole deck someday. He reminded himself just what was at stake, and this was no time to fold his cards and walk away.

CHAPTER TWENTY-ONE

Chet had never considered how lonely and threatening silence could be, and he did not like this introduction to it. On most days, Stormy was as chatty as could be, except for the down times right after losing a baby. He attributed her silence to grieving. How could it be anything beyond that?

"Let's get the most unpleasant task out of the way first," Stormy directed. "Head to Lambent's Funeral Home. According to Deputy Whillson, they keep an attendant there during the daytime hours of the holiday season. Let's just hope he knew what he was talking about."

Chet parked in the space closest to the front door of the mortuary. He opened the passenger door for Stormy, and extended his right hand to help her out since they were in town. There was no telling where spying eyes might be hiding.

Opening the front door of the funeral home, Chet followed Stormy into the lobby area. Looking up, Stormy noticed the sign on the wall and the arrow pointing toward the office. She stepped next to Chet and slipped her hand inside his right arm. "Everything for show," Stormy reminded herself. "Actually, everything for Mommie."

Tracie Sudder, a former classmate of Stormy's, looked

up from her computer screen as Chet and Stormy entered the receptionist's office. Stormy quickly reminded herself why she did not venture into town very often as she had not particularly liked very many of the students in her graduating class. The girls were extremely cliquish, and the boys hadn't really matured past the locker room. None of them had fared as well as she had done post-graduation.

Rolling back her chair and rising to greet Chet and Stormy, Tracie approached Stormy to give her a hug and express her condolences regarding Jantzi's passing. When Tracie extended her arms toward Stormy, she stepped backwards signaling no hugs accepted, causing Tracie's arms to fall down to her sides.

"Please accept our most sincere sympathy regarding your mother's death," Tracie said graciously. "Please have a seat and let us know how we can help you. That's what we are here for. We have been able to help so many families for many years as they deal with tragedy."

Exhibiting his most gentlemanly behavior, Chet pulled the chair out for Stormy. She sat down, crossed her legs, and set her purse on the floor.

"We are thankful that you are here to help us, Tracie, because we don't know which way is up at this point and really need some direction," Chet explained.

Stormy's rebuke was swift, "Chet, we're not so stupid and inept that we don't know which way is up. Even a two-year-old knows which way is up and which way is down. Be silent and let me handle Mother's affairs."

As Chet glanced down at the top of Tracie's desk, he could see that her folded hands were trembling slightly. Reaching over and picking up a ballpoint pen from her collection in the black mesh container on top of her desk,

Tracie began asking questions on a preprinted form, and taking notes as to Stormy's preferences for her mother's services. She was very patient as she showed Chet and Stormy the large notebook containing the various memorial accessories that could be used for the funeral.

"I thought your sister Sarita would be helping you decide the appropriate arrangements," Tracie commented. "Is she still working for Dr. Diller?"

"Since the obligation and duty goes to the oldest child in the family to handle such important matters, it was unnecessary for Sarita to accompany us today. Mother would want a lot of outdoor-type things for her special day. I am just sure of it. Although we never talked about any of this, because she was not supposed to die so young, I just know I am doing the right thing. I want the most expensive and ornate casket that Lambent's has. One of your lower-level employees needs to ride into the high country and cut some fresh juniper branches. Mother wasn't into all of those colored flowers that folks in town use for their funerals, so we won't bother with that. Can we go into that back room that you mentioned and pick out her casket? Oh, and before I forget, I think you should print at least 1,000 of those little *In Memory Of* papers that you showed me. Everyone absolutely loved Mother, thought the world of her, and highly respected her. I am sure they will attend her service in droves so we need to be prepared. I want everyone in attendance to have one so they can remember her for the magnificent person that she was."

"Stormy, are you sure you want to purchase the most expensive casket that they have?" countered Chet. "There are going to be a lot of expenses, so I think you need to be careful how much you spend on everything because we haven't even gone to the bank yet to see what funds might be available."

Seething as she jumped up, Stormy yelled, "Chet Castins, may I have a private word with you this minute? Go out in the hallway."

Hanging his head, Chet walked to the far end of the hallway where Stormy reprimanded him in a hushed voice. Tightening his jaws to keep from saying a word, Chet followed Stormy as they reentered Tracie's office.

"If you are ready to take a look at the caskets, we can go to that room now if you like," Tracie offered. "No rush. Please take your time. Days like these can be very draining and emotional to say the least."

"I'm ready now," Stormy demanded. "The sooner we get all of this over with, the better. This has already taken far longer than I thought it would. It should be pretty straight forward how someone is buried. It can't be that complicated. It takes a much higher IQ to run a huge cattle spread than a funeral home."

Tracie led the way as the three of them walked down the long hallway and entered the room where the caskets were displayed.

"Show me your most elaborate one with the largest price tag," directed Stormy. "Mother would be horrified if I cut any corners and spared any expense on her. A loyal daughter always does the very best for her regal mother."

Tracie walked to the far corner of the room and showed a very ornate white casket with white lining to Chet and Stormy, who reached down and rubbed the satin between her fingers.

"Yes, this is the one," agreed Stormy. "Mother was as pure and honest as the driven snow. She deserves to be buried in something that exemplifies those attributes. Never mind what the cost is, just write up a bill, and we will settle up when all of this is done."

Tracie continued, "We will need some clothes for your mother so if you could plan to bring those into town right away that would be most helpful."

"I will go to the ranch and select something appropriate for the burial of a queen and send it into town with Chet. You have my home phone number in case you think of anything else. I am quite fatigued and have other business to tend to, so I am finished here for now."

Chet extended his right hand to shake Tracie's hand and thanked her for her help. Stormy pivoted on the ball of her right foot and departed from the building.

Stepping up his pace, Chet unlocked his pickup using his key fob since Stormy was already standing next to the passenger door. He was not looking forward to the drive to Cattlemen's Central, even though it was only a short distance away.

"Chet Castins, if you ever make a fool out of me in public like that again, you are finished. Do I need to leave you in the car like a dog while I go into the bank or do you think you can behave and do what you are told? Maybe I should get a roll of duct tape from your tool box in the bed of the pickup and tape your mouth shut before I take you into the bank with me. Now behave like a good husband or else."

A sound could not be heard from Chet. It was as if he was a robot chauffer. If he played his cards just right, he knew he would come out ahead at the end of the game. Now was not the time to fold and lay his hand down, even if there was a Joker in it.

CHAPTER TWENTY-TWO

As Chet drove in total silence to Cattlemen's Central, he wondered if other men who married into wealthy families had to endure such treatment. There was no such thing as a perfect marriage, but the way Stormy acted toward him sure wasn't the way his mother had been toward his dad. Chet surmised that he was soon going to be in charge of the Sabblonti spread, so if silence was what it was going to take that would be just fine with him. No problem. There was a price to pay for everything. Sometimes it was top dollar.

"Don't forget that we are still in this Podunk town and on parade, Chet. Get out, get around here, and open my door like a good country gentleman should."

Chet did as he was instructed, and followed Stormy into the lobby of the bank. With no one in the line ahead of them, they approached the counter. Lance, one of the local tellers, looked up from where he had been counting money in the drawer. "Hello, how can I help you today? Did you have a nice Christmas? I certainly did!"

"You must not know who I am," replied Stormy. "I am Stormy Sabblonti Castins, and I need to see a bank manager or assistant manager right now. And don't tell me you don't have a manager or assistant manager in here because it's the Christmas season."

"We are required to have a manager or an assistant manager in the bank every day that it's open so that's not an issue. Since it's the noon hour, I am unsure if Mr. Sanders or our assistant manager, Lonnie Browne, is here right now. Can you please take a seat in the lobby and I will find someone to help you? There's hot coffee if you would like a cup. Please make yourselves comfortable."

Stormy chose to sit in the lobby as she commanded Chet, "Get me a cup of coffee, and if it's extra hot, put one cup inside the other, and don't dump too much of that creamer goop in there so that I won't like how it tastes. The least you could do is see to it that my needs are met."

Chet looked around to determine the location of the customer coffee since he deemed he better not speak and ask someone where it was. He ventured into the area between the office alcoves where a large table had been supplied with coffee decanters including all of the extras. Reading from left to right, and trying to decide what flavor would help to soothe Stormy, Chet randomly selected a medium dark roast. He guesstimated that three of the small containers of creamer should be sufficient. How was he to know? He drank his coffee straight and lots of it. His favorite was the sheepherder style made around the campfires during branding season or the fall roundups. He was not familiar with all of this froofy stuff they offered in town. He started to walk across the lobby to hand Stormy her cup of coffee when it began sloshing down the sides. A few drops sprinkled on his right hand so he quickly switched the cup to his left hand, and shook the droplets off his right hand. Looking up to see if Stormy was watching him, Chet relaxed somewhat when he realized she had her nose buried in *The Ridgemonte Rider.*

Midway across the lobby, Chet turned around quickly and headed back toward the coffee bar. At least this outfit served hot coffee, and none of that lukewarm tasteless brown liquid. Chet doubled two new cups, poured the contents of the prior one into the new one, and slipped the first cup with about an inch of leftover coffee in the bottom into the lined trash can underneath the table. Such finesse, and from a country boy at that! It was flat out amazing what one could do under pressure. Collecting himself, he began his second attempt at serving coffee. Chet walked toward Stormy once again. Knowing full well that she was aware he was standing in front of her, Stormy ignored Chet and made him stand there with a cup of coffee held out for her for a couple of minutes. This was taking humiliation to a whole new level. It was a good thing it was the lunch hour, two days after Christmas, and there was not much activity inside the lobby of Cattlemen's Central. For a fleeting moment, Chet entertained the thought of dumping the coffee in Stormy's lap but restrained himself. Cattle empires were not acquired via such behavior.

Feigning surprise that Chet was standing in front of her, Stormy looked up and purred, "Why, Chet, darling, how thoughtful of you to serve me coffee while we wait."

Chet sorted through the magazines on the square table in the middle of the lobby and found one featuring cattle, ranching, and grazing. Perhaps there would be enough money in Jantzi's checking accounts to order a subscription in his own name. When it arrived, he could take it down to the barn and read to Beebee, Blue, and Blitz.

Chet and Stormy waited for a half hour in the lobby. Chet was totally immersed in his magazine when Lonnie Browne, the assistant manager, entered the lobby where he and Stormy were sitting. "Hello, I am Lonnie Browne, and I apologize for making you wait. It seems when the bank is closed for just one day it takes us a week to catch up. My office is down the hall and to the left. Please follow me. You can bring your coffee with you if you like."

Inside Lonnie's office, he shook hands with Chet and Stormy. "Please have a seat and let me begin by saying that I am very sorry to hear of the death in your family. That's never easy, and with it happening this time of year, it makes it harder to deal with. How can I be of assistance?"

Stormy did all of the talking. Chet immediately transitioned into mute mode. "Lonnie, my mother never mentioned a word to me about her and my father's financial matters, and it never occurred to me to ask. Chet and I have had everything a person could ever want provided for us since we got married. Every month, a sizeable sum was automatically deposited into our checking account. It was as if we were trust funders, but we weren't in the technical sense of the word. I need to know what to do now. I have to pay for Mother's funeral and who knows what else from this day forward."

"That's what we are here for, Stormy. Cattlemen's Central has been in these parts for over a century, and we have helped many families with their transitions and the changing of the guard. You mentioned the words *trust funders.* Did your parents have a trust set up for you? Do you have siblings? What was your mother's full name? I will pull up her accounts on my computer and we will see what everything looks like. Hopefully there was someone else's name added to her accounts who had authorization to sign checks and so forth. If not, that's when the delays begin until her estate is probated. Is your father still living?"

"If you would stop in between your rapid-fire questions and give me time to answer you, that would be most helpful," chided Stormy. "I have one sister who lives in town. Her name is Sarita Sabblonti, and she works for Dr. Diller. My father died in 1993. I have no idea what is set up for my sister and me and have no clue what a trust is. I know what the word trust means, but not how it applies to legal matters or financial things. My mother's full name was Jantzi Belle Siddonz Sabblonti."

Typing a few different entries on his keyboard, Lonnie was able to locate Jantzi's accounts. "Let's look for the most important thing first, which is the signature on file for someone authorized to sign on these accounts. There's your dad listed here, but of course you indicated he passed away some years ago. Wow, this one goes way back! Do you remember your mother having you sign any paperwork for the bank when you were in high school? These records indicate that you have been on her account since 1978. You could not be more fortunate than that if I say so myself. It's a good thing Cattlemen's Central keeps these kinds of records going back decades. That's one of the benefits of sticking with one financial institution throughout family generations."

"High school seems like a long time ago and I have tried to forget most of it. Mother had a good business head on her for which I am thankful. I have never signed a check drawn on the Sabblonti accounts. Can I please see that paper that I signed?"

"Sure, no problem. Sign your maiden name, Stormy Suzanne Sabblonti, on this blank piece of paper for me, and I will print a copy of the paper you signed all those years ago. We will see if the signatures match."

"Are you trying to accuse my family of something, Mr. Browne?"

"Not at all. You are the one that seems to have some hesitation about signing a bank document twenty-one years ago."

Stormy signed her name on the blank sheet of paper, *Stormy Suzanne Sabblonti,* complete with all of the scrolling *"S's"*. She had forgotten how she enjoyed seeing her dramatic flowing signature as it appeared on paper.

Feeling confident that the handwriting matched, Lonnie stated, "Yes, those two signatures certainly seem to be the same. It takes a real artist to put all that fancy work into those letters."

"Can we quit horsing around with all of this handwriting malarkey and get serious about our appointment? I have had precious little sleep the past couple of days. This trivial stuff bores me to tears, and it's not like I haven't shed enough of those lately."

Lonnie thought to himself, "When a family has this kind of money and it bores them to tears, heaven help the rest of us!"

Looking toward Chet, Lonnie commented, "Chet, you sure are a quiet guy. Don't you ever talk? You have not said one single word since I met you. Cat got your tongue, or something?"

Flashing a grin, Chet just laughed out loud, and shrugged his shoulders.

"Let's see, your mother had several accounts set up here," explained Lonnie as he continued to type and tap the number pad on the right side of his keyboard. "So, it looks like just your dad's name, your mother's name, and your name appear on these accounts. Are you older than your sister? What's her name again? I apologize, but I have been concentrating on these accounts, and her name did not register with me."

"Her name is Sarita. I am four years older than she is." Stormy started to mention the fact that her sister did not get along particularly well with her mother, but restrained herself. There was no need to hang the family's dirty laundry where it could be viewed by the bank employees. Jantzi Belle would be none too happy with anything of the kind. Chet was sitting there waiting for the bottom line, not the clothes line.

"So, I am going to take a cursory read of these accounts. You can let me know if you want to transfer any money today while you are in here," Lonnie offered. "Are Lambent's taking care of things for the funeral? We have a great working relationship with Larry Lambent which just makes it easier and smoother for everyone. Of course, you could use Calvin's Funeral Chapels over yonder, but if you want to stay in county, you just can't beat Lambent's for assistance."

"I have decided on Lambent's," Stormy informed Lonnie. "They were most helpful when we stopped in there earlier today."

"Okay, so for the main checking account, there is $536,872.04 in there as of today. Jantzi called this one her operating account. Then she had a general account, a household account, a CC account, a miscellaneous account, three savings accounts, and five interest bearing certificates of deposit. The saving grace for you is that Cattlemen's Central revamped their policies a few years ago to where if someone was already authorized to sign on one account, the signature was acceptable on all accounts, unless the bank had been instructed otherwise. I did not see any of those types of instructions on these file notes. This is one of the beauties of an independent bank. It looks like a large sum was withdrawn earlier this month from one of the savings accounts, and it was taken out in cash. There's a note typed in here by our manager, Stewart Sanders, that your mother made a substantial withdrawal as she was going to make several large cash gifts this year for Christmas. Lucky for those family members! Oops, I am sorry. That was very unprofessional of me. Please forgive me as I should not have said that. Gauging from the size of some of these deposits the past few years, there must have been truckloads of cattle sold." Turning to face Stormy, Lonnie informed her, "Stormy, it looks like you and your sister will be well taken care of in the future. Your mother was a very good, long-range planner."

"Lonnie, this really helps a lot. I think I will just leave the existing amounts in the different accounts as they stand today. There should be enough in the operating account to pay Lambent's Funeral Home. Once we sort through the mail at the ranch house and check the current bills, I will have a better idea of what I need to do. When you reeled off the various accounts, the names of one of them jumped out at me. You mentioned a CC account or some such. What is that if you don't mind me asking?"

"Great question, Stormy, and please feel free to ask away. I want to make sure that you feel secure when you depart Cattlemen's Central today. It will take me just a minute to get back to that account. Let's see — CC, where are you? I just had you on my screen a couple of minutes ago. Are you hiding from me? Oh, don't mind me. I tend to be a verbal processor who talks to himself! Okay, the CC account officially reads, *Chet Castins Account*. Wow, Chet, you even had your own account inside the Sabblonti accounts! You must have been held in very high esteem within the family. Yes, then it appears that money was transferred monthly from that *CC* account into your personal account that you have with Chet. So, does that help to answer your questions, Stormy?"

"Yes, Lonnie, that explanation is most helpful. I will be able to follow the flow of funds from one account to another."

Chet could feel every muscle in his body relax. He did not realize what a large lump had formed in his throat until he tried to swallow.

With dollar signs in their eyes, Chet and Stormy rose to their feet and left Lonnie's office.

As Lonnie sat back down in his chair and stared at the computer screen, he said to himself, "Well, I guess it takes all kinds. Stormy's set for life. One would think the least she could do was offer thanks to those who helped her." Maybe, just maybe, some of those rumors he had heard about the hoity toity rich ranching folks were true. Perhaps he was being too hard on her since she had just lost her mother. It bothered him, though, that Chet acted the way he did and never opened his mouth. Granted, silence can be golden at times. Also, the heart of man cannot be determined by the size of a bank account, even a soon-to-be transferred or inherited one.

CHAPTER TWENTY-THREE

Sitting inside the cab of the pickup, Chet and Stormy waited for the interior to warm up and windows to defrost a bit.

"What do you want to do now?" Chet inquired in a barely audible voice. "I could sure eat a good warm meal somewhere. Do you want to stop in at the local greasy spoon and grab a bite to eat before we head back to the ranch?"

"I have very little appetite for anything right now. And the dead dog last thing I want to do is to sit in some drab country café where everyone can stare at me. Polished people don't do such things three days after the matriarch of a family dies. Chet, I never realized how uncouth you were until now. Maybe there is some truth to that saying, 'Love is blind.' It's high time to take my blindfold off, see things for what they really are, and get on with my life. Drive to The Shadowy Merc. I will wait inside the pickup while you get yourself something to eat. You can fix your own meals in the kitchen at the ranch house. Do not lollagag around in the store. Get the lead out of your cowboy boots."

"Do you want anything from The Merc? I am going to get some canned goods to tide me over for the next few days until things smooth out a bit. When I looked inside the pantry there was a whole lot of nothing in there. I guess I should have paid closer attention to how my mother cooked a pot roast and a few other things. Well, at least I can scramble eggs and cook bacon. I forgot my checkbook at the house. How do you want me to pay for the groceries?"

Opening her wallet and selecting a $100 bill, Stormy handed it to Chet. "Use this wisely and don't buy anything extravagant or junk food. I don't want you growing one of those pot bellies. You need to plan to eat lean and stay thin. With all of the manual labor that I will have you doing at the ranch, rest assured you will not become overweight. Leave the engine running so I can keep warm and don't plan to be inside for very long. You don't want to suffer through a scene if I have to come inside and get you."

During the time Chet was inside the store, Stormy looked through the cab of his pickup to see if there was a little tablet or something she could use to start making a list of what she needed to do. Not finding any writing material, she looked through her purse, but could not locate anything suitable. A mental list would have to suffice for the time being.

Walking up and down the grocery aisles, Chet was like a kid in a candy store. He longed to fill his cart with some packaged sweets, chips, and snacks, but was unwilling to incur the verbal wrath that would follow when the groceries were unloaded at the ranch house. Lost in his thoughts, he jumped when he heard a voice behind him, "Well, hi Chet! What brings you to The Shadowy Merc so soon after Christmas?" Turning around while holding the grocery cart with his right hand, he remembered meeting Salina Bevvins, who had started working at the store about a year ago.

"Salina, you about scared the daylights out of me

coming up behind me like that! How did you know it was me?"

"Oh, I saw the left side of your face when you were making the turn at the top of Aisle #13."

"Well, you sure do have a good memory since you were working as the clerk one of the few times during this past year when I happened to be in the store purchasing supplies before one of my mountain treks. How do you like working here?"

"It's a great job for me because I am a real people person. I moved here about this time last year at the invitation of my aunt and uncle, Denny and June Slader, who live about thirty miles west of town. I needed a fresh start coming off a bad relationship where I lived previously. There must be something about Ridgemonte because it has offered the healing I needed! It might be the good ol' mountain air and the wide-open spaces. My days at The Shadowy Merc just fly by. You know what they say, 'Time flies when you are having fun!' I do a little bit of everything here. Sometimes I work in the back in the lumber and hardware part of the store. I prefer to work up front in the grocery and sundry area. There are more women to talk with as they are the ones who purchase most of the supplies so they can prepare meals for their families and so forth. Oh, I am so sorry. I forgot to mention that I heard that your mother-in-law had a bad accident and passed away a couple of days ago. Are you doing alright?"

"It's been pretty tough going the past few days. Death seems to come calling when we least expect it. As you can tell from what's inside my cart so far, I will be fending for myself for a while. At least I can cook breakfast meals. Sheesh, I just might end up fixing those three times a day.

Hopefully some of these hungry country man meals are as good as they look on the outside of the can."

Giggling, Salina offered, "Well, just buy lots of shredded cheddar cheese and sprinkle some of that on the top of whatever you are eating. It helps to add a lot of flavor and is good protein. Oh, and don't forget catsup! I have heard that cowboys like catsup and mustard on most all their food."

"I like the cheese idea a lot. But it's probably got too much fat, and I have been instructed by the wifey that I cannot get fat and sport a spare tire. I am ordered to stay lean looking."

Skewing her face a bit, Salina responded, "Well, it must be working. You look pretty lean to me. It seems to me that working men should be able to eat most anything they want. But what do I know?"

"Are you sure you're not from Jupiter? I didn't know they still made women who were nice, kind hearted, and still lived on planet earth."

Salina felt a sudden blush flushing her face. "Maybe I should just tell you that I fly my non-existent long distance space travel jet into work every morning from a land far-far away. Actually, I drive my Aunt June's pickup in the winter since it has four-wheel drive. Coming down the mountain, it's the first ten miles that are the most challenging. I grew up on the beach wearing my flip-flops while playing volleyball in the sand. Never in four life times did I ever think I would end up in a small town, but it's been a wonderful adventure so far. Now, I am just a lonely country girl. And for the record, I don't even know your last name, not that it matters much."

"My last name is Castins. Since I am only part way finished with my grocery shopping, I had better put it in high gear."

"Shopping carts like the one you are pushing don't have gears. We have a few of that kind in the store that you can ride which are designed for older or handicapped people. Thanks for the short visit, and, again, I am very sorry to hear of the death in your family. If you like, I can wait on you when you are ready to check out."

The words *check out* seemed to hit a raw nerve in Chet's brain. He would have liked to check out somewhere for a while so his head could stop spinning, and he could begin to think clearly.

Pushing his loaded grocery cart toward the checkout stand, Chet looked down and suddenly wondered if the $100 bill that Stormy had given him would be enough to pay for the items. What an awkward moment that would turn out to be if he came up short!

Salina continued her bantering back and forth with Chet as she scanned his purchases, placed them in large brown paper bags, and stacked them inside the cart. When she hit the total key on the cash register, it read $127.14.

"Salina, this is one of the most embarrassing moments of my life. I am glad there's nobody in line behind me. I have only a $100 bill so I will need to put some of these groceries back on the shelf, and in the dairy and meat sections. You can tell that I don't shop a lot and my eyes are bigger than my wallet. I am just mortified."

"Be kind to yourself, Chet. Please stay right here and I will be back before you can say, 'Bob's your uncle!'"

Returning to the checkout stand, Salina placed a $20 bill along with a $5 bill, two $1 bills, one dime, and four pennies into the cash register. "Okay, all settled, and you are good to go." Holding up the cash register receipt in her left hand, she asked Chet, "Do you want to put this in your wallet or shall I place it in one of the brown sacks?"

"Salina, I can't let you pay for part of these groceries. After the funeral, I will drop by the store and repay you. That's the least I could do. I don't know what else to say or do right now. Please place the receipt inside the sack."

"Chet, don't concern yourself with reimbursing me. In the community in which I grew up, when someone had a death in the family or something bad happened, the beachfront neighbors prepared meals and took them to the family to help comfort them. Just consider it as my way of helping to comfort you and your family."

"Thank you, Salina. I guess it's the little things in life that mean the most. I am thankful that you were working in the store today."

Salina could have sworn she saw a mist forming in Chet's eyes and that he was fighting back a tear or two.

As Chet pushed the grocery cart across the parking lot, he was very conscious of Salina's act of generosity. Compared to the holdings of the Sabblonti Ranch, her net monthly income seemed so insignificant, and yet, a small dose of kindness could sure help to sustain someone through a rough ride. He reminded himself that he did not want to misplace the receipt for the groceries so that he would know how much money to take with him on his next visit to The Shadowy Merc.

Arriving at his pickup, Chet gingerly opened the rear door on the driver's side and began stacking the groceries on the floor and back seat. He braced himself for what might follow if Stormy deemed he had spent too much time obtaining his victuals. Glancing quickly in her direction, he smiled when he realized she was napping. She had rolled down the window on the front passenger side about four inches and was out like a light.

When Chet closed the pickup door Stormy lifted her head upon awakening from her cat nap. Turning around and looking at the large brown sacks placed on the back seat, Stormy questioned Chet, "You bought all that for $100? They must have been having some holiday specials or something. Of course, if you don't have to buy meat, you can stretch money a lot further." Chet knew if he tried to explain anything at this point, he would end up in hot water. He acted like he did not hear her.

"Anything else before we leave town?" Chet wanted to know. "I would like to get back to the ranch before dark now that I have two sets of winter chores to do. I am running short on time."

"I am done in this rat hole," hissed Stormy. "I never could stand this town, and the older I get, the less I can tolerate it. You will be taking care of everything in Ridgemonte from now on. After Mother's funeral, I plan on driving down county to find a new beauty shop and whatever else I need. It will take decades for these local tongues to stop wagging. It's all so juvenile. I am so far above all of it. Yes, yes, wealth has its distinct advantages. It's hard to be firmly in control without it."

CHAPTER TWENTY-FOUR

"How about I drop you off at the main ranch house, take the groceries inside, and then drive home to get the feeding done early?" suggested Chet. "Since there are more outside lights here, I can do the chores after dark if necessary."

"Initially, I had not planned on spending the night at the main house until it was cleaned up. While you were taking so long to purchase your groceries, I had time to rethink my plan. With there being plenty of guest bedrooms, I will stay here. When you go home, empty my closet and dresser drawers into large green garbage sacks. Bring them to Mother's when you return. Don't wad my clothing into a big ball; otherwise, you will get the one easy lesson on laundry. You need to beat feet as you have a lot of ground to cover between now and your bedtime tonight. And don't expect me to put away your groceries, either. Such duties are for servants, and I am no servant. You are the hired help in case you hadn't been paying attention for the last few years."

"Take it easy," Chet reminded himself as he felt his face turn bright red and his blood pressure rise. Wow, the price to pay seemed to be awfully expensive these days!

Chet packed the groceries inside, placing the perishable

items inside the refrigerator. There was part of him that wanted to walk up to his wife, grab her in his arms, give her a big hug, and tell her that he loved her. But, then again, he did not want to get bit in the process. "Bide your time, Chet, ol' boy, as it will all be worth at the end of the game," he silently coached himself.

Driving to the lower ranch house, Chet had some quality quiet time to process the past couple of days along with the last nine years. To his way of thinking, it appeared as though he had been living a dream for nine years, and then three days ago suddenly his life became a nightmare. One thing about nightmares, they go away when you wake up.

Chet had driven the road so many times between the main ranch house to where he and Stormy lived at the lower ranch house that he could almost turn his pickup on auto pilot. It was virtually as straight as an arrow. His mind parked briefly on the grocery store encounter earlier in the afternoon. He asked himself, "Was Salina Bevvins as nice to every other customer who frequented The Shadowy Merc as she had been to him? Would she have gone to the break room of the store, opened her own purse, and taken money from it to make up for a deficiency for any other person?" Chet nodded his head affirmatively as he drove. Sometimes you can tell a book by its cover. Salina seemed to have a heart as big as all outdoors, or at least, as large as Shadow Butte County, and that was quite vast.

Chet's welcoming committee, Beebee and Blue, met him at the edge of the front yard as he pulled in and turned the pickup engine off. As soon as he got out, he bent down, petted both dogs, and rubbed their faces affectionately. "You mutts better not have been up to any mischief after I left here this morning," warned Chet. "My plate is already overloaded, and I don't need any shenanigans from you two. I just want you to know, though, that a dog really is a man's best friend. No doubt about it. Since there are two of you, I've got two best friends. Can't beat that with a stick! Let's go down and check on the hosses, shall we?"

Beebee and Blue tagged along behind Chet as he made his way to his horse barn. As soon as he opened the door, Braezee, his mare, whinnied as if to say, "It's about jolly good time you checked on me!" The ripe smell reminded him that it had been several days since he had cleaned the stalls. Speaking of hired hands, he needed one right about now.

Chet measured out the grain and hay for his horses inside the barn. He would be glad when spring was here again so that he did not have to dry lot his herd. When he filled Braezee's feed bucket, she bent her head down and just sniffed the grain. She lifted her head and looked intently at Chet. Setting his feeding bucket down, Chet walked closer to his mare and noticed that she was not applying any weight on her right hind foot. Walking carefully around her side and patting her gently, he picked up Braezee's hind foot and let out a gasp. "Good grief, Braezee, where on earth did you pick up that nail? That blasted thing has penetrated the center of your frog! Stand real still and let me see if I can gently apply backward pressure on the head of that rusty nail and dislodge it. Grrrr! It took some doing to get that thing out of there." Applying pressure to the area, Chet could not get it to bleed. "Okay, girl, let's get your halter on and see if you can take a few steps."

Braezee stepped gingerly inside the horse barn for a couple of minutes. Chet cleaned her foot, soaked it in warm water, dried it off, and put her back in the stall with some clean straw bedding.

Chet walked to the house, unlocked the front door, and walked inside. He thought he saw something scurrying across the kitchen floor. Sure enough, he caught the glimpse of the tip of a mouse's tail as it flattened itself and squeezed under the pantry door. It had left its calling card in one corner of the kitchen next to the refrigerator. Chet did not want to ask himself what could go haywire next.

Since Braezee took precedence over a mouse any day of the week, Chet grabbed the phone book to look up Dr. Shaw's number. When he dialed the phone, it rang six times, and went to voice mail. Chet could only hope that the vet checked his messages periodically. Not wanting to leave the house for fear of missing Dr. Shaw's call, Chet busied himself with cleaning up the mouse's mess and heating up another can of beans. "A loaf of bread!" exclaimed Chet. "That's what I forgot to get at the store today. Oh well, no bread and butter with my beans. I will survive without it."

"Mobile phones would sure be nice," Chet reminded himself. "Let's just hope they get that cell tower built out here in the boondocks sometime in the next one hundred years. There better be some peanut butter in that pantry so I can set a trap for that two-bit mouse. What we really need around here are some cats, but we just can't seem to keep any. No use looking for any cheese because I know there's none of that. Cheese makes a belly look like a pot according to Stormy."

Chet dug through the junk drawer and managed to find an old mouse trap. Baiting it with peanut butter, he placed it in the far-right corner of the pantry behind the empty potato bin. "You better like your peanut butter chunky," hoped Chet.

With dusk fast approaching, Chet placed a call to Stormy at the main ranch house. After dialing the number, the phone rang innumerable times but no one answered. Chet hung up the phone and dialed the number again. He was just about to hang up when Stormy picked the receiver up.

"This is Stormy Sabblonti," she said icily.

"Stormy, there have been some complications at our place. My best mare, Braezee, ended up with a rusty nail in her foot, and I need to try to get the vet out here tonight to take a look at it. I placed a call to his office and left a message, but still haven't heard from him. I don't know if he went out of town to visit his family for Christmas or what. I need to stay down here at the ranch until I hear from him. Can you walk down and feed the horses and heifers in the barn and lean-to just for tonight before it gets too dark? There's good outside light if you turn on the yard lights. I really need you to help me out with all of this. Can I count on you?"

"I just woke up from a power nap. I don't know where any of the food is for the animals, so they can go without for one night. If there was a famine in the land, they couldn't eat every night anyway. They will survive. You fuss way too much over the four-legged creatures. Why don't you just plan to stay down there tonight? Now that I have gotten my second wind, I need to start going through some things here at Mother's and can't be bothered with what you deem is an emergency or overly important. I don't need you underfoot for one night. I can't really concentrate on what's important with you being here."

"Do whatever suits you best. It would appear to me that it's the four-legged creatures that have kept the Sabblontis in the manner to which they have become accustomed for the past few decades."

"Wow, such eloquent speech from a top cow hand. Maybe you were actually paying attention in your high school English class. I thought you concentrated more on those high-minded rodeo queenettes. I am learning something new every day these days."

"What's a queenette?" inquired Chet.

"You know. It's someone who fancies herself as queen material some day in the future, but doesn't have a prayer of becoming one. It's sort of like an amateur wannabe. This section of the country is full of them." Stormy slammed the receiver down, which caused Chet to jump back and pull the receiver away from his ear. He had no sooner hung up the phone after talking to Stormy when the phone rang again.

"Chet, here."

"Hello, Chet, this is Dr. Ben Shaw. Sorry I missed your call earlier. My assistant has been on vacation this week, so I am the only hand in town. In your message you said something about a bad foot on one of your mares."

"Thanks, Doc, for calling me back. Braezee seems to be off her feed, and when I lifted up her right hind foot, I discovered she had stepped on a rusty nail. I got the nail dislodged but could not get the foot to bleed. She was able to take a few steps. I cleaned her foot and put fresh clean straw in the stall. I know it's getting late, but is there any way that you could get out here tonight? We're down at the lower ranch house. Since you moved to Ridgemonte, I don't think we've ever had to call you down here. If my memory serves me correctly, you've just been to the barn at the main ranch house. It will be after dark by the time you get out here, but Braezee is in her stall in the barn, and the lighting is good inside there."

Dr. Shaw replied sympathetically, "Before I forget about my manners, Chet, when I had to check on one of Toppens' cows earlier today, Merna mentioned that you had lost your mother-in-law. I only saw her a couple of times at the ranch since moving here. I can only imagine that it's a real difficult time for all of you. Please accept my sincere sympathies for your loss."

"Thank you, Dr. Shaw. Night has run into day, and day has run into night. I don't know how I am still walking around to tell you the truth. I need a good night's sleep."

"We country vets seem to be like the old-time country medical docs. We just keep going until we have the critters taken care of, and then we can call it a day or night or whatever it happens to be. I will be out there as soon as I can. Is there anything I can bring you from town? I have to go to The Merc to get some milk. I am like a bull calf when it comes to my milk. I have got to have it every day! If I get a move on, I can get to the store before they close."

"Yes, there is something you can pick up for me, Doc. I plum forgot to get any loaves of bread when I was in there earlier today. I like that buttermilk kind if they have it. I would imagine that three loaves ought to take care of it for now. And, speaking of milk, can you pick up about four gallons of the whole kind? I can cut you a check to reimburse you when you get down here to the ranch."

For a fleeting moment, Chet thought about asking Dr. Shaw to make his check payable to The Shadowy Merc for $27.14 above the total amount for his groceries to repay Salina Bevvins while he was in there. Life was complicated enough right now. There was no use making the water any muddier.

CHAPTER TWENTY-FIVE

Dr. Shaw grabbed his keys, checkbook, jacket, hat, gloves, and headed out the door. Forgetting to lock the back door to his clinic, he trudged back to secure it. He deemed most folks in cattle country to be as honest as the day was long, but the landscape seemed to be changing. All of his valuables were located in his clinic, including his most comfortable bed along with his electronics.

Pulling into the closest parking space next to the entry door of The Shadowy Merc, Dr. Shaw saw someone's hand putting the keys into the lock. Bailing out of his pickup and running toward the front door, he motioned for the person to open it. "Wow, that was a close call! Are you officially closed?"

Salina responded, "Normally we would be, but you look like you need some supplies in a big hurry. I can let you in to get a few things. It's a good thing I am substituting for Cannaleah late this afternoon. She would have locked the door in your face."

"Really?" Dr. Shaw said as he stepped inside the door. "Obviously, she must not be as considerate as you are. Thank you so much for doing this for me. Actually, it's not just for me. Did you hear that the Sabblonti's had a death in their family? I just got a call from Chet. I need to go check on one of his mares that is having a problem with her foot. Infection can set in very quickly, so I am headed out there tonight. You know how it is. No rest for the weary, and the righteous don't need any. Chet needs me to purchase some bread and milk for him, too."

"You must be the local vet," replied Salina. "I had heard about the death in the family. Chet was in here earlier today to get some groceries, and I expressed my condolences to him then. He sure is a nice guy."

Dr. Shaw continued with caution, "Do you know Chet and his family very well? Would you mind turning on a few more lights in here for just a couple of minutes so I can find my way around the store to get the things we need? Since I don't shop here much, I don't know my way around that well. I am far more familiar with the back part of the store than the front."

Salina continued to pry, "Who normally does your grocery shopping for you? Pardon me. That line escaped from my mouth before I put the stop sign up. I would imagine that your wife takes care of those duties."

Dr. Shaw pulled a cart from the small storage area adjacent to the checkout stand.

"I thought you said you only needed a few items," Salina said as she studied Dr. Shaw. "We have these little baskets that you could carry in each hand so you don't have to bother with that big cart if you don't want to. I am watching the clock." Salina tried to contain herself, but started giggling.

"For the record, I don't have a wife who does the grocery shopping for me. Believe it or not, my assistant, Jacobe Davone, does most of it and takes my supplies back to the clinic. I virtually live there. I have a nice bed, TV, radio, and the whole set up. I don't think I could even make a meal from the things in my cupboard or refrigerator. Why am I telling you this personal stuff anyway?"

"You are telling me this personal stuff because I was kind enough to let you inside The Shadowy Merc after closing time to do some grocery shopping," reminded Salina. As Dr. Shaw inquired about the location of items within the store, Salina gently pulled his grocery cart behind her as she helped him load it.

"Back to the subject of the Sabblonti family," Dr. Shaw continued, "You didn't answer my question. You mentioned earlier that Chet was a real nice guy."

"I've lived in the Ridgemonte area for a short period of time so I am still trying to figure out the lay of the land," Salina explained. "This county is pretty wide. The country is even wider. There are not that many people who live around here, but they are very spread out because the cattle ranches are so huge. Most of the women don't come into town that often, and when they do, they shop for about three months at a time. There's neither rhyme nor reason as to the days of the month they seem to come in here. When I am working in the back of the store, I rarely see them as it's mostly the ranchers themselves that tend to those sorts of things sold back there. I have only seen Chet a handful of times inside the store. There's something so mysterious about him. His mouth can't seem to say what's going on inside of him, but his eyes speak volumes. Why did you ask about Chet?"

"Oh, no real reason," Dr. Shaw said with reservation. "I have been called to the ranch a few times to treat their cattle and horses. I had seen Chet along with some of their other hired hands. But that Mrs. Sabblonti, and I can't recall her first name right now, was something else again. It was a real different sort of name than I had ever heard before. Judging from the way she spoke to her hired help, I was amazed she could keep any one of them for more than a week at a time. After she barked orders to that son-in-law of hers and those other guys, they scurried around like ground squirrels. I had never seen anything quite like it in all my days working as a vet. I am not trying to speak disrespectfully of the dead, but it just stopped me cold in my tracks when I observed it. After tending to their cattle, horses, and especially those old breeding bulls they had out there, Mrs. Sabblonti never once invited me into the house for a cup of coffee or anything. In fact, I don't think she ever thanked me for going out there and taking care of their animals for them. All Mrs. Sabblonti ever said to me was, 'Send me the bill.' Then she would do an about face and stomp toward the ranch house. It was just the strangest thing! Not that it's fair to compare ranching families in these parts, but whenever I get called out to the Toppens, Merrills, or most any other ranch, the Mrs. usually invites me in for dinner or supper. To tell you the truth, that's where I end up eating a lot of my meals. All of them know I don't have a wife, so they spoil me. I start talking to some of them and can hardly get away. 99% of the people in this area are the best ever!"

"Okay, Dr. Shaw, your few minutes have almost become a full hour. Let's get you taken care of so you can be on your way. Chet needs you at his ranch to look at his mare. Please tell him hello for me."

"Salina, there's no use setting your hat for Chet Castins. He is a married man. You better be looking elsewhere. There are some other eligible bachelors in these parts."

"I am not setting my sights on Chet Castins, Dr. Shaw,"

Salina pushed back. "I try to be kind to everyone. It just seemed to me that he is really hurting and his wounds are not just superficial. Speaking of kind, I will place your cash register receipt inside one of your brown grocery bags and Chet's inside his. Life is all about the little things, you know."

"Even if his wounds are deep, they're not for you to treat," warned Dr. Shaw as he helped to place his groceries inside the sacks and Chet's in separate ones.

A sly smile graced Salina's face as she challenged, "Dr. Shaw, I have a suggestion. Why don't you tend to the wounds of the four-leggers and let me tend to the wounds of the two-leggers?"

"Thanks for your help, Salina. I need to save my brain cells for doctoring animals. I don't have a comeback for you right now."

Leaving town, Dr. Shaw wondered what that dialogue was all about. He reckoned maybe it was a good thing he had his assistant tend to most of the purchasing of supplies. Jacobe could not return to Ridgemonte soon enough.

CHAPTER TWENTY-SIX

"Nothing in life goes faster than time or money," Dr. Shaw muttered to himself as he drove to the Sabblonti Ranch. "Those old timers always had a saying for pretty much everything. I should have been on the road an hour ago. I sure hope Chet was not blowing hot air when he told me that he had good lights inside his barn."

Driving past the main ranch house, which was pitch black, Dr. Shaw pondered the death of Jantzi Sabblonti. He reminded himself, "Life is but a vapor and can end at any time. Every day is a gift."

Chet was more nervous than he realized as he looked through the kitchen window watching for headlights. He felt his shoulders relax and his facial muscles loosen at the first sight of spotting of them. "Beebee and Blue, let's hope this is the good doctor headed our way."

Dr. Shaw pulled into the driveway of the lower ranch house as Chet walked outside to meet him.

"Good to see you, Doc, and thanks a million for coming out so late tonight. I left the inside and outside lights on so we can get down to the barn quicker."

"No problem, Chet," responded Dr. Shaw as he grabbed his metal box full of basic supplies and hastened his pace toward the barn. "Who are these two characters?"

"Oh, they're Blue and Beebee. Blue was my father-in-law's dog. My mother-in-law kept him at the main ranch house. After she passed away the other night, I brought him down here so he would not have to be alone and neither would Beebee. They have gotten along just great."

Opening the door and walking toward Braezee's stall, Chet announced, "Braezee, the real doctor just arrived to take care of you." Picking up the bloodied rusty nail, Chet continued, "As near as I can tell, I don't think it penetrated more than about ¾ of an inch. For the life of me, I can't figure out where it came from because this barn is not that old."

Dr. Shaw approached Braezee's head and stuck out his hand to allow her to sniff it. As he rubbed her forehead, he said, "Well, girl, let's see how that foot is looking." After donning his head lamp, Dr. Shaw eased his right hand down Braezee's right hind leg and lifted her foot. "I can see a small slit in the plantar cleft of the frog near the heel bulb. Hopefully the nail did not go deep enough to cause any real damage. It's a good thing you got it cleaned up right away. I need to go to my truck again and get some additional supplies. I will be right back."

Returning with equipment to thoroughly cleanse the wound site, Dr. Shaw continued to work. He cleaned the area well, dried Braezee's foot and treated it with sugardine. After applying the wrap, he added duct tape to the bottom of the wrap for extra protection. He asked, "Chet, is Braezee current on her tetanus shots?"

"She's never had a tetanus shot, Doc."

"Okay. I will give her one tonight. Also, I don't think we need to take any x-rays to determine the extent of her injury, but if she develops a fever or you notice any lameness, we will need to take x-rays. One more trip to the truck. Back in a flash."

Returning with a tray loaded with syringes, medicine bottles, etc., Dr. Shaw continued with his treatment. "Chet, I will inject Braezee with an antibiotic tonight and she will need to have the same thing daily for 8 more days. How comfortable are you with giving shots to your horses? It's paramount that you give the shots in a major muscle area like the rump or the neck, and do not hit any bone when injecting, or Braezee will let you know about it in a hurry! I can leave you some syringes."

"I am used to giving the cattle their vaccinations," Chet said. "I will call you if I run into any trouble."

After collecting his supplies, Dr. Shaw suggested they sit on the straw bales in the corner of the barn for a short while. "Chet, there are a few other things that you will need to do for Braezee. She will need to rest in her stall and walk a little bit every day inside the barn. Put some more duct tape on the bottom of that wrap each day to keep it dry. Don't let it get wet. See if she gets back on her feed and shows any sign of discomfort. Watch for decreased appetite and diarrhea. You will need to take her temperature and if it's above 101.5, call me right away. Several things can cause a spike in temperature such as weather, stress, excitement, etc. I may need to put her on an additional antibiotic in a few days. We will wait and see how she is doing. I will come back later and do a wellness check on her and cut that bandage off her foot."

"Sounds good, Doc. I so appreciate you driving here tonight."

Dr. Shaw recalled, "Chet, I completely forgot about your

groceries in the cab of my truck. Speaking of such, I was going to tell you about an unusual experience I had at The Shadowy Merc when I stopped in there to get our supplies. If I would have driven into the parking lot a minute later, I would have come up empty handed. This young lady named Salina had just put the key inside the lock and was ready to turn it, when I walked right up to the front door and motioned for her to open it. She opened it alright and then proceeded to turn into quite the chatter box. I told her I needed to get out here tonight so I could treat one of your horses. When I mentioned your name, she became overly interested. What is her story anyway?"

"Doc, it's entirely a coincidence that you should mention her. I might have seen her a total of five times, maximum, since she moved to Ridgemonte. Keep in mind that I rarely go into the grocery store part of The Shadowy Merc. If I have to go to town, I usually need something from Clinker's Feed Store. Stormy does the grocery shopping, if and when she decides we need to eat."

"It doesn't look to me like you have missed too many meals, Chet. I mean, you're not overweight or anything, but you certainly would not be considered gaunt by any stretch of the imagination. Who is Stormy?"

"Stormy is my dear wife. We have been married nine years. My mother-in-law didn't like to cook either. It was kind of a standing joke with the women folk in the Sabblonti family. They could not cook a decent meal if they had to, so I've eaten from a can the majority of the time. Anyway, back to Salina. When I was getting a few groceries this afternoon, she was drawn to me like a bear to a pot of honey, and it made me very uncomfortable. All I was trying to do was buy some food and get out of there. I don't think she is one of those super-needy types. She lives with her aunt and uncle, Denny and June Slader. Salina said she moved here on the heels of a bad relationship. Those kinds of vague explanations make a guy wonder. Look before you leap, still water runs deep."

"Chet, from just a first impression, I think Salina would glom onto you if you weren't already taken. I reminded her that you were a married man. I can't vouch for the happily part of the married business, but I do see your wedding ring. I am surprised that you wear it working with your cattle and all."

"For safety reasons I usually just wear my wedding band when I get dressed up to go someplace. I put it on to attend Christmas Eve dinner at my mother-in-law's house before everything went south. It's been a hectic few days, and I completely forgot to take it off."

Dr. Shaw rubbed his right jaw which caused Chet to ask, "Do you have a toothache or something?"

"No, my teeth are fine now," replied Dr. Shaw. "Some high school kids came into the clinic about six weeks ago selling homemade popcorn balls and all types of goodies. I bought a dozen of those pink and red ones because they've been my faves since childhood. Well, I bit down too hard on one and broke part of my back molar off. I have had four appointments with Dr. Diller to get a crown put on there. I've had to chew on the left side of my mouth which feels so odd. After this molar debacle, I got so disgusted with those popcorn balls that I just chucked them into the trash can. The downside of all of this business has been the dent to my checkbook. The upside is that there's a very quiet, kind, and attractive lady who works in the front office named Sarita. Each time I have had an appointment with Dr. Diller, I find myself showing up fifteen minutes early just so I can enjoy the scenery. My normal inclination is to try to at least be on time for any appointment anywhere, but most of the time I am running a half hour late. Trying not to bore a hole through Sarita when I look at her, I find that I am really drawn to her for some reason. The last time I was in there I did not see any rings on her left hand. Of course, she doesn't work with the dental instruments or anything. She's just in the front office. Do you know anything about her or who she is? You know how those medical outfits are, and the powers to be have their policies in place where you can't find out anything about the employees. Maybe it's a blessing in disguise that my back molar broke off because it had been a while since I had a dental exam, teeth cleaning, and so forth. You would think I would pay more attention to my own teeth since I clean horses' teeth for a living."

"Small world in which we live, Dr. Shaw," Chet started to explain.

"Hold that thought, Chet. Let me walk over and check Braezee's temperature one more time just to be on the safe side." Sitting down again, Dr. Shaw reported, "It appears she's fine as her temp is 99.8 and her pulse is 40 bpm."

"How long have you been in these parts, Dr. Shaw?"

"Not that long actually. I bought the practice from the former vet because he was ready to retire. Since your outfit does a lot of its own vaccinating and so forth, I've not been summoned to the ranch very often. A couple of the calls were to treat that aged bull at the main ranch area. It's a good thing a separate corral had been built for him. Your mother-in-law or somebody must have ordered their supplies elsewhere because they sure didn't come into the clinic to purchase them. Maybe she drove to Ignee County to get them."

"There's no telling with her," Chet opined. "Jantzi treated me very well after marrying into the family, but I never asked a lot of questions about anything. I just did what I was told when I was told to do it. Jantzi didn't like questions of any sort and considered inquiries the same as insubordination. At least that's the way she explained it to me."

"Everything comes with a price, I guess."

"Dr. Shaw, you asked about Sarita. Believe it or not, Sarita is my sister-in-law! She is Stormy's younger sister. She went to work for Dr. Diller after her dad died a few years back."

"Sarita is your sister-in-law?" responded Dr. Shaw as he reared his head backwards. "There aren't a whole lot of people in these sagebrushed parts, but I never would have guessed that to be the case. Boy howdy! That puts a whole new spin on top of that one! I thought I might like to ask her to go on a ride in the country with me. Do you think she would be at all interested in such an outing with a country vet?"

"I am probably not the best person to ask about such romantic matters," Chet replied cautiously. "Even though I have been married for awhile, a guy sort of forgets about all that courting this and that. The other thing in the mix is that there's a cow hand who works for the Toppens who is really sweet on Sarita. As near as I can tell, she's head over heels in love with him, too. He's a nice enough guy, but doesn't even own a vehicle, and Toppens are letting him live in their bunkhouse. My mother-in-law was sore displeased that Sarita set her sights on a saddle tramp. Oh, his name is Wyn Moreland. He grew up in a boy's home and is pretty much a drifter. I suppose you could wait until she gets off work some afternoon and meet her in the parking lot or something. I don't think Dr. Diller's office takes too kindly to dating calls and all that mushy stuff."

"Thanks for the information, Chet. I will have to give some thought as to how to play my hand. Your wife is probably wondering what's taking so long down here at the barn tonight."

"No concerns regarding Stormy. She's staying at the main ranch house. I called her when I discovered Braezee had a problem with her foot. I didn't have time to make the trips back and forth to bring Stormy back down to the lower ranch house."

Dr. Shaw started to ask, "Couldn't she drive herself back down here tonight?" but then caught himself before a word spilled from his mouth. "I am going to head home now. Get some rest, Chet. Again, I am sorry for the death in your family. Please let me know if any of you need anything else. I would be more than happy to lend a helping hand. I will set your groceries on your kitchen counter."

Securing the compartments in his truck and double checking to make sure everything was in its proper place, Dr. Shaw left the lower ranch house and drove toward the main house. Steadying the steering wheel with the top of his right knee, he lifted his cowboy hat with his left hand, and scratched the top of his head with his right hand. He was lamenting the fact that Sarita seemed to have already set her sights on a beau. As he approached the main house, he slowed down to ten miles per hour. In the distance, he saw the top floor of the Sabblonti Ranch house lit up like a Christmas tree. What was going on during the midnight hour, pray tell?

CHAPTER TWENTY-SEVEN

Meanwhile back at the main ranch house, Stormy jumped to her feet in the family room as the clock struck one. She did not realize that she had fallen into such a deep sleep. Wrapping a denim lap quilt around herself, she ventured into the kitchen. "Hopefully that half-baked husband of mine had the presence of mind to buy some decent food at The Shadowy Merc," she muttered to herself as she selected a can of soup from the pantry to heat it in the microwave. After brewing herself a cup of coffee, she sat down in the dining room to mentally plan her strategy and put the heavy scope on the inside of the house since she was alone.

Stormy reminded herself that there were distinct advantages to living in the boondocks where they virtually had to pipe daylight into you. She sensed she was going through a major metamorphosis. She verbalized her concerns, "Is this what happens to the oldest child following the death of both parents?"

Polishing off her bowl of food and savoring her coffee, Stormy felt warm enough to shed the lap quilt and laid it across the couch.

Walking up the long flight of stairs to the third floor, Stormy immediately realized that every light was on. She reminded herself that she had not even gone up to the top floor after Chet let her off at the house. Who or what had turned all of those light switches on? She checked inside each room to see if her mother had timer switches attached to any of the lamps or main light switches and discovered that she did not. Just as Stormy turned around to walk back down the hall after checking the last room at the end of the hallway, she heard hastened footsteps. Was she imagining things? Whirling around, she literally saw the southern window open about two feet and then close tightly again. Oh, my stars and garters! Stormy wished that Chet was there with her at that very moment. Did he prefer his animals over her? She made a decision that as soon as they buried her mother and got her financial affairs in order, she would need to tune him up and jerk the slack out of his country western jeans. Perhaps there was a method to her mother's madness after it was all said and done. Time would tell. Stormy encouraged herself, "Keep your head about you and get to work girl. You might as well make the most of drinking that caffeine at one thirty in the morning."

During all of their childhood years and beyond, Jantzi Belle had one hard and fast rule for her daughters — they could never go to the third floor of the house. Having been raised with that regulation for as long as she had a memory, Stormy never questioned it. She did not suspect anything morbid or unusual. She just attributed it to the fact that her mother was an extremely private person; therefore, it was only natural that she reinforced those strict boundaries. In addition, Ace had kept guns in the master bedroom, and Jantzi Belle didn't want her daughters near any of them. Stormy wished her father had never owned a gun.

When they were growing up, Stormy and Sarita had full

run of the second floor of the house. On the very rare occasions when their grandparents, aunts, uncles, cousins, and other relatives visited, all of them stayed on the second floor as well. Speaking of visits from relatives, Stormy could remember very few from either of her maternal aunts, Jonsey and Jillian. She much preferred Jonsey to Jillian, who said children should be seen and not heard.

Easing into each of the rooms on the third floor, Stormy drank in the ornate cherry wood furniture and accessories. Who slept in the two extra bedrooms on this floor?

All of the rooms were open except her dad's office. Above the door hung a piece of wood with the black inscription of *Ace's Place.* A hole had been drilled in each end of the 2 x 4 and barbed wire had been strung through the ends of each one in order to hang it above the door. Stormy started to open the door and then reconsidered. Somehow, she sensed there was nothing in there that would help her right now.

Not wanting to revisit the master bedroom at this exact moment, Stormy turned to her right, and stopped in front of the first door on the right. Stepping inside, she looked at the pictures on the wall. Why would Jantzi Belle have plastered this room with pictures of her parents, her wedding, Stormy's individual school pictures, and Stormy and Chet's wedding? It must have been because this is where Jantzi spent most of her days. This would explain why no one else ever really saw her out and about, in town, or on the ranch. Stormy remembered her mother mentioning one time, "All administrators need a command control center." Suffice it to say, this must have been hers.

Jantzi had placed her oak roll-top desk to the left of the window on the east side of the house which afforded a peaceful view of the pine and quaking aspen trees. The office chair was facing west as Stormy looked at it. Obviously, her mother had turned around in her chair, stood up, and walked out of the room without having turned the chair back around and pushed it against the desk where it would normally belong. Stormy was struck by how neat and tidy the office appeared. There was a place for everything, and everything was in its place.

A row of filing cabinets lined the wall on the left-hand side of the desk. Stormy hoped these were not locked, as there was a keyhole in the top drawer of each one. They looked older than the hills and were a faded dark green color. Pushing in a button that protruded out about a half inch from the top drawer caused the drawer to release and open. Stormy relaxed somewhat. She conjectured that she probably could have ultimately found a key to open the filing cabinets, but did not want to burn up the precious time looking for one in the wee morning hours. This was premium time and she needed to cash in on it without interruptions.

Brushing her left hand across the file folders in the top drawer, Stormy quickly surmised that her mother began this filing system the first year her parents were married. Each file was alphabetized, and after each title appeared the numbers — 1958. Opening the drawers beneath the first one, and viewing the contents therein along with the files in the various cabinets of the succeeding rows, Stormy found the last ones which read — 1999. Jantzi Belle had her pulse firmly on the Sabblonti enterprise since the day she married into it. The drawers were very heavy to open and close. Small wonder, Stormy reminded herself, these were fireproof storage cabinets. They might well have belonged to her paternal grandparents. It would have been a real project to haul those cabinets to the top floor.

Sitting down in her mother's office chair, Stormy turned around and scooted her feet along the plastic floor mat to get closer to the roll top desk. She deemed it odd that the roll top part of the desk had been pulled down flush with the top of the desk, as if her mother had said good night to it, but her office chair was at the end of the long plastic mat which extended eight feet in length. Shouldn't the chair have been next to the desk inside its little cubby hole area? Maybe those footsteps she heard in the hallway had something to do with the misplacement of the chair.

Lifting the roll top portion of the desk, Stormy enjoyed grabbing hold of the white knobs on the little drawers, pulling them out, and discovering what was inside each one. Even the paper clips were organized by various shades of colors. In the center of the small drawers there was a row of four vertically stacked shelves for file folders. They were empty. Stormy conjectured her mother was ready to close her business and financial year even though she was not ready to close her life. Above the little pull-out drawers on each side of the top of the desk were seven vertically shaped slots in which to place envelopes, bills, and similar items. Nothing was inside the seven slots on the left-hand side. Six on the right-hand side were empty, but there were several envelopes and papers stuffed into the far-right hand slot.

Stormy's left knee bumped against the side of the desk, which drew her attention to the row of four drawers on the left-hand side. Reaching down to the first one, she opened it. "This is exactly what I am looking for!" exclaimed Stormy. Each of Jantzi's checkbooks was neatly lined up, one behind the other in the top drawer, and each checkbook was a different color. Stormy spent some time examining each one of them. The color of the checks matched the color of the checkbook cover. The Sabblonti brand was printed on each check along with the designation of the particular account, such as the Operating Account. Stormy thought it a bit odd that her mother had her full name, Jantzi Belle Siddonz Sabblonti, printed on all of the checks. That would be a very long signature to sign each time, and her mother was the check writing queen. None of the checkbooks contained a register. How did her mother keep track of how much money she had to spend? Ace and Chet made the money, and Jantzi spent it. That's the way it was until a few days ago. Who would get to spend the money from now on?

Looking through the other drawers in the bottom of the roll top desk yielded only basic office supplies and accessories. In the bottom drawer on the right-hand side, there were letter sized pastel colored file folders. This seemed odd because Jantzi always said, "Paint in bold colors, not pale pastels." For someone who had lived her life in bold colors, why did she choose pastel office supplies? She must have been attempting to strike a balance.

Skimming through the folders, Stormy noticed one that read *1999 Tax Info for Accountant*. Because how to spell *accountant* was the only thing she knew about financial matters, she quickly closed the drawer. Resting her elbows on the desktop and propping up her chin with her hands, Stormy came to the sudden conclusion that she would need someone to help her sort all of this out. She was not particularly close to anyone but her mother. Following the events of Christmas Eve, she did not want to involve Sarita. Grammy Mabel was dead so she could be of no assistance.

Her father had been gone for a number of years. Chet didn't seem to be really comfortable with financial matters. His strengths were working with the cattle, managing the range, and all that encompassed. He was exceptionally good with horses. Before they were married, Chet had a job breaking horses to ride, and he also worked at a race track. Stormy didn't press him for the details of this specific part of his life. In her estimation, only low lifes spent time at a race track squandering their money. Chet had better never even entertain the idea of getting into horse racing in any way, shape, or form, and definitely not chariot racing.

Pushing the chair back from her mother's desk, Stormy started to stand up when the tip of bright white caught her right eye. She reached for the handful of envelopes and assorted papers crammed into the far-right slot above the little pull-out drawers of the desk. A couple of the unopened envelopes fell onto the desk. Holding the items in her left hand, Stormy began to sort through them with her right hand. There was a bill from the utility company, the telephone company, Clinker's Feed Store, along with a gas company located in Ignee County. Gathering the envelopes that had dropped onto the desk and combining them with the ones in her left hand, Stormy started to place them back into the wooden slot, when a single piece of white paper folded into thirds fell out. She could tell that it pertained to something in her mother's handwriting. Stormy wondered who her mother could be penning a personal letter to this close to the end of the year. It was probably specific instructions for her accountant.

Stormy unfolded the piece of paper as she started to sit down. Her eyes just about bugged out of her head when they fell upon the first few lines which read,

"Last Will and Testament

Of

Jantzi Belle Siddonz Sabblonti
I, Jantzi Belle Siddonz Sabblonti, being of sound mind, do hereby make my last will and testament."

Stormy sunk down in her mother's office chair. She wondered what time it was. How long had she been upstairs? She carefully folded the piece of paper and gently tapped it against her left hand several times. Was her mother of sound mind when she recently penned this will? This was just a piece of notebook paper. It wasn't even a real will, or was it?

A folded newspaper clipping had also fallen from between the stack of envelopes in Stormy's left hand. It had been removed from the October 1999 issue of *The Ridgemonte Rider* and was titled, **"Inheritances: Avoiding Utter Chaos at the Worst Possible Time."** This was a four-column lengthy article that Stormy had no intention of wasting her time reading.

Stormy looked around the room for a wall clock. Her mother watched time like a hawk, so there had to be one somewhere. Scanning the walls again, Stormy noticed an object that clearly resembled a wall mirror. When she looked the first time, it appeared as a mirror, mirror, on the wall. She blinked and the surface became a clock which registered four in the morning. She blinked a second time and the clock face disappeared.

Stormy opened the top drawer on the left-hand side of the roll top desk and placed her mother's will behind the row of checkbooks. She slowly closed the drawer as red-hot tears welled up inside her eyes and spilled onto the desk. She wanted to call Chet and tell him to drive to the main ranch house this minute, but maybe he had not gotten much sleep because of being up so late with Braezee. Well, too bad, so sad. Someone else could take care of that stupid horse now. Stormy decided she had better get Chet's to-do list written and get him out of bed and on task. The sooner he found out who was now in charge, the better. Besides that, he needed to deliver Jantzi's clothing to Lambent's Funeral Home. Stormy sensed the next few days were going to be stormy.

CHAPTER TWENTY-EIGHT

Chet had fallen into bed a little after three that same morning. He did not hear the phone ring when Stormy called him at four thirty. She dismissed his lack of answering and attributed it to the fact that he was a very sound sleeper. She used to tell him that he could sleep through an earthquake. Speaking of such, there was about to be an earthquake alright, but not due to the normal shifting of the tectonic plates of the earth. The main quaking and shaking would be occurring on the Sabblonti cattle spread and surrounding area.

Stormy trudged down the hallway and opened the door to her mother's bedroom. She cringed as she looked around the room. She was not about to muck it up. That task would fall to the cleaning crew, and if one could not be scheduled, it would be one of the first things on Chet's list. Sorting through the clothes in the closet, she selected a bright red sweater, ankle length red suede skirt and matching jacket. While she lived, Jantzi was always in control. Why should it be any different now that she was dead? Surely, she could still control from her grave. Red was the color worn by women who were fearless and operated important headquarters, even if it was on the third floor of a main ranch house in the mountains of a remote county. Perception was everything. Reality was entirely different.

Those worlds often clashed.

Even the thought of preparing people for their funerals creeped Stormy out. Reminding herself that her beloved mother needed to look her absolute best in her lovely white satin casket, she selected her makeup, complete with a bright red shade of lipstick labeled *Regal Red*. With Jantzi's funeral clothing and makeup in hand, Stormy made her way down the three flights of stairs and placed the items inside a brown grocery bag from The Shadowy Merc.

Chet answered the phone on the eighth ring. "Hello," he said groggily as he rolled over in bed.

"Chetter, honey," Stormy cooed as she added the sweetness to her voice. "You sound so sleepy. What time did you get to bed, lovey?"

"The last time I looked at the clock it was sometime around three. After Doc left, I had to stay up with Braezee to make sure she was okay. She's my special mare and I just couldn't bear it if anything happened to her. I have had her since she was a baby. I broke her, trained her, and the whole horse deal."

Stormy bristled as she listened to Chet drone on about his horse. She lit into him, "Listen to me, Chet Carleton Castins, you need to wake up. Mother's funeral is tomorrow, and you still need to take her clothing and accessories into Lambent's Funeral Home. I have all of the stuff picked out and have placed it inside a bag here at the main house. Get your chores done so you can be here by ten thirty and drive into town to get this taken care of. Time is flying by like an arrow."

"Wow, you used my full name so I must be in real trouble, even though I haven't done a single thing to warrant it! I didn't know you remembered my full name. You must have seen it somewhere recently or something. There are times when I just don't comprehend you women folk."

"Never mind us women folk. You better not be late because you don't want me driving down there to get you. Trust me when I tell you that. And while I'm thinking about it, be sure to tell Mr. Lambent or whoever is working today that we want all of mother's jewelry and the gold from the crowns in her mouth. None of it goes to the grave with her."

"You have got to be kidding me, Stormy! Extracting gold from a dead person's teeth is just hideous. Don't you want your mother to rest in peace and leave her mouth alone?"

"With gold averaging around $300 per ounce, you can bet your bottom dollar I want every bit of it. Those funeral home folks can just extract it, melt it down, give it to you, and we will pretend that it didn't come from Mother's mouth when we spend it. I would rather they do that than sell it to Dr. Diller to use for one of his patient's gold crowns. If you behave yourself, I might let you have some of the money to buy a new little foal. I will make a mental note of how you perform in public over the next few months before I make my final decision. Let me clarify my offer. Whatever the gold will fetch on the open market after extraction from Mother's mouth is what you can have to purchase your next horse. That might give you some incentive. Have you too quickly forgotten that it's my signature that carries the authority on all of the bank accounts? She who owns the gold and the money is who makes the rules, and rules the roost, along with the rooster."

"Stormy, you saw the figures of how much money is sitting in your mother's various bank accounts at Cattlemen's Central, and you're worried about some gold in her mouth when she is dead? I think you have flipped your cooker lid. Well, that can't be since you don't like to cook!"

"Don't get smart mouthed with me," warned Stormy as she slammed the phone down.

Chet let the phone dangle from its cord along the side of his bed. He pulled the covers to his chin and fell fast asleep.

Beebee and Blue were barking in unison outside Chet's front door. "Alright, alright, canine alarm clocks," yelled Chet as he got out of bed. His right leg brushed against the dangling phone. "Well, I guess that's one way to prevent incoming calls," he said laughingly. A few minutes later he opened the door and welcomed his best friends inside. "Shall we go down and see how Braezee is faring this morning?"

As soon as Chet opened the barn door, his mare began to whinny. A large smile appeared on Chet's face as he approached Braezee, wrapped his right arm around her neck, and pulled her close to him. "Glad to see you're doing better this morning, girl! You had me plum worried last night. Good thing the doc was able to make it out here after hours. How about some oats? I'll give you the good stuff first before I have to be mean to you."

Braezee munched her oats leisurely as Chet gently lifted her right hind leg to check on her wound. He surmised from the way she was applying a little more weight on her back foot that the healing had already begun. "Now that you are finished with that treat, I need to tie you a little closer to the front of the stall so I can give you the injection. Beebee and Blue, I sure wish you could help me, but I realize your limitations. Nothing personal."

Chet rubbed Braezee's rump as he administered the antibiotic to her. He applied some additional duct tape around her hoof and took her temperature which was still below 100. "Okay, girl, you have the good day. I have business to tend to in town."

After cooking some scrambled eggs and downing one half pot of coffee, Chet got cleaned up so he could head to the main ranch house. He fed his pooches and double checked to make sure the house and barn doors were locked. Ten minutes or so into the drive, he remembered that he had wanted to be sure to take his checkbook so he could stop by Dr. Shaw's clinic and pay him for the groceries. Well, that would just have to wait until another day.

Having totally lost track of time during the morning, Chet was seemingly in no hurry to arrive at the main ranch house. He wondered if he could just sort of slide into the house, grab the bag of Jantzi's belongings, and drive into town without really being noticed. No such luck.

As soon as he walked onto the front porch, dropped the four large bags of Stormy's clothing, and opened the door, Chet knew he was in trouble. Was he seeing clearly or was Stormy's face as red as it appeared?

"Have you been crying, Stormy? Your face is as red as Rudolph's nose."

Stormy shoved the brown grocery sack into Chet's chest. "Do you even know what time it is, you dunce? Take this stuff into Lambent's immediately and don't dawdle around. Watch your step or else we will be conducting double funerals the same day. Be careful how you handle that brown bag. The heirloom photographs I've selected for the programs are inside. Remind Tracie to print at least 1,500. Even though it's winter, people will turn out in droves. I don't want to be embarrassed by not having enough. Sabblontis lack for nothing. It's high time everyone in these parts recognizes the top horse."

Chet drove into Ridgemonte and took the sack of Jantzi's personal belongings inside the funeral home. Walking slowly down the hallway, he entered Tracie Sudder's office. "Hi, I was hoping you would be working today," announced Chet. "Oh, sorry, your back was toward me so I didn't see you were on the phone."

Since Tracie was on hold with another business in Ridgemonte, she placed her hand over the receiver and replied in a soft voice, "Hi Chet, no worries, I will be finished with this call in a couple of minutes. Please have a seat. You can set your grocery bag on the chair next to you if you like."

After completing her call, Tracie came around the side of her desk and extended her right hand to Chet. "How are you doing today? I know these circumstances can be so hard on families. You look like you could use a hug, but how about a handshake instead?"

Chet hadn't been offered a hug in quite a while and didn't realize how much he missed one. He had established proper boundaries in his married life and maintained them even in the most contrary of circumstances.

Standing up, Chet said, "I appreciate your kind words. Stormy sent these clothes and whatever else in the sack for my mother-in-law's funeral tomorrow." He shifted nervously from one foot to another. He thought he was going to fall in the middle of the floor if the elongated toes of his cowboy boots happened to tangle with one another.

"Is there something else, Chet? You seem a bit nervous. Take your time. Sit down for awhile if you need to. I am in no hurry. Jantzi's funeral is the only one we have scheduled for tomorrow, so we have plenty of time. Spring, summer, and fall months are far busier for us with respect to conducting funerals because that is when it seems folks are working cattle, rodeoing, and all that related stuff."

"Well, now that you mention it, there is something else, but it's sure a strange request. I would be in a horse trailer load of trouble if I drove back home and did not mention it. Stormy would take the horse whip to me, for sure."

"Chet, you are just being silly! Why, you are a grown man! It's not as if you are a five-year-old boy that needs to be disciplined, and certainly not with a horse whip!" Tracie looked deeply into Chet's eyes and could have sworn she saw pain floating within.

"Oh, I just use horse racing terms every now and then since I used to work at the track when I was younger. Don't put a whole lot of stock into what I say since it doesn't really count for much these days."

Tracie was of the opinion that what people tended to say when they were nervous was worth taking note of as it usually had some element of truth to it. Walking back around to take her seat in front of her desk, Tracie opened a manila folder. "Go ahead, Chet, and I will make some notations before the service tomorrow."

"Well, uh, SSSSS, SS, SSS, Stormy wants to have all of the gold removed from her mother's teeth before she's placed in her casket, and then she wants you to give it to her after its melted down. She also wants all of her jewelry. It was so hectic Christmas Eve night at the ranch that I can't even remember what Jantzi was wearing or anything. It all happened so fast and was like something unfolding from a horror movie. Oh, and one last thing. The other day when we stopped in here to see you, did Stormy tell you how many of those little funeral programs she wanted you to print? She told me this morning that she wants 1,500. She's firm on that number."

Tracie had been writing some notes on a blank piece of paper inside the folder she had marked for Jantzi Belle Sabblonti. "Let's see here, I thought she said 500, and that's what I have written down. I may have made a mistake, so I am glad you verified the number."

Chet continued, "Stormy's convinced that even though the weather has turned cooler there will still be lots of folks who will attend, and she wants each one of them to be sure to have something in hand to remember her mother. Good thing we are having the services inside the school auditorium since it's heated. None of the churches around here are big enough to hold everybody that's going to show up, and Sabblontis aren't church going people anyhow. I assume Mr. Lambent called Stormy to get the information for the service. I never even thought about it until now as to who is going to speak at Jantzi's funeral. There would be so many people to choose from, so I don't know who Stormy settled on to do that."

"I don't have much information in this file regarding the particulars for the service. Mr. Lambent or one of his assistants usually takes care of that. Let me check to see if he is in his office."

Chet was too exhausted to be thinking about much of anything. He never dreamed that he would lose his mother-in-law so early into his marriage to Stormy.

Tracie returned within a few minutes to inform Chet that Mr. Lambent had everything in hand and that he had telephoned Stormy to collect the necessary information. She added that Mr. Lambent had dispatched someone to the mountains to gather the juniper branches, twigs, and berries to decorate the outside of the casket. "The services have been scheduled for two in the afternoon, which gives everybody ample time to drive in from the surrounding towns and counties as well. I can remember that your father-in-law's funeral was very well attended in the big meadow on the Sabblonti Ranch. Lots of the local business people came to Ace's funeral. I think it was held about the same time in the afternoon with the general idea in mind that people required extra travel time. Of course, he didn't die in the winter, and some of the outlying roads might be bad this time of year. I haven't heard what the weather's been like in Ignee County."

Chet thanked Tracie profusely for her help and kindness.

"Don't give it a thought, Chet. I like to help people. I discovered that I have lots of mercy to give out like bouquets of flowers during the storms of life."

"You definitely do have mercy. It's kind of goofy to think that a man could be given a bouquet of anything. What do you call those single type flowers that men wear at weddings?"

"It's called a boutonniere. It's a real funny word."

"A boot what? I wear cowboy boots, but I have never heard of a boutonniere. Stormy was the only one that had flowers when we got married and she carried a bouquet of beautiful wildflowers from the high country. But, rest assured, you have given me a bouquet of kindness today for which I thank you."

Could that have been the early mist of a tear forming in Chet's right eye or had the reflection of the lights in the ceiling played a trick on Tracie's eyes? She was confident it was the former.

After Chet departed from her office, Tracie stood watching out her window and pondered the last half hour's visit with Chet. Something did not seem quite right. She chocked it up to the family trying to process grief, which was never an easy thing to do in anybody's world anytime.

CHAPTER TWENTY-NINE

Wednesday, December 29th, dawned crisp and clear. Neither Chet nor Stormy had slept well the night before. There was not a great deal of difference in the temperature inside the cab of Chet's pickup compared to the outside, despite the heater being turned on full blast. Chet tried to no avail to engage Stormy in meaningful and comforting conversation en route to the Ridgemonte High School auditorium.

Stormy had tried to eat a bite of late breakfast, but had no appetite. Chef Chet's frying of bacon had just about fried her last nerve. She chided him for gorging himself as he mounted his defense that he had not had much to eat for the past several days. He also reminded her that it was going to be a long day, and, unlike after Ace's funeral where Jantzi hired the country western caterers in Blunte County to put on the big spread, there would be no meal after the funeral. Stormy advised Chet to use his head for something besides a hat rack as funerals conducted during the winter presented far more of a challenge.

Chet pulled into the high school parking lot at ten minutes past one. Reminding himself that he was once again on public display, he straightened his vest as he walked around the side of his pickup to open the passenger door for Stormy.

"I did not realize how scraggly you looked," scolded Stormy. "When was the last time you stopped in to see the barber? You need to shave your moustache off and not plan to let it grow again. I don't want to be married to someone who looks so old and decrepit. Take your time when you escort me inside the building since I am wearing a long skirt."

"It's not like I've had a lot of free time on my hands the past few days. If my memory serves me correctly, you told me not that long ago that you liked my moustache."

"Well, that was then, and this is now. Comes the revolution with the new chapters of the Sabblonti family."

"It's a good thing I don't read much," Chet retorted.

As soon as she stepped foot into the auditorium, Stormy began to weep uncontrollably. Chet ushered her to a chair immediately to his left. "Why don't you sit down here for a little bit while I round up Mr. Lambent?"

Chet's eyes swept the entire room as his heart swelled with profound appreciation for all that the funeral home had done in preparation for Jantzi's services. Everything looked so uniform along with the ornate white casket serving as the perfect focal point. Chet thought to himself, "Dead or alive, Jantzi would be so pleased that she was still the center of attention." The juniper wreath decoration heavily laden with berries covered the top of the casket and was the ideal accent needed. The song titled *Your Permanent Rest On That High, High Desert Mountain* could be heard through the sound system while Chet walked down the adjacent hallway looking for Larry Lambent and his staff.

With only about a half hour remaining until the funeral was scheduled to begin, Chet wondered where everyone was hiding. Surely the funeral directors would not be eating a late lunch and shaving it so close to the start of the service. He finally spotted someone round the corner of the hallway. "For a minute there, I thought I was going to have to conduct this funeral," said Chet. "I walked all around inside the building and couldn't scare anybody up. Where's Mr. Lambent?"

"He had a last-minute change of plans and advised me he would not be able to be here today, so he sent me and a couple of our associates instead," Travis Fisen explained as he extended his right hand to Chet.

"Pleased to meet you, Travis. Have you done lots of funerals before? I sure hope so because my pretty wife would be most unhappy with anybody but the best. She's pretty particular with anything pertaining to her mother, God rest her sweet soul."

"With the adjustments happening so quickly earlier today, I did not have time to notify anyone. Rest assured, I have been a mortician for almost twenty years. I moved here from the southwest five years ago at the request of Mr. Lambent. I really like the community. There are an awful lot of nice folks who live in these parts."

"I was going to say that I don't remember you from Ace's funeral back in 1993, but then again, you hadn't moved here yet so that makes perfect sense. Could we head back inside the auditorium so you can give me the run down on what's going to be happening when? Stormy, my wife, is really struggling as you can only imagine. It's real tough to bury your mother."

"Chet, I am so sorry for your loss. I have not yet had to say a final goodbye to my precious mother, so I can't totally relate. I will do my very best today and hope that all of you are well satisfied. I think that's about all anybody can ask of someone else."

"I am sure you will do just fine, Travis. Can I take a look at one of those programs for a second? I did not see any of them when we first entered the building."

"Sure, please follow me." Handing the 4.25-inch x 5.50-inch light sage green colored paper to Chet, Travis excused himself to go put the finishing touches on a couple of remaining items.

Chet was struck by the photo Stormy had selected to be placed in the oval frame on the outside of the paper. It was of Ace and Jantzi on their wedding day in 1958. Granted, it was her mother and she could select any picture she wanted. He sure as the world wasn't going to bounce her about it now or ever. He had been walking into a strong head wind for days now and would be relieved when the wind died down. When the calendar turned to 2000, Chet was confident that it would.

The line beneath Ace's and Jantzi's wedding picture on the front of the funeral program read,

In Loving Memory Of
Jantzi Belle Siddonz Sabblonti
"Queen of Diamonds ~~~ Queen of Our World, Forever"

Chet deemed it odd that it did not list Jantzi's year of birth or her year of death. Oh well, no biggie, he was not in charge of supplying any information in this regard.

Opening the program, Chet stared at the two photos on the left-hand side. The top photo was Stormy's high school graduation picture, and directly beneath it was Chet and Stormy's wedding photo.

The information on the right-hand side of the program was quite scant as it listed the date, time, and location of Jantzi's funeral with Lambent's as officiating the services. There were no pallbearers or honorary pallbearers. Raising his eyebrows and glancing toward the casket, Chet made a mental note that it looked quite heavy. No worries. He would leave the heavy lifting to Lambent's. After all, that was what they were being paid to do.

Turning to the back page of the program, Chet was somewhat surprised to see the following:

Stormy had regained her composure to the point where she could at least approach the casket. It was as if her mother was still speaking to her, "Stormy, darling, remember that you can catch more flies with honey than you can with vinegar." Generating some sugar substitute deep within her, Stormy released it into the atmosphere. "Travis, would you be so kind as to please remove the gorgeous juniper wreath from Mother's casket so that I can view her? I want the casket to be open before the funeral starts so that when people pour in, they will be struck with her elegance. She was so magnificent in real life, and I want everyone's last memory of her to be likewise. By the way, where are all of the beautiful arrangements sent by other people? I know the floral shop is open today."

"Lambent's didn't receive a call from the floral shop notifying us that there were any potted plants or flowers ordered by anyone else for the services today," Travis explained as he quickly removed the oversized juniper trimmings, and gently laid them across four of the folding chairs arranged close to the casket. Chet crept behind Stormy quietly and placed his hand on the small of her back, which caused her to wince and jump forward. "Get your hands off me, Chet. The last thing I need today is you trying to smother me." Chet was secretly hoping that Travis had not heard what Stormy had said.

"I will get this opened so you can see your mother, Stormy," offered Travis. "I think you will be well pleased with Lambent's efforts."

As soon as the casket was opened, and Stormy saw Jantzi, she let out a gasp, "Oh, Mother, you look absolutely radiant! Are you sure you are not still alive? Travis, she looks extraordinary! The red against the white satin backdrop is the exact effect I was hoping to achieve. Would you and Chet mind leaving the auditorium for a bit so that I can have a few private minutes with my mother? I need to ask her a few things. Thank you."

Travis shot Chet a quizzical look as Chet just shrugged his shoulders and walked toward the exit doors into the long hallway.

Touching her mother's right hand, Stormy began, "Oh, Mother dearest, I know that you can hear me. You might not be able to communicate with me right now, but I am sure you will figure out a way to send me messages in the future."

Stormy had thought of two additional things she wanted to say to her mother, but she looked up and saw Sarita enter the auditorium, walk forward three steps, and then stop abruptly. Stormy looked inside her mother's casket. Time seemed to stand still. Who would make the next move?

Chet and Travis entered the auditorium from the far side and walked toward Sarita. Chet hugged his sister-in-law and introduced her to Travis. Chet then extended his right elbow, and Sarita took his arm as he escorted her to Jantzi's casket. Sensing the chill in the room, Travis stepped away to check the sound system.

"At least you had the decency to leave that saddle tramp of yours home today, Sarita, and not disgrace Mother's funeral by bringing him here. I will not concern myself with some scraggler who will always embarrass me."

Chet started to address Stormy, but reminded himself that he was trying to avoid the verbal horse whip. Stormy had been standing near the center of the casket, but now moved to the far left and closer to her mother's head. She rubbed her mother's hair softly. Sarita stood at the end of the casket in total silence. She turned and walked toward the chairs.

"Sarita, please have a seat in the front row as that has been reserved for family," Travis explained. "Mr. Lambent wasn't exactly sure how many family members would be here today, so we reserved the first four rows on each side of the aisle. Do you know how many relatives will be attending?"

"I have not talked with my aunts or anyone from my daddy's family to know if any of them were able to make the trip. Stormy would be the one to ask about all of those details."

Checking his wrist watch, Travis noted that it was exactly two o'clock. He opted to not ask Stormy regarding the attendance of her relatives. Walking to the back of the auditorium, Travis checked the volume of the music, which could be heard just fine. He mustered his nerve to approach Jantzi's casket one more time. "Stormy, it's two now. How much longer would you like to wait until we start the services?"

"We need to wait a few more minutes at least. People are really busy between Christmas and New Year's. All of the roads are in good shape, and those traveling from surrounding counties might not have allotted enough time. I will let you know when I am ready to have you start the services. When I take my seat on the front row that will be your signal. Don't plan on starting a minute before then."

Sarita chose to sit toward the end of the first row on the right-hand side. Spotting the portable coat rack after she had sat down, she got up and hung her well-worn ankle length wool dress coat on a hanger. Dr. Diller had expressed his sympathies to Sarita concerning the loss of her mother and had said he was sorry that he would be unable to attend the services because there was an emergency extraction of a patient's wisdom teeth scheduled for the same time.

Deeply engrossed in looking at her mother's funeral

program, Sarita did not see Dr. Ben Shaw walk into the auditorium. Chet spotted his white beaver Stetson and walked over to greet him. "Wow, Doc, how nice of you to come today to show your support for the Sabblonti family!"

"I was hoping there would be no sudden critter emergency so I could be here. How's Braezee?"

"She seemed fine the last time I checked on her."

"That's good news, Chet. I am sorry I didn't arrive sooner. Since I was running late, I tried to enter through the back doors of the auditorium, but they're locked up tighter than Fort Knox. Glad I got here before the services started. Look at this place! Somebody went to a whole lot of work to get all this set up. Very nice. Where is everybody?"

"You tell me, Doc. The roads are clear and there have not been any recent storms. Maybe folks are out of town for the holidays or holed up at home. I appreciate you taking the time from your busy schedule to stop in. Oh, how would you like to say *hello* to my sister-in-law? I am quite confident I am not the only reason you are sporting your Sunday best today. One small suggestion, I think you should remove that rattlesnake hide hat band and go with something a little friendlier before you play your next card."

Sarita stood to her feet as Dr. Shaw and Chet approached her. "Sarita, I am sure you've met our outstanding vet, Dr. Ben Shaw. He is a God-send in these parts. When my best mare was struggling to stand the other day, Doc and I pretty much pulled an all nighter to save her."

"It's nice to see you, Sarita, and please accept my deepest sympathies following the loss of your dear mother. I can only imagine how difficult the past few days have been. You probably remember me from Dr. Diller's office. I am the *Popcorn Ball Patient*." Dr. Shaw made a mental note of the lack of any rings on either of Sarita's hands at that moment.

"Thank you, Dr. Shaw, and it's nice to see you again, too. It is so kind of you to attend the funeral."

Chet located Travis within the auditorium. "Are we about ready to roll this wagon train?"

"We will be when your wife sits down and sends me the signal. Not a moment before then."

Chet wondered if Stormy was sending smoke signals these days since she seemed to be burning up inside most of the time.

A dark whirlwind blew through the front doors. Salina Bevvins was dressed from head to toe in jet black, complete with black wool cape, black fringed hat, black leather gloves, and black knee length boots. Everyone played the statue game as Salina hung her cape on a hanger and walked toward Chet. Oh my, no time to dodge this bullet! Dr. Shaw turned to Chet, "Better you than me, pardner! I have my sights set elsewhere."

"You think I don't! I am not the budding bachelor in this building!"

Pouring on the charm, Salina wrapped her long arms around Chet's neck. "So sorry I am late, and glad the main event has not already started. Please accept my deepest condolences on the death of your mother-in-law." She placed a firm kiss on his left cheek, which left a bright red outline.

Dr. Shaw burst out laughing and quickly covered his face with his Stetson. He turned sharply to his right, walked to the coat rack, placed his hat on the top shelf, and walked to the front row of seats. Since Sarita was sitting in the seat next to the last one, he opted to sit beside her. "Do you mind if I sit here? You look like you could use some company."

"I'm sorry, but I don't feel like talking to anyone."

Dr. Shaw stood up, looked around at the auditorium full of empty seats, walked to the back of the room, up the far outside of the left aisle of seats, and sat in the end seat on the front row.

Travis had helped to officiate innumerable funerals over the past several years, but none quite like this one. Granted, each one unfolded differently.

Chet had spent some time in the *Cowboys* restroom trying to remove the red lipstick marks from his cheek. He was able to get most of it off, but there was still some residue that remained. His long-sleeved white shirt with silver colored pearl snaps just accentuated his bright left cheek.

At long last Stormy stepped back and sat in a chair in the front row a few feet from Jantzi's casket. Chet sat to her left as he was quite confident Stormy had not taken in the whole hug in the aisle business. He reasoned that his cheek would be less noticeable if he sat to her left during the lengthy funeral service.

Travis stepped to the microphone, reached down under the podium to retrieve his black officiating notebook, and placed it on top of the podium. He cleared his throat, and began to speak, "Good afternoon everyone . . . "

Salina slid into the chair on Chet's left side. He could feel Stormy stiffen as never before as she arched her back and shot him a left sided peripheral death glance. Salina placed her right knee visibly close to Chet's left, which caused him to inch closer to Stormy, who in turn moved to the next chair on her right. This little game continued for the next few minutes. Travis, losing his composure, turned away from the microphone and feigned checking something inside Jantzi's casket before resuming her funeral service. When he returned to the podium, four of the five people in attendance were sitting to his far left on the front row of chairs bunched up like a small herd of cattle. There was one stray on the far-right hand row. This gave new definition to uncomfortable. Granted, this was one for the funeral record books. With 1,500 open chairs in a country sized auditorium, Travis had not witnessed a seating arrangement quite like this one.

Travis cleared his throat again, "Well, now, if everyone is comfortably seated, we will resume the afternoon funeral service for Jantzi Belle Siddonz Sabblonti who was born . . ."

Following the reading of Jantzi's short obituary, Travis decided to offer the microphone to anyone who would like to make a few comments. Chet's heart skipped several beats on this one. Travis did not realize that no one took license or liberty with the Sabblonti women. Chet was confident that Travis would find that out in short order. No one in attendance approached the podium.

Travis was saddened by the fact that there were no prayers requested for Jantzi's services. Private interment was scheduled for later that afternoon at a secluded location on the Sabblonti Ranch next to where Ace was buried.

Soft western music played in the background as Chet and Sarita thanked Dr. Shaw and Salina for attending the funeral. Salina embraced Chet once again as she prepared to depart from the auditorium.

Sparks flew as Stormy lashed out, "I would remind you that Chet is a married man. Have you no manners, especially during a public funeral? You should be highly ashamed of yourself. I would suggest you enroll in a finishing school of some sort and work on your etiquette."

Leaning her head backwards, Salina laughed uproariously. "Tsk, tsk, now Mrs. Castins. Don't let your fur fly too far across the room. I just might have to brush it off my black satin garments if it sticks to them. Yeah, I could look into a finishing school alright while you work on your marriage before it's finished. As far as etiquette goes, plan to polish yours a bit, too. Speaking of polish, maybe you could help your handsome cowboy husband polish that lipstick off his left cheek. It looks like he could use a little feminine help. Chet, if Stormy does not know how to remove lipstick, I would be happy to oblige. Oh, my, now, that would give me a little bit more one-on-one time with you and I would really like that!"

Sarita was biting the inside of her right cheek to keep from bursting out laughing. Chet blushed crimson at this point. Taking a step forward, Salina pulled the brim down of her oversized fringed black hat, curtsied, and headed to the front door with a, "Good afternoon, Gents, and Miss Sarita! Y'all know where to find me on any given day."

Sarita thanked Travis for all of his assistance with her mother's funeral services and started toward the front door.

Chet suggested that all those interested go to the Sage Hen Café for a quick lunch. Sarita politely declined and drove back to her apartment.

"Thanks for the offer, Chet, but I had better get back to the clinic. My prime assistant, Jacobe, isn't due back from visiting his relatives for another week, so I am running a one-man rodeo down there now. I would offer to help you with that cosmetic removal, but as you know, my expertise lies elsewhere. And, remember, that lipstick anywhere near a white shirt collar always spells problems, especially for a married man."

"We'll miss you during lunch, Doc. Speaking of the lipstick, ah, yes, I need to head to the *Cowboys* room one more time."

"Do you want me to give you a lift to the café, Chet?" offered Dr. Shaw. "It might be a whole lot safer riding with me than the Mrs. She doesn't look any too happy right now. That Salina Bevvins is one brazen woman to be sure. I think I might have just figured out why she has not been branded yet."

"Thanks, Doc, but I better plan to drive Stormy to the café. I need all the brownie points I can get."

"Travis, do you need help with anything here or are we pretty much finished for right now?" Chet asked.

"Lambent's staff can take care of dismantling everything inside the auditorium, and we will plan to meet you in a couple of hours for the interment on the ranch."

Chet and Stormy drove in complete silence. His left cheek did look rather strange. He hoped the café would be completely empty so no one would notice.

"There's no parking close to the café," commented Chet. "I wonder what else is going on in town that so many people are here."

Opening the front door to the Sage Hen Café, it sounded like half of Ridgemonte was sitting inside. Even the banquet room was overflowing.

Chet spotted a couple of seats at the counter and suggested he and Stormy sit there.

As they walked past the tables and wide-open banquet room, they noticed Tom and Merna Toppens, Nelson and Marita Merrill, Wyn Moreland, Blake Benson, Stewart

Sanders, Lonnie Browne, Chara Tankton, Denny and June Slader, Larry Lambent, Tracie Sudders, Priscilla Fletcher, and several other families from Shadow Butte County. There were even some from Ignee County. Surely all of these people had known that Jantzi Belle Siddonz Sabblonti's funeral service had just concluded. None of them even bothered to look up when Chet and Stormy walked by.

CHAPTER THIRTY

No sooner had she sat down on the cracked, orange, plastic-covered stool at the front counter of the Sage Hen Café, than Stormy rose to her feet, slung her purse over her left shoulder, and headed for the front door, lifting her head high in the air as if sniffing smoke from a fire. Chet followed her like a puppy dog.

"Are you marrying into that Sabblonti outfit, Wyn?" challenged Blake Benson, the Southwest Division Brand Inspector. "Let's hope the girl you are engaged to isn't anything like that one. Small wonder nobody attended the family funeral."

Merna Toppens immediately rose to Wyn's defense, "Now, Blake, didn't your mother ever teach you that unless you had something nice to say, you don't say anything at all? Wyn will be marrying Sarita very soon, and she is a lovely young woman. Why, maybe we could even have the wedding next year at the Toppens' Ranch! How would you like that, Wyn?"

"It would suit me just fine, but since Sarita's the bride to be, she would be the one to ask about all those details."

Blake continued, "Wyn, considering that you will be a member of the Sabblontis soon and very soon, is there some reason you didn't go to the services?"

"By the time we finished with everything at the ranch

and our business in town, we flat ran out of time."

Blake thought it a tad strange that the Toppens' family had time for a late lunch inside the Sage Hen Café, but did not have time to pay their respects to their ranching neighbors. Oh, well, what did he know? Were the customs in the remote west different than he thought they were?

Exiting the café, Chet extended his right arm to escort Stormy to his pickup. "Put your arm down, Chet. I am fully capable of walking. Actually, I am going to stand here on the sidewalk and wait for you to give me curb service. Get going."

Looking up from his lunch plate, Wyn winced as he saw Stormy standing there and Chet walking off.

"I need to . . . ," Chet started to say.

"You need to what? Don't tell me you need to stop at The Shadowy Merc for one single thing. I don't have time nor the patience right now for you to explain that whole Salina Bevvins side show to me, but you had better be on the up and up. If I find out that you are switching horses on me, you can expect to find a horse head in your bed when you wake up some morning. I can put you out to pasture when I decide the time is right. There are lots of men in these parts from whom I could choose. Most of them would give their eye teeth to be married to me. Consider yourself a most fortunate man, Chet Carleton Castins. Any questions?"

"No questions. I started to say that I need to get a move on and get to the top of the Sabblonti Ranch to meet Lambent's for the interment. We are burning daylight."

"You are burning more than daylight at this point, in case you were unaware."

Stopping briefly in the street in front of the café so Stormy could get comfortably situated in his pickup, Chet commented, "Well, I see the mares' tails forming in the air."

"What do you mean by mares' tails? I did not realize that I married someone who was so unrefined. I am not sure at this point that there's a dime's worth of difference between you and Wyn Moreland. I don't think either one of you has an IQ that's larger than the circumference of your belt buckles. Matter of fact, your combined IQ's would probably not exceed twelve."

"Cirrus clouds are sometimes called mares' tails. And that's not an old wives' tale."

"Don't try to be humorous with me, school boy."

"It's been a long time since I was in school."

"Obviously."

"Sometimes the mares' tails signal a change in the weather. I feel like there's a big storm heading our way."

Chet turned off the main highway onto the road that led to the upper part of the Sabblonti Ranch. Stormy rested her head on the top portion of the passenger seat and appeared to be napping. Chet drove the steady incline for about the next fifteen minutes.

All of a sudden, the pickup engine died on a narrow curve of the road. Chet turned the key in the ignition several times to no avail. "What it the world is going on?"

Stormy lunged forward as she lifted her head. "What happened? What's wrong with your pickup?"

"I don't know. I can't get it to start. First, Jantzi dies on me, and now this thing keeps dying on me."

Chet put the parking brake on, pulled the hood latch underneath the steering wheel, and stepped onto the road. Lifting the hood, he looked to see if anything appeared to be amiss. Finding nothing obvious, he got back inside the cab. "Beats me, but considering everything else that has gone haywire in the past couple of weeks, nothing surprises me anymore. It feels like the hordes of hell have been unleashed against me lately."

"When is the last time you filled your pickup with gas, Chet?"

Turning the key in the ignition to the point where the gauges would register, the gas tank read below 'E.'

"That just might be the problem. I think we have run out of gas."

"You cannot be telling me the truth. You have been so sidetracked by Salina and her side winding that you couldn't even remember to put gas in your vehicle. One would think you were sixteen again and this was your first rodeo. Have you never mentally graduated from there? It is beyond time to hire some new help and lock you up in the corral permanently. I will have to make a final decision on that one later. Now what are you going to do? Do you have any extra gas in the back?"

"No, I don't. Remember that we are driving my pickup today and not the one we use for ranch work."

"We will miss Mother's interment. It's getting dark. What will we do now? I never dreamed I would be in this predicament. Mother will never forgive me for this."

∞∞∞∞∞∞∞∞∞∞∞∞∞∞

Travis and the other two assistants from Lambent's

Funeral Home waited inside the hearse with the heater running. Thankfully, they had driven the one designed for burials in the mountains. Surveying the sky and looking down at his watch, Travis commented, "I can't imagine where Chet, Stormy, and Sarita are. I asked them to be here no later than five o'clock. We still have to shovel the dirt after we lower the coffin into the ground. At least the backhoe operator piled it all in one spot for us."

With just enough daylight remaining to lower the casket into the ground, pile the dirt on top and smooth it out, Travis was startled at the mournful extended squawks that were released into the atmosphere. "Vultures, vultures, everywhere. Get out of here, bird choir! Well, I guess since no other mourners showed up to say good bye, you are filling the bill."

Turning to his associates, Travis suggested, "Let's get back down the mountain, post haste. It's an eerie feeling up here. I hope this is the last time I have to bring a body to the mountains. No wonder Mr. Lambent farmed us out on this project. Maybe we'll get a year-end bonus for this one! How about one of you two offer to drive back here to update the headstone with Jantzi's date of death and then this project will be completed? I will plan to phone in ill when that assignment comes due."

"This has been one strange day to say the least," opined one of Travis' assistants. "No disrespect intended, but I still wonder what happened to the fifteen hundred people who were supposed to attend the funeral. We moved heaven and earth to get that auditorium set up with all of the special effects."

Travis braked heavily as he rounded the sharp corner to avoid running into Chet's pickup. "Wow, another coat of black paint on that pickup and we would have collided!" Lowering his window just as Chet lowered his, Travis inquired, "What's up, Chet? You dead on the road? Is there something wrong with your vehicle? Looks almost new to me."

"I ran out of gas, Travis. I've been overwhelmed the past few days and completely forgot to check the gas gauge. I don't suppose you have any extra fuel with you?"

"In a hearse? Not so as you would notice! You want us to give you a lift back to the main ranch house or somewhere? There's room for the two of you in the back seat. You can be nice and cozy back there."

"Sure, that would be most appreciated."

Chet helped Stormy get out of the cab of his pickup and gestured for her to get into the back seat of the hearse.

"Chet, you get in first. I am not sitting next to someone I don't know. Are you a complete twit or what is your story lately?"

Double checking to make sure his pickup doors were locked, Chet climbed into the back seat of the hearse. His knees reached his chin when he sat down. Stormy sat on the end of the right rear passenger seat.

Chet apologized, "I am sorry that we did not make it to the interment, Travis. I will have to drive back up there right away to pay my final respects to my wonderful mother-in-law."

"That's not a problem, Chet. In our business, we roll with the punches."

"Say, Travis," continued Chet, "there is one thing that I would like to ask you about if you don't mind. I thought for sure that Mr. Lambent would be in attendance today. If he had time to go to . . ."

Stormy reached around and backhanded Chet's right cheek.

Travis and his two attendants flinched in their seats.

"Chet, I don't know what happened," explained Travis. "All I know is that when the three of us arrived at the funeral home this morning, we were told that we were in charge for the day. Then Mr. Lambent left his office. This is going to be one long day as we still have some final clean up to do at the school auditorium. Great way to end the year, wouldn't you say?"

"We really appreciate all of your help with Jantzi's services," Chet offered. "I will have to admit that it would have been super nice to have some support from the community. I just don't get it. All kinds of folks showed up to pay their respects to Ace. Of course, the weather was much nicer when he died, and the Christmas holidays are so busy for everyone and their families."

As Travis drove to the Sabblonti main ranch house, he thought to himself, "The weather looks just fine to me. If I can drive on these roads this time of year, anyone can, and the holidays are not that busy. It's all about priorities in life. People make time for what's important to them."

Chet continued, "Any other funerals scheduled before the end of the year, Travis?"

"Not that I am aware of. Sometimes if there's a real large one in these parts, the funeral home in Ignee County will call and ask us to help. So, it looks like we will have a calm and quiet New Year's Eve, which would be nice. I can stay home and enjoy my ever lovin' as we usher in the New Year."

Arriving in the Sabblonti driveway, Travis turned the ignition off and turned the dome light on. "We'd offer to help you get back to your pickup and put some gas in it, Chet, but we still have about three hours of work ahead of us. I hope you understand. And, Chet, take care of those cheeks of yours. It's been a tough day for both of them."

"Oh, I understand. Thanks so much for the lift down here and for everything else that you have done today. We appreciate all of you so much. As for my cheeks, well, I don't spend a whole lot of time looking in the mirror."

The attendant in the front passenger seat of the hearse started to open his door so that he could open Stormy's rear passenger door for her. "Don't bother. Stay in your seat and close your door. I can fend for myself," she snapped.

Chet tipped his hat to Travis and his helpers as they left the driveway.

As Travis drove the hearse down the lane toward the main road, he commented to his associates, "I think there is wisdom in saying, 'Never approach a bull from the front, a horse from the back, or Stormy Sabblonti from any direction.'"

Chet headed into the house to round up some help to rescue his stranded pickup.

Looking in the phone book, he located the number for the Shaw Vet Clinic. After placing the call, the phone rang inside the clinic several times. Just as it was about to go to voice mail, Dr. Shaw answered.

"This is Dr. Shaw. How can I help you?"

"Hey, Doc, this is Chet. If it wasn't for bad luck, I wouldn't have any luck at all these days!"

"Now what's going on?"

"My pickup ran out of gas while I was driving to Jantzi's interment late this afternoon. Never did make it there. Travis had to give us a lift down to the main ranch house in

Lambent's hearse. Anyway, could I convince you to lend me a helping hand? I could really use one right about now."

"Sure. I could use some Wednesday night company. I'll be right out."

Chet located a five-gallon gas can inside the shop and filled it from the storage tank located north of the barn. He carried it into the front yard and sat down to wait for Dr. Shaw to arrive.

After reflecting upon the events of the day, Chet went inside the house. "Stormy, are you on the main floor?"

"Yes, I am in the bathroom changing my clothes."

Emerging a few minutes later, Stormy walked into the family room and slumped down in a recliner.

"Stormy, honey, I would like to give you a big hug. I know that you have been through a lot, and human touch and encouragement are vital during these times."

"I don't want a hug from you or anything else from you. Don't try to give me this *human touch* song and dance. That's probably just a way for you to try avoid explaining your carryings on with that Salina. She can't even be classified as a lady. You don't want to know what I would call her. You are as guilty of wrongdoing as guilty can be. Why else would some woman attend a funeral of another woman she does not even know and kiss a man in public that she supposedly does not know? I would much prefer explanations of truth to fake embraces."

"Alright. Have it your way."

"You better know I will have it my way. It's my way or no way!"

Chet walked into the silence of the front yard, sat down, and waited for the set of headlights to appear down the lane. He was too exhausted to argue with Stormy.

Dr. Shaw pulled into the driveway, rolled down the passenger window, smiled, and offered, "You need a ride, cowboy?"

"I sure appreciate you driving out here to help me. You can just add this to my ongoing tab. Let me get this gas can loaded into the back."

"Think nothing of it. I could use a good unwinding as we head up the mountain road. Uh, Chet, have you looked in the mirror recently? It looks like you were smacked on the cheek."

"My cheek met the back of Stormy's hand while we were riding in the back of the hearse heading down to the main ranch house. It stung like the dickens. Travis and his helpers must have been horrified. It was really quiet inside the hearse from that point forward."

"She actually struck you, Chet?"

"Yes, Doc, she did. She's never done anything like that in the entire time I have known her. I have not done one single thing to provoke her to act that way toward me. Ever since Jantz died, it has been like a night and day difference in Stormy. It's as if she turned a switch on that was labeled *EVIL*. She has become like a constant storm wreaking havoc in my life. She has not been the same person the past couple of weeks. I don't suppose that fancy degree you obtained so folks could call you Dr. Shaw allows you to practice psychology as well as treat critters, does it?"

"Unfortunately not, Chet. I am trained to treat animals and that's about it. I deem you need to give it some time. I doubt there's any such thing as the perfect marriage or the perfect woman. But, hey, since I have never been married, I am far from the marital expert."

"Well, working this Sabblonti spread, especially after

Ace died, has been an all-consuming venture. I am hoping it pays huge dividends some day."

"Well, it sure should. How many kids did Ace and Jantzi have?

"They had only the two daughters, Stormy and Sarita."

"After the estate is probated, you and Stormy should get half of the whole shootin' match. That's not too shabby if you ask me. I mean, after taking just a casual look at that whole operation, dollar signs end up in both eyes. Granted, there's more to life than money. In the area in which I grew up, there were some very affluent people, and some of them were the most unhappy people I have ever known. Their money did not assure them happiness by any stretch of the imagination. Money is nice, but it's not the panacea."

"The what?"

"The panacea. You know, the remedy for all difficulties. It's like saying it's the magic bullet or cure all."

"Oh. It's a strange word and sounds like some body part."

"You are probably thinking of *pancreas*. That's got to be your pickup on the side of that curve. Fine place to run out of gas!"

"Like I am operating on all cylinders lately, Doc!"

"I'll stop here and put my lights on bright so you can dump that gas into your tank. Then I'll go up ahead and try to find a place to turn around so I can follow you back down to the main road."

"There's a place to turn around a couple of miles up the mountain. One of the shoulders is wide enough that I think you will be okay." Shaking hands with Dr. Shaw, Chet said, "Happy New Year, Doc. Stay in touch. I need to get down to the lower ranch house, check on Braezee, Beebee, Blue, and the rest of the bunch."

Driving back to his ranchette three miles south of Ridgemonte, Dr. Shaw voiced his one man's opinion to his invisible audience, "If I was a betting man, I would wager that Chet spends the night at the lower ranch house while his wife stays put at the main ranch house, and I know I would win that bet. Can't say as I blame him any. Who would want to be stung by Stormy, the Scorpion? Not me. I would not put up with being treated shabbily by my wife for all of the money in this world."

CHAPTER THIRTY-ONE

On his way to his clinic Thursday morning, Dr. Shaw stopped by Clinker's Feed Store. The large cow bell hanging over the front door announced his arrival. July Clinker, now eighty-two and somewhat hunched over, looked up and flashed a crooked grin. "Good morning, good doctor, how can I help you today?"

"I am looking for a small strip of old sleigh bells. Would you happen to have something like that in your antique section? I sure hope so!"

"Sleigh bells, gee, I don't rightly recall if we do or not. The little gal that helps us part time in the store isn't here today. I don't suppose many folks will be coming in right about now, so I will lock the front door. Let's go dig around and see what we can scare up, shall we?"

"How long have you owned your store, Mrs. Clinker?"

"We opened it in 1932. It was my husband's idea. It's been a lot of work, but a real blessing, too. Now that he's gone, it's much harder. At least I have my son and grandson to help me. They handle all of the feed for the animals and related things."

July flipped the light switches on which revealed a menagerie of antiques.

Dr. Shaw realized it could take some time to try to locate a set of bells if there were any to be found. "Do you mind if

I help you look inside some of these boxes underneath the wooden benches?"

"That would be just fine. I can always use an extra set of helping hands."

Dr. Shaw was getting quite discouraged from failing to locate what he wanted.

"Why, bless my sweet soul!" exclaimed July. "If this set of bells would have been a snake it would have bitten me! They were turned upside down."

"Boy, howdy! That's exactly what I need. Thank you so much. I was concerned that I was only going to be able to locate a set of bells and a separate strap, and would have to figure out how to marry them up to be one unit. This is my lucky day."

"Speaking of married, are you hitched yet, Dr. Shaw?"

"No, I am still unhitched, but looking to get hitched. Do you have any good ideas?"

"Well, as a business owner in a ranching community, I do keep my ears pretty close to the ground. Also, I have a lifetime membership to the Long Ear Society."

"Long Ear Society? Is that for rabbits or some such? Surely there's not a real organization that goes by that name, is there?"

"You just might be surprised! You book-learning folks really do need to be countrified. We may look pretty plain, but we don't miss out on much. Especially us older folk. There are a few young eligible women in these counties, but match making is not my cup of tea."

"Do you have any holiday cards back here? I need one of those, too."

"Are you mailing a belated Christmas gift or something?"

"I am not technically mailing anything. I need to put together a little something for one of my potential customers."

"Oh, I get it. You are working on a little customer relations project."

"Yes, I guess you could call it something like that."

"I don't know exactly what our clerk, Janelle, has here at the counter. Some people like to give antiques as Christmas gifts, so she might have some of those *To – From* tags you could use. You are welcome to look through that box of assorted cards and what have you."

Dr. Shaw flipped through an old cowboy boot box containing greeting cards. He could have sworn that some of them dated back to the 1940's or earlier. Well, this was an antique store! What did he expect? The very last card in the box was exactly what he had hoped to find.

"July, could I get you to gift wrap those sleigh bells for me? I know I don't have any holiday paper at my clinic. You can include that in the total charges."

"Doc, can you come behind the counter and see if you can help me find some? I can't bend very far down any more. I'll make you a deal. If you can find some wrapping paper, I won't charge you for my wrap job. How's that?"

"Sounds like a deal to me. Let's see, there are about four rolls standing up in this box. Can I choose whatever color I like?"

"Sure, sonny, it's your gift. Now you did not specify if this was for a male or female. But I guess that emerald green with gold accent colored paper could go either way. Oh, silly me! Of course it's for a female. Look at the front of that card. You'd think I was born yesterday."

July struggled to lay the paper flat, make the proper creases in it, and square the corners to make it look just right. She could only imagine if she were going to be the one to receive such a gift. Her mind traveled back in time to her courting days with her husband. He had a soft romantic side to him as well.

"Here you go, Dr. Shaw. This is about as good as I can do today. I have arthritis in my hands, and some days it acts up worse than others. Today I can barely bend my fingers. A cold front is probably getting ready to roll in. My joints are far better weather forecasters than those characters on the TV. Sometimes they're spot on and other times they miss the forecast by a country mile."

"You've done a wonderful job, July, and I appreciate it so much. It's not every merchant that would lock the front doors to help a customer in the back part of their store.

Happy New Year to you and your family. All the best in 2000!"

Oh, how Dr. Shaw wished Jacobe had not asked for time off to visit his family during the holiday season. As he continued to walk a few more steps, his conscience was struck at the very thought of it as he reflected upon his selfishness. His assistant was more than entitled to take a vacation.

Turning the key inside the lock of the front door of his clinic, Dr. Shaw remembered that he had locked the door the night before. "Wow, that's odd. This door is unlocked. I could have sworn that I locked it before I left. In fact, I know I did because I have not had time to make a deposit at Cattlemen's Central the past few days." After pushing the door open, he heard the radio playing in the back room. "Hello in there! Who is my mystery guest? Identify yourself, please."

Dr. Shaw walked into the kitchen area of his clinic to discover Jacobe bent over rummaging through the bins of the old refrigerator. "Doc, you must have recently gone grocery shopping. This package smells like women's perfume. Is there something that you would like to tell me?"

"Jacobe Davone, how are you doing, old timer? What are you doing back in town already? I did not expect you until Monday the 3rd. Did your mother run you out of her house?"

"Ah, Doc, what's with this old timer business? Last time I checked, I was a whole lot younger than you are. Naw, too many relatives showed up at my parents' house this year. The older I get, the less I like an overflowing house crawling alive with people during the holidays. I decided to drive back a few days early. I hope you don't mind. I needed some peace and quiet. Besides, the young cowgirl I had designs on decided she did not like my breed of horse, so I was unable to lasso her."

"Sorry to hear that, Jacobe, but I am really glad you are back early. I need to enlist your help with a little New Year's Eve project."

"Uh, oh, this sounds serious. Are you planning a big blowout party here at the clinic or is there a barn dance somewhere out in the boonies that everyone's invited to?"

"Not that I am aware of right now. It's been a strange few days here in Ridgemonte since you left. Nothing personal, but I don't have time to fill you in on all of the details right now. Let me write inside this card, and then I need you to take it over to Dr. Diller's office and deliver it."

"Anybody in particular over there at Diller's?"

"Yes, it's the lady named Sarita who works at the front desk. All I want you to do is deliver it. If she's not there, just leave it at the front counter. Yesterday was her mother's funeral, so she might not be in the office."

"Her mother's funeral? Who was her mother?"

"Jantzi Sabblonti from the Sabblonti Cattle Ranch."

"You mean to tell me Jantzi Sabblonti died? How? Good grief, I leave town for a couple of weeks, and everything falls apart."

"Well, not everything fell apart. I'm still here and in great shape," laughed Dr. Shaw. "At least I was the last time I looked in the mirror and stepped onto the animal scales."

Dr. Shaw located an ink pen and carefully wrote inside the holiday card,

Sarita ~~~ the distinct pleasure of your company is requested on Saturday, January 1st, for a horse drawn sleigh

ride in the high country. Extra warm blankets and a thermos of hot chocolate will be provided along with the superb company of a fine country veterinarian. The favor of your reply is requested.

Happy New Year,
Dr. Ben Shaw

Jacobe held the package containing the sleigh bells and card in one hand while turning the door knob to the dentist's office in his other one. Approaching the front counter, he inquired, "Are you Sarita?"

"No, Sarita is on personal leave," explained Molly. "How can I help you? Do you need to make an appointment with Dr. Diller? If so, it will probably be the first part of February before I can get you one. The winter months in here are busier than busy."

"I am Jacobe Davone. I don't need an appointment right now. On second thought, maybe I should go ahead and book one anyway. It's been a while since I have had my teeth cleaned and x-rays taken. I've been too busy cleaning animals' teeth. Can you please give this to Sarita? Do you know when she will be back in the office?"

"I am uncertain if she will be back tomorrow or not. She may have taken an extra day off. We are only open a half day since it's New Year's Eve. I will be sure to give her the package and envelope when I see her. I misspoke a moment ago. I do have an appointment opening on Monday afternoon, January 31st at three o'clock. Will that work for you?"

"Sure, go ahead and pencil in that appointment for me.

I can always call and change it if I need to. Can you please write that information on one of those little appointment cards?"

Jacobe drove back to the clinic pondering the death in the Sabblonti family. He had noticed throngs of people in Ridgemonte when he drove back into town late yesterday afternoon. Well, that would explain why as they would have attended Jantzi's funeral, or so he assumed.

"Mission accomplished, Dr. Ben Shaw; however, Sarita was not in Diller's office as she was on personal leave according to the lady working at the front counter. You know, the one that bats her eyelashes all the time and is obviously in search of a groom, and by groom, I don't mean the kind that works at the race track."

"Thanks, Jacobe. Did the receptionist say when Sarita was returning to work?"

"She said she was unsure as to exactly when Sarita would be back. They are open half a day tomorrow, since it's New Year's Eve. Sure wish there was some action in this town for the last night of the year."

"When I was visiting with July Clinker, she informed me there are several eligible young cow girls in these parts. I have not seen them, but then again, I am usually too busy treating the four-legged variety, so I don't have much time to devote to the two-legged ones. Pull up a chair, Jacobe, and let's chew the fat for a bit. I will regale you with the tales of the last two weeks."

Jacobe listened intently as Dr. Shaw apprized him of what he knew of Jantzi Sabblonti's death, her funeral, treating Chet Castin's mare, and other happenings. "For you see, Jacobe, Ridgemonte is no different than any other place carved out on the planet somewhere. There's more going on than meets the casual eye, so keep your eyes peeled at all times."

"I would say so, Doc. I thought this was just some quiet sleepy high country. Are we working all day tomorrow?"

"If everything goes as planned, we will be working just half of the day. Can you arrive a little early so we can get the jump on the day, say around 7:30ish?"

"Yes, that works for me. I need to stop by The Shadowy Merc and buy some steaks."

"Speaking of The Merc, you better keep a sharp eye out for the grocery clerk named Salina. She appears to have purchased a new high-powered scope to assist in her husband hunting game. I would not allow her to put her cross hairs on you. That's just a friendly suggestion from an employer to his employee. Of course, some guys don't mind being in the cross fire, I mean the cross hairs."

"Thanks for the advanced warning, Doc. The one thing I do not need is some needy gal latching onto me like a pack of fleas. I heard a story one time about a country western chic like that and it about scared the wits out of me. I really don't think my mother would approve of such a daughter-in-law."

"I am not trying to taint anyone's reputation, Jacobe. You are several years younger than I am. Good things come to those who wait. I already told you what happened inside the Ridgemonte High School gymnasium. If I would have been wearing false teeth, they would have fallen to the floor. Salina's conduct was bold and then some. You just don't walk up to a married man, drape yourself around him like a lamp shade in broad daylight, and place a big smacker on his cheek. That's not even supposed to happen after dark. Just sayin'. It looks like we have got to tighten the personal fences in these parts of the high country, and not just for the horses, cattle, and sheep."

"You better know it, Doc."

Dr. Shaw opted to stay at his clinic overnight rather than drive to his place in the country. It would afford him more time to get an early start tomorrow morning. Looking through the closet in the back part of his clinic, he was greatly relieved to discover that he had a clean pair of jeans and a new blue plaid country western shirt.

After frying himself a cheeseburger along with some red spuds and onions, Dr. Shaw sat down to eat. His appetite vanished as he picked at his food. He felt like he was back in school again and has asked a girl to the Friday night dance. The butterflies in his stomach were boxing with his dinner which was not winning.

∞∞∞∞∞∞∞∞∞∞∞∞∞∞∞

Sleep eluded Dr. Shaw as he tossed and turned during the night. He dreamed that he was comforting Sarita as she laid her head on his shoulder and cried a gallon milk bucket full of tears.

When Jacobe arrived at seven fifteen the next morning and walked into the back of the clinic, he let out a loud whistle. "Whew - ee! It sure doesn't smell like antiseptics or animals in here right now. And look at you, Doc! It looks like you are all dressed up and have someplace to go."

"Good morning, Jacobe. I need several shots of straight caffeine this morning to get my horses galloping. I hardly slept a wink last night."

"Sorry to hear that. I slept like a ton of hay. Traveling wipes me out, so it's been good to be back in my own bed the past couple of nights."

"I dreamed off and on about Sarita all night long, which left me exhausted. "

"Let's hope today is your lucky day and next year your best ever."

"Wouldn't that be nice? I need to keep a sharp eye on the clock and not let time get away from me. I've got a list of calls you need to make for me this morning, please, and then some clean up around the clinic. Let's hope there are no animal emergencies. That would nix my whole plan. Can you please let me know when it's eleven thirty?"

Jacobe busied himself in the clinic with his assignments from Dr. Shaw, who was as nervous as a cat on a hot tin roof. Jacobe had never seen him so fidgety. It would be disastrous if an animal needed some serious care in the next couple of hours, because it sure would not get it from this veterinarian. Dr. Shaw observed how well Jacobe handled the public, and his phone etiquette was impeccable. Perhaps he should give him that raise he had been contemplating.

"Five-minute warning, Dr. Shaw. Take one last good long look in the mirror, don that snappy white good guy hat, and away you go!"

"Thanks for being my personal coach and timer this morning, Jacobe. Hold down the fort 'til I get back."

Dr. Shaw drove to the parking lot of the dentist's office and parked at just the right angle so he could still remain out of sight if someone exited the front door. At five minutes until high noon, he got out of his truck and gently closed the driver's door. What if Sarita had taken the morning off work?

Several of Dr. Diller's employees walked out the front office door, got into their cars, and drove off. Dr. Shaw waited for a few more minutes. Suddenly he caught a glint of something metal. Turning around, he saw Dr. Diller and Sarita leaving the building. Sarita walked toward her Bronco parked about thirty feet away. Dr. Diller had already rounded the corner and was out of sight since he had parked on the opposite side of the building.

"Hi, Sarita! I was hoping to catch you as you were leaving work today. Did you get my holiday card?"

"Yes, Dr. Shaw. That was so sweet of you to think of me and offer to take me on a sleigh ride. Any other time, I would have jumped at the chance. It's such a romantic gesture, especially this time of year. I have never been on a sleigh ride before."

"I wasn't trying to be insensitive since your mother passed away so recently. I thought it might help cheer you up a bit and help to take your mind off a few things. There's nothing like good clean mountain air to help blow the cobwebs from our minds. Oh, that was pretty graphic. Excuse me, please."

"It's fine, Dr. Shaw, really it is. I owe you an apology of sorts, I think." Sarita gently removed her royal blue and white checkered wool mittens. Flashing her left ring finger, she explained, "I am officially engaged. I just now realized that you would have no way of knowing that since I was not wearing my ring during Mother's funeral services. I had taken it to the local jeweler to have it enlarged just a wee bit. Since I type so much during the day, it was slightly constricting my left finger. I wanted to have it fixed right away."

Feigning ignorance, Dr. Shaw queried, "Oh, please forgive my poor manners. I certainly did not intend to be untoward in any way, shape, or form. Who is the lucky guy?"

"Wyn Moreland," Sarita replied blissfully. "We haven't set an official wedding date yet, since he just proposed to me recently."

"Well, it looks like Wyn is the winner! Congratulations to both of you. I will just ride into the sunset and wait for a new horizon somewhere. Oh, and just in case things don't work out, there's no expiration date on the sleigh ride offer."

"Oh, things will work out for sure between Wyn and me. Even if my mind tries to tell me something else, I plan to follow my heart, which belongs to Wyn."

Dr. Shaw nodded his head, tipped the brim of his white Stetson toward Sarita, and walked back to his pickup. "Sometimes you win, sometimes you lose, and sometimes you just don't ask the dealer for extra cards," he reminded himself as he drove back to his clinic.

Jacobe was just turning the *OPEN* sign to the reverse side so it would read *CLOSED* as Dr. Shaw reached the front door.

"Uh, from the look on your face, Doc, I would guess that the cow didn't even get out of the chute."

"True story. I completely struck out. Sarita is engaged to one of Toppens' cow hands. A guy named Wyn Moreland."

"Gee, I am sorry, Doc. I guess we are both back to the drawing board at this point. I've met a couple of the hired hands when I've been down at the Toppens' corrals, but I don't think I recall a Wyn Moreland. It's interesting that he made a play for Sarita since he is just a cow hand and her lashup is loaded. I am surprised that her family approved of him."

"All's fair in love and war, Jacobe. And that includes range wars, water wars, and women wars. I am not the warring type, however. Some fine young filly will ride across my trail someday soon. I just know it. The same will be true for you. Who knows, maybe they will be twin sisters and we will eventually marry into the same family? Why, we could even have one of those double country weddings."

"Thanks, Doc, I hope you are correct. I've just got to make sure that I stay on the straight and narrow between now and then."

CHAPTER THIRTY-TWO

"Brent, since we're closing early for New Year's Eve, will you please call the number on this slip of paper?" requested his father, Delbert Dawson.

"Sure, Dad. Are we open tomorrow, or did we decide to close up shop for the day?"

"Since a lot of folks were in town during the week and stopped by to look at our new truck models, I am going to give our employees the day off. We'll plan to open bright and early again Monday morning. I would imagine there are several New Year's Eve celebrations that have gotten started a little early, as usual."

"The partiers can party on if they want to, but I'm heading home and staying off the roads."

"Can't say as I blame you there. I'm getting way too old anymore for all of that stuff. Oh, before I completely forget about it, I also need you to call the auto parts store in Ignee to see if they have struts that fit that used red 4 x 4 we took in the first part of this week. I need to pop into Cattlemen's Central really quick before they close for the day. I've got to talk to my thick buddy, Stewart Sanders."

Brent dialed the phone number that was handwritten on the yellow paper, but no one answered immediately. He was just about to hang up.

"Hello, Tom Toppens of Toppens Ranch."

"I am sorry, but I must have dialed the wrong number."

"Who were you calling in the first place if it wasn't me?"

"The name on the paper reads Wyn or Wine, not sure how you pronounce it."

"Oh, you must mean one of our hired hands. He goes by the name Wyn, you know, like you win a card game. He lives down at the bunkhouse. I don't know that number right off hand. My better half is taking a nap, and I don't want to disturb her. Do you want to give me your number so I can give it to Wyn? Who's calling anyway?"

"This is Brent Dawson and the number is 549-0078. It's the same prefix, of course."

"Is there a message for Wyn, or do I just tell him to call this number and ask for you?"

"Yes, please, that would be great. Wyn can ask for my dad, Delbert, or me. Either one of us can help him."

"Wait a minute! Dawson. Let me see. Is this the same Dawson that's the truck dealership in Ridgemonte? Is Wyn finally getting ready to buy a truck or some such?"

"Well, something like that. Just have him return my call today if possible."

"Sure thing. I'll put the hustle on it right now and get down there to the bunkhouse. The ranch hands don't usually start their chores for another hour or so. I should be able to round somebody up."

"Thanks, Tom, and Happy New Year. Let us know when you want to trade in your old one ton for a new one."

"Will do, Brent. It's operating just fine right now, so it may be a while. I want to get some running lights on my next one though."

Donning his winter coat, hat, and gloves, Tom made his way down to the bunkhouse. "Any of you fellers awake in there?"

Wyn answered the door, rubbing his eyes to help him wake up. "Have you been standing out here very long? I just barely heard you. The other guys must have started their chores early."

"Here's a message for you, Wyn. Brent from the dealership called and said he needs to talk you. I did not know you were truck shopping. If you would have asked me, I would have gone with you to give you some advice. Delbert, Brent, and the rest of the crew are all real straight shooters, but I could help you with a little fatherly assistance, if necessary."

"I'm not sure what all of this is about, but I will call Brent back. I am definitely not in a financial position right now to buy a truck, new or used."

"Brent might have gotten his wires crossed, but, then again, he did ask for Wyn. He asked if your name was Wyn or Wine. I thought that was sorta funny."

"There have been other people that have mispronounced my name over the years. It took the man in charge of the boy's home a long time to remember that it was win instead of wine. Okay, thanks, Tom. I will call him back in a little bit or maybe I will just wait until the first part of next week. The last thing I need is someone pestering me about buying a truck when I don't have the money to make a down payment on a free lunch."

"Suit yourself, Wyn. I am merely the messenger."

"Happy New Year to you and Merna."

"You, too, Wyn. I hope next year is a real bonanza for everybody!"

∞∞∞∞∞∞∞∞∞∞∞∞∞∞∞∞∞∞∞∞∞∞∞∞∞∞∞∞∞

Shane and Spence, two of Toppens' hired hands, entered the bunkhouse, and the flurry of activity began.

"What finally woke you up, Wyn?" Shane asked. "When we left the bunkhouse, you were sawing logs, and your chain saw was buzzin' up a storm! You must have been tired to have been snoring so loudly."

"Tom came down to give me a message."

"Is everything alright, Wyn?" Spence questioned on a serious note.

"Sure, Spence, everything is fine. It was a message to return a call to that truck dealership in town. Like I can really afford to get a set of wheels right now."

"I hear ya," echoed Shane and Spence simultaneously.

"What I can't figure out is how they got Toppens' phone number with my name attached to it. I've never had anyone call me at Tom and Merna's."

"Neither have I," Shane and Spence chimed in unison.

Shane continued, "Well, if you think about it, this is a big broad county, but news seems to travel pretty fast. Most folks around here could probably tell you the day we signed on with Toppens, the color of shirt we were wearing that day, and the wages we agreed upon. It's not that it's a bad thing. It just requires that we keep a sharp eye on happenings, and just might have to sleep with one eye open."

"Shane, you've been sitting by the stove reading too many of those western stories," kidded Spence.

"Wyn, are you headed over to the big New Year's Eve shindig at Merrill's Ranch tonight? Shane and I are going. They're supposed to have barbeque beef with all of the trimmings. I don't know who all will be there, but it might be nice to get to know some more of our neighbors and see how the rest of the world lives. It seems like folks always have a few year-end yarns to spin. I might have to spin one or two myself."

"I didn't even know there was anything going on tonight at Merrill's. I hadn't planned on going anywhere. It's been a long couple of weeks, and I wouldn't mind having some peace and quiet."

"Just about plum forgot, Wyn," Spence continued, "You are a branded man as of Christmas! You and Sarita could put in an appearance if you wanted to. I am sure the Merrill's would not mind."

"Thanks for letting me know about it, Spence. I have not seen Sarita for a couple of days. I was thinking I might call her tonight so we could visit. Hint, hint, it will be nice to have you cow pokes parked at the neighbors so I can have some privacy. How are you getting to the festivities anyway? Are you going to attach headlights to your horses' bridles?"

"I asked Tom if we could borrow the old tan pickup," Shane explained. "He told us he would be happy to loan it to us as long as we brought it home in one piece."

"Let's hit the showers, Spence," directed Shane, "and see who the most handsome top hand is after we put our efforts into the clean up."

"Who will be the tie-breaker?" challenged Spence. "I guess it will have to be Wyn."

With the rustic coffee table propping up his stocking feet, Wyn could have sworn that he smelled a skunk. He walked to the front door, opened it, and scanned the front area of the house, but didn't see a moving black and white object. Closing the door, he sat back down on the well worn green and brown plaid couch. The smell was nauseating. Wyn walked around, opened the windows up along with the front door, placing a log wedge in the crack to keep it open.

Shane sauntered into the living room, admired himself in the mirror, and slicked back his hair one more time with his pocket comb.

"Yetch! It's you, Shane!" exclaimed Wyn. "I thought I smelled a skunk so I opened all of the windows and the front door. Where on earth did you get that aftershave? You better take another shower to see if you can't wash that stuff off. That smell will drive everyone from Merrill's barn."

"Take a chill pill, Wyn. Cowboys are supposed to be calm, cool, and collected. There's nothing wrong with my cologne."

"Is that what you call it, cologne?"

"Well, yes. I brought it with me when I signed on here. The official name is *Double Lariat.* It comes in a real snazzy bottle with a little lariat tied around the neck of it. I am confident it will attract the cow girls."

"It's all a matter of opinion, Shane. I would suggest you get a second opinion from Spence. Trust me when I tell you that you might have problems lassoing anyone with a lariat at the Merrill's barn. After you walk inside, and people get a whiff of that stuff, there will be no one left inside that barn!"

Spence entered the living room all decked out in his country best. "Oops, just about forgot the most important thing. I need to get my cowboy hat. Can't go anywhere without that. It's the hat that counts, forget everything else. What is that odor? Have we been visited by some black and white striped critters? Is that why the windows and front door are open?"

"I rest my case, Shane. That's two of us that think your cologne smells like a skunk."

"Cologne, Shane? Seriously? Flush that stuff down the can and pitch the bottle outside in the burn barrel. I hope that odor does not jump onto me."

"Spence, it's all in your head. I can't even smell it. Let's get going so we can arrive at Merrill's before all the good grub is eaten. Wyn, enjoy your talk with your sweetie. If we don't return in time, please cover the morning shift for us."

"You two cow hands will be back in time, or I will send out a search party."

With Shane and Spence on their way, Wyn dialed Sarita's number. "I only hope she answers," he reassured himself, which she did on the third ring. "Hello, My Sweet, it seems like forever since I talked with you. I had to wait until Shane and Spence left for the big doins' over at the Merrill's barn tonight."

"I had not heard that Merrill's were hosting anything. I came home after work and took a much-needed nap. There is something that I need to tell you right away because I don't want you hearing it from anyone but me."

"It sounds urgent. What happened?"

"We only worked part of the day today. When I walked

outside to get inside my vehicle, Dr. Ben Shaw met me in the parking lot."

"Why would he need to talk to you? Is something wrong with one of the Sabblonti's cows or horses? Why didn't he contact Chet or Stormy?"

"It's nothing to do with any of the animals. It has to do with me personally."

"Uh, I don't like the sounds of this already."

"Keep your six shooters in your holsters and let me explain to you what transpired. After you surprised me with my elegant engagement ring on Christmas, I wore it to work on Monday, but discovered that it was too tight on my finger when I was typing. So, during my lunch break, I took it to the local jeweler and he enlarged it just a smidgen. I wasn't able to pick it up until Thursday; therefore, I was not wearing it during Mother's funeral. Dr. Shaw attended the service and did not see anything on my left hand, so he must have assumed I was fair game."

"Dr. Shaw attended your mother's funeral?"

"Yes, along with Salina Bevvins, Chet, Stormy, and myself."

"There were only five people there?"

"That's it other than Travis Fisen and two other associates from Lambent's."

"Who is Salina? Is she one of your cousins?"

"Hardly. She works at The Shadowy Merc in town, and that is a story and then some. I will tell you later."

"Before we continue, Sarita, I need to apologize to you for not attending the funeral. I probably should have been there to support you, but I just could not bring myself to do it. I hope you understand and don't want to break our engagement just because of my no show."

"Apology accepted, Wyn, but there's no need to apologize. It was no secret that my mother did not care for you one iota. Now back to Dr. Shaw, who sent his assistant, Jacobe Davone, to Dr. Diller's office to deliver an envelope. When I arrived at work this morning, I opened it, and there was an invitation to a sleigh ride in the high country. That's why Dr. Shaw was waiting for me in the parking lot. I removed my winter mitten and showed him my left hand. I explained that I was engaged to you. He was quite embarrassed and apologized profusely for asking me to go on the ride since I was spoken for. He was very gracious about it, and I tried to be as well."

"Thanks for explaining all of that to me, Sarita. It's best I hear it straight from the horse's mouth. Not that you are a horse, mind you! When the news of our engagement whips through Shadow Butte, Ignee, and Blunte counties, I am sure there will be all sorts of folks wonderin' why you signed on with me. They could easily speculate that I made a play for you since you are a wealthy Sabblonti. The real riddle would be why you would settle for some ranch hand like me."

"First of all, Wyn, it's no one else's business what we do with our lives. Secondly, I am following my heart which is in love with you, and your heart, which is as big as all outdoors. End of conversation as far as anyone else is concerned. End of game playing as far as anyone else is concerned, too."

"That's sweet music to my ears, Sarita. What a relief! I don't have anything against Dr. Shaw. I have not been around him that much at all. He seems like a nice guy. He's doctored a few of the cows for Toppens in the past. The strangest thing happened a little bit ago. Tom came down to the bunkhouse to tell me that I needed to return a call to Dawson's Dealership. I ran out of time to call back before they closed. They're probably trying to unload some of their last year's inventory. I don't have that kind of money for sure."

"Don't concern yourself so much with money, Wyn. We will figure it out as we go along. My old Bronco is paid for, which will help a lot. Say, I have an idea! Do you think it would be okay to drive out to Tom and Merna's tomorrow since it's New Year's Day? Maybe you and I could sit in their den and have a little time to discuss some personal business. I would offer to bring something for supper, but I don't have much at my apartment. I am sure that The Shadowy Merc will be closed since it's a national holiday."

"It's not that late right now. I'll walk up to their house and see what's cookin' for tomorrow. I would rather talk to them in person than call them. If you don't hear from me again tonight just assume that all systems are go. What time were you thinking of arriving here tomorrow?"

"I want to sleep in tomorrow morning and have some time to concentrate on a few other things. When I have major decisions to make, I like to write things down. I make two columns, one for positive and one for negative. At some point in the not-too-distant future, I will need to go to the ranch and speak with Stormy. It's very important that you get time off work that day to come with me. Actually, it can be in the evening so neither one of us has to miss any work."

"That sounds like a good plan. Good night, Happy New Year, and I love you the universe full!"

"Gee, that's a lot of love, Wyn. The feeling is mutual."

CHAPTER THIRTY-THREE

By the time Shane and Spence arrived at the Nelson Merrill ranch and made their way to the barn, the year end barbeque was well under way. Marita Merrill, standing just inside the opened double doors, welcomed them heartily. "Come on in and grab some good beef! We've got plenty for everybody. There's lots of hay bales to sit on, too. Will there be anyone else from the Toppens' Ranch joining us tonight?"

"Thanks, Marita," said Shane. "Probably not. Since Wyn got hitched to Sarita Sabblonti at Christmas, he bowed out for tonight. I checked with Merna, and she told me that she and Tom were going to spend a quiet evening at home."

"When I called Merna the other day to extend the invitation to all of you, she did not mention anything to me about one of their cow hands getting involved with the Sabblontis. Of course, I only talked with her for a couple of minutes because I was in a hurry."

"That's an odd way of putting it, Marita," challenged Spence. "Getting involved with the Sabblontis. Is that a bad thing? Shane and I are relatively new in these parts. We used to buckaroo in the Lone Star State and made our way up here for a change of pace."

"Are you on the run from the law?" asked Marita as a

concerned look formed on her pretty face.

"Of course, not!" exclaimed Shane. "What gives you that idea? Tom Toppens never would have hired us if that was the case."

"Well, how would he know, really? Considering some of the things that have happened to us over the past few years, we tend to be a whole lot more careful nowadays than we used to be when we first started ranching. Excuse me, please, there are more neighbors arriving, and I want to greet them. Make yourselves at home. Enjoy your evening."

"Shane, check out that strawberry blonde over there by the cider press, will you? I've suddenly developed a powerful thirst."

"You go ahead, Spence, my stomach is talking to me. I am going through the food line first before all of that prime beef is gone."

Priscilla Fletcher dumped the bucket of freshly pressed cider into a larger barrel. "Wow, there are some cider lovin' folks here tonight!"

Seeing no one else within earshot of Priscilla, Spence stood directly behind her, "Who are you talking to?"

She jumped forward upon hearing his deep baritone voice. Turning around, Spence noticed that her cheeks just about matched her pink leather jacket. "I was talking to myself, I guess."

"Allow me to introduce myself. I am Spence, one of the ranch hands who works for Tom Toppens. Do you know Tom and Merna? Also, I apologize. I should not have stood behind you and tried to startle you like that."

"Hi, Spence. I am Priscilla Fletcher, and I do accept your apology for attempting to spook me. You have one low voice!"

"Yes, I have been told that more than once."

"Are you alone or did Tom and Merna accompany you? They are some of the sweetest people in these parts. I have not seen them for quite awhile. I would love to visit with Merna."

"No, can't say as they are here. Merna stays right beside Tom. I want to find me the good wife like her someday."

"Well, maybe you will. There are lots of young ladies here this evening."

"That's great news!" Just as Spence turned around to join Shane, the heel of his left cowboy boot caught the edge of the tray into which the cider was flowing, causing it to flip over, and wash across Priscilla's pink boot. Spence was clueless as to what he had just done.

"Spence! Look at what a mess you have made! Can't you walk and talk at the same time?"

"What mess did I make?"

"Look at the floor, Spence, and look at my new boots! Talk about sticky!"

"Gee, how did I do that?"

"You tell me, Spence! Takes real talent, for sure. Oh, it's alright. I don't get uptight about simple things like that. I would ask you to tend the cider press while I go clean my boots off, but I had better find somebody else."

"You don't think I am capable, do you?"

"I didn't say that. I think it's best you go locate your ranching buddy and have something to eat. It seems like men are always hungry."

"Now that's a true statement. When you live in a bunkhouse and are batchin', yes ma'am, hunger is a real issue."

"Batchin'? Did I hear you correctly?"

"Yes, you know, not married up. Single, in other words. What do you call a guy who is unmarried?"

"A possibility, providing he comes with the correct qualifications. I have very high standards. Excuse me. I really need to get these boots cleaned off. They are quite gunky. Yuck!"

Spence spotted Shane sitting at the very end of the row on the far side of the barn. He filled his plate to overflowing and sat down next to him on the adjacent hay bale.

"Shane, let's eat, and get out of here ASAP."

"What's your hurry? I am just settling in and am working on my third plate of food. These are some good groceries. Best I've had in a long time. Neither Wyn, you, nor I can cook much at all, so I am enjoying my handsome little self here for awhile."

"I just made a complete fool of myself with that pretty petite blondie over there by the press. I stepped in that cider collecting gizmo gadget, and flipped the fresh cider over her new pink ropers that match her new pink leather jacket. Talk about a dude! I just want to go hide somewhere."

"Look around, Spence. Do you see a lot of places where you can lose yourself? This place is lit up like the professional rodeo palace at night! You are just exaggerating. Nothing ever seems quite so bad on a full stomach, trust me. Say, did you see the way Marita Merrill acted when we mentioned Wyn got engaged to Sarita Sabblonti? What's up with all that?"

"You expect me to know? We've been in this county the exact same amount of time, which has not afforded us much of an opportunity to get the scoop. Wyn didn't say *boo* before he got engaged. He's as quiet as a church mouse anyway. Poor guy. I would have hated to have grown up in a boy's home. If the Sabblontis are as flush as rumor has it, how will it square with him marrying one of their daughters, anyway?"

"Aren't both parents dead now?" asked Shane.

"Oh, yeah, I guess they are. Plus, Wyn and Sarita are both adults so no big deal. Sarita can do as she pleases. Wyn's probably just marrying her for her money. I overheard somebody say here tonight that Sabblontis own more land than they know what to do with it."

"What did you say about Sabblontis?" inquired Priscilla.

Spence jumped up and nearly dumped his plate onto Priscilla. "Priscilla, allow me to introduce you to my cow poke buddy, Shane."

Shifting his plate to his left hand, Shane extended his right hand to shake Priscilla's hand. "Pleased to meet you, Priscilla. Your boots look just fine to me."

"Oh, the boots! Did Spence tell you how he baptized my new ropers? I thought it was hilarious! Do you mind if I join you after I fill my plate? You've got a nice quiet corner way down here. I am sure Spence can round up a separate hay bale for me."

"We'd be delighted for you to have the pleasure of our company," winked Spence. "I'll be right back with a bale."

"What did I tell you, Spence? Don't be so queasy in the country. Take a deep breath. Enjoy your evening."

"Well, would you look at that? I have my very own bale between you two handsome cowboys. Can life get any better than this? Maybe this is a snapshot of what the next year will bring."

"You country girls sure don't eat much," bantered Shane. "I guess that's where they get the saying, 'doesn't eat enough to keep a bird alive.'"

"You might say that I graze rather than eat. I take little samples of this and that during the day."

"Well, it's sure not much of this and that as far as I can tell," opined Spence.

"So back to the Sabblontis," pressed Priscilla.

"What's your obsession with that family, anyway?" Shane asked.

"I would not call it an obsession. Obviously, you two have not lived around here very long. It's past time you learned the lay of the land. Also, you need a basic cattle country history lesson."

"I never did care much for history," Spence countered, "but go ahead. It's best to show good manners. Speak on."

"I was born and raised in Shadow Butte County. My daddy passed away when I was in high school, so I went to work in the county recorder's office to help my mother financially. This would have been seven and half years ago, so it was the year 1991. I still live at home.

"The elected recorder, Betty Lou Bradford, has been a great mentor to me. Since I had taken a lot of office skills classes, she hired me two weeks after I graduated. I know she took pity on Mother and me, but it is what it is. Not every day is a mountain top experience even though we are surrounded by mountains. There seems to be a lot of deep valleys, too. Are you guys with me?"

"We're with you," replied Shane and Spence resoundingly.

"One hot summer day in 1994, Jantzi Belle Sabblonti blew into the recorder's office. Betty Lou had traveled down south for her annual vacation, so I was holding down the fort. The other two part time employees were also gone that afternoon. So, it was just me, myself, and I.

"Jantzi informed me that she had been out riding the range wherein she discovered a boundary stone marker that she did not know previously existed. She asked to see the legal descriptions of the adjoining ranches. I presumed she was a very slow reader because she seemed to pour over them like she was memorizing them. About that same time, a new land owner came into the office, so I needed to help him.

"One other thing about Jantzi — I had been warned to give her a very wide berth because she had a reputation of breathing fire and wreaking havoc with anyone or anything that got in her way. Keep in mind, I was only twenty years old at the time. So, when she asked me to make copies of the deeds, I thought nothing of it. She paid the required fees in cash. Before she left, Jantzi asked me how long Betty Lou was going to be on vacation and the work schedules of the other employees. I acted like a scared little bunny rabbit and told her the precise times and dates.

"You could have almost set your watch to the exact hour and minute one week later when Jantzi paid me a second visit. You guessed it! I was all by my lonesome in the recorder's office again. She asked to see the original deeds to the Sabblonti, Merrill, and Toppens' Ranches for the second time. I was in the middle of making sets of copies of other documents for an upcoming county commissioner's meeting, so I was not paying much attention to Jantzi. I had my back turned to her the whole time because I was assembling and collating the stacks of copies.

"All of a sudden, I spotted some dark purple liquid on the floor. When I turned around, I discovered that it had spilled on the counter across one of the deeds and had made a royal country mess! I did my best to clean it up as Jantzi apologized all over herself for her clumsiness. When I asked what the liquid was, she informed me that it was a country elixir that she had ordered through the mail. It was guaranteed to make one live a very long life. Jantzi informed me that she wanted to live to be at least one-hundred years old, so she drank this purple goop by the gallons, undiluted, and carried it with her everywhere she went. She had some lame excuse that she had failed to secure the lid on the bottle tightly, so it spilled all over the papers on the counter. Also, the elixir rendered the original deed unreadable. It's strange that the spill did not occur anyplace else. I think it's called intentional.

"I excused myself for a minute, walked down the hall to the break room to get a bottle of spray cleaner along with a new roll of paper towels, and returned to the office. After wiping down the counter twice so I had a clean and dry work surface, Jantzi suggested that since the original deed was not salvageable, I should go ahead and record the copy I had made for her the week before. Because I gave into fear of man, or woman in this case, I recorded the copy of the deed and filed it back inside the safe. I didn't know what to do at the time. In retrospect, I should have told her to come back the next week and Betty Lou could deal with her. Also, I was afraid of losing my job, which I desperately needed, so I did not tell Betty Lou about Jantzi's two visits. I should also add that a portion of the counter had to be replaced because the purple elixir left a permanent stain."

"This next part of the story is Marita Merrill's account as told to my mother, who in turn filled me in.

"In late August of 1995, one of Sabblonti's hired hands cut the five-strand, barbed wire fence of Merrill's ranch in order to allow the Sabblonti's cows and calves to drink from

Alder Creek which runs right through the heart of Merrill's ranch. We were experiencing quite a drought that year so water was scarce and vital. Nelson Merrill drove to the ranch and confronted Jantzi, who informed Nelson to recheck the legal descriptions and boundaries of his ranch.

"For many years before he died, Jantzi dispatched Ace to Merrill's Ranch I don't know how many times to lean on Nelson to sell, but Nelson was of the firm belief that one does not sell the land one inherits from one's father. Ace should have known this since he inherited the Sabblonti Ranch from his father. Ace coveted that part of the Merrill Ranch that had the stream running through it.

"During one of Merrill's fall roundups, some of Ace's loose-lipped hired help talked to one of Merrill's hired hands as they sat on horseback across the fence from one another. According to one of them, Ace used to lie on the couch for hours at a time in the main Sabblonti Ranch house and face the wall. He would pidge, pout, and moan that he did not own the Merrill Ranch, or at least the portion of it where Alder Creek was located. Jantzi assured him to bide his time as one day she would acquire the part of the ranch containing Alder Creek. Marita said she was surprised that Jantzi did not make her bold move to get it for Ace before he died. She was amazed she waited so long to cook up her brew of deceit.

"Thankfully Betty Lou was present in the county recorder's office the day Nelson Merrill came in to check the official deed for his ranch. Unfortunately, he had never asked for a copy for himself. All we had to rely upon was the recorded copy of the deed, but Nelson could tell right away that the doctored deed was not the accurate legal description. The revised land area did not include the portion of the Merrill Ranch where Alder Creek was located. Nelson said he thought the seller's signature was a forgery and that the seller had been dead for decades.

"Nelson paid Jantzi another visit to inform her that he was onto her game of how she had pirated his land and stream from him. She countered that he had taken leave of his senses. He threatened to file suit against her. She quickly informed him that she kept Dunne, Dunne, & Dunne, Chtd. from Ignee County on retainer. Jantzi further advised him that if he wanted to keep even one acre of his ranch, he'd better carefully count the cost before he went to war with her. Nelson, keenly aware of the Dunne legal eagles, did not pursue legal action. Marita told my mother that although Nelson relished a court battle to recapture his land, he realized what that would cost. Marita was of the mindset, 'Why line the lawyers' pockets with our hard-earned money?' It looks like she prevailed.

"Suffice it to say, I am not the only one who is not keen on the Sabblonti outfit. There are many other ranching folks who were not born yesterday and cannot be sold a phony bill of goods. This whole incident has made all of us keenly aware of the enemy and how he or she operates."

"I would have never dreamed somebody would be up to those sorts of shenanigans in these parts," commented Spence. "Thanks for the warning about those Sabblontis. Are there any of them here tonight? I suppose you know that Wyn Moreland just got engaged to Sarita."

"I just found that out tonight when Marita told me. I could hardly believe it! Does he know what he is getting into? Well, he's probably just marrying her for the family moulah. To answer your question, there's not a Sabblonti in sight tonight, which suits me super fine. I've talked your ears off so I better scoot for now. Maybe I will see you around sometime." Priscilla proceeded to find Marita to ask if there was anything else she could do to help out for the evening.

"Spence, you are not going to be too pleased with me right about now, but I have developed a huge gut ache," complained Shane. "I feel like I am going to upchuck right here on the spot. I've got to get some air. I'm heading outside."

"Get gone! Give me your plate first. There's no maid service around here tonight. We have to clean up after ourselves. I will be outside in a minute. Small wonder, you gorged yourself on three plates of food piled sky high along with five large cups of fresh cider. Just the thought of all that churning around in your stomach makes me nauseous. I can hear the gurgling sound clear over here."

Priscilla was making the rounds collecting odds and ends of trash and placing it inside a large can. "Here, Spence, I will take your trash from you. Where's Shane?"

"He had to step outside for some fresh air. His stomach is acting up quite a bit or so he said."

"That's too bad. I hope he gets to feeling better soon. I took note of how much he ate. I couldn't eat that much in a month!"

Spence headed outside to check on Shane, who was lying on the ground moaning like a bloated cow. "I could find a round piece of barn wood and stick it in your mouth to help you let the air out like we do for the cows when they bloat up."

Shane was in too much misery to say a word.

"Okay, too bad, so sad. Looks like it's time to end this roundup. I could stay here for hours, but you look like you could use a nurse maid. I will expect a bail out or a payback from you sometime, pal. Just when my evening looked like it had some promise, you go and ruin it for me. Oh, never mind me. I know I am being too hard on you. If I was in the same predicament, you would do the same for me. Let me say goodnight to my newly found cider girl, then I'll come back, load you into that old tan job, and we will be on our way. What an exciting New Year's Eve. Not!"

"Priscilla, it's been my distinct pleasure to meet you this evening. Thanks for taking time to visit with Shane and me. He really is in a world of hurt, so I better get him back to the bunkhouse. Happy New Year, and send me a cleaning bill for your ropers if you feel so inclined. I would be happy to pay it. Take care until we meet again."

"The pleasure has been mine, Spence. Please tell Shane I hope he gets on the mend very soon. I can tell that you are a loyal person because you take good care of your friends. You will make some young woman a great husband someday. Happy New Year to you, too. Oh, wait just a second! I forgot to give you these two jars. They're a little something from Marita to give to Merna. Can you please deliver them?"

"Will do," agreed Spence. "Wild Plum Gumbo and Currant Conserve. Never heard of those two. I am sure Merna will know what to do with them."

"The Currant Conserve is delicious with roast beef. There's no shortage of that in this country. Enjoy!"

CHAPTER THIRTY-FOUR

Merna was sitting in her rocking chair crocheting a burgundy afghan when she heard a knock on her front door.

"Why, what a pleasant surprise, Wyn! Please come in and make yourself at home. You can hang your jacket on the coat tree there by the wood stove if you like. Is everything alright?"

"Thanks, Merna. Yes, everything is okay. I just wondered if you had a few minutes that I could talk with you about a couple of things? Where's Tom?"

"Oh, he went to bed quite early tonight. I think he's just overly tired for some reason."

"I hope he's okay. Has he seen a doctor lately?"

"Tom, go to a doctor? Shake yourself! These old ranchers don't think they need any help from any kind of doctors unless it's an animal doctor. I think he might have wrenched his back again. I offered to take a look at it, but he said he just wanted to go to bed. Would you like a nice piece of fruit cake with a cup of hot chocolate or coffee? Does anything like that sound good? Then we can sit in the living room and visit if you have time."

"I've got nothing but time and that's real hospitable of you, Merna. Is the fruit cake the kind with all of those chunky dried fruits, nuts, and stuff in it?"

"Yes, that's why it's called a fruit cake!"

"Uh, no thanks on the fruit cake. I heard a lady one time at the boy's home say that fruit cake belongs at the city dump along with pickled beets and canned pears. I guess you could say that cake was not her favorite."

"Let me see what else I might have in my cupboard. Oh, I just remembered! Since the red velvet cake was such a big hit for our Christmas Dinner, I made another one and have kept it in the refrigerator. Would you like a piece of that?"

"Sure would. You can treat someone else to that fruit cake if you don't mind. I don't want to sound ungrateful or anything. And can you make it an extra big chunk of the red velvet one?

"What about something to drink?"

"Could I have a large glass of cold milk with my piece of cake, please?"

"You sure can, Wyn. You are just like a son to me, especially after losing my one and only son, Toby, who drowned in the stock tank when he was two years old. What mother would not give her children a little something extra special every chance she got?"

"Well, my mother obviously did not. She took me to the boy's home and dumped me off there. To make matters worse, I never knew my real father."

"I am so sorry, Wyn. I did not mean to say something that would bring back painful memories. Please forgive me. I should not have said that."

"It's alright, Merna. I do forgive you. I have never taken time to work through the pain of the abandonment. I don't know how to do that, and I don't want to take it with me into my marriage to Sarita. That's not fair to her."

"Speaking of forgiveness, Wyn, it's very important that

you forgive your mother. When you do, you will feel a great release and your healing will begin. Forgiving her does not change what she did to you, but it helps you to move on with your life. Holding onto unforgiveness is like being hogtied. And, in fairness to your mother, you don't know everything that was going on in her life at the time when she felt that she was doing the best thing for you by taking you to a boy's home. If there's one thing I have learned in life, it's that not everything is as it appears. There are usually several layers or chapters to any given thing at any given time. Also, we don't always get to choose who and/or what we can keep in this life."

"That's a great word picture, Merna! When you said that, what I saw in my mind's eye was myself all bound with heavy ropes. I guess I had never thought what hanging onto unforgiveness was doing to me. It was binding me. If I forgive, it's like all those ropes unwind, fall off me, and I walk free! That helps me a whole lot. That's not what I came up here to talk to you about, but that's just the icing on the cake, not that the icing on this red velvet cake isn't good enough by itself. Yum! Could you please give this recipe to Sarita so she can make it for us after we get married up?"

"Yes, and speaking of marriage, what are your plans, or have you made any as of yet?"

"We have hardly had time to talk about anything following Jantzi's death. Part of me feels very badly for not attending her funeral, but in all honesty, I could not bring myself to attend. Sarita knows that her mother could not bring herself to be civil to me, so I know it was okay with her that I was not in attendance."

"I am sure Sarita did fine at her mother's funeral. She has a lot of inner strength and resolve. She's a wonderful young woman. You two will be very happy together."

"I feel so inadequate since I grew up in the boy's home and did not have a fair shake at life. At least that's the way I feel about it. If it wasn't for you and Tom, I don't know where I would be right about now. It took me forever to save up enough money to buy Sarita's engagement ring, and I know that kind jeweler took pity on me when he discounted the price. Why, I don't even own a pickup truck! I sense I am the laughing stock of the whole county. I was amazed that Sarita even accepted my marriage proposal. I am as poor as a church mouse, and she comes from such a wealthy family."

"Don't be so hard on yourself, Wyn. You have had a lot of obstacles to overcome, and I am really proud of you for saving your money to buy Sarita's ring. The two of you will work it out. I am sure of it. Not to be disrespectful of the dead or anything, but since Ace and Jantzi had two daughters, each of them will probably be given half of the estate holdings, which are substantial to say the least. Once Sarita takes possession of her share, you will be in good shape. Just stay in your saddle for a while and you will do fine."

"The Sabblonti's money is not why I asked Sarita to marry me. I could care less about how much money anybody has. I have a plan to buy a cattle ranch of my own someday. All hard work brings a profit."

"Yes, it certainly does. Tom and I worked very hard to purchase our ranch and maintain it. It's been a real struggle at times, but we did not give up. Keep in mind that my husband did not inherit his ranch like Ace Sabblonti did."

"Merna, why didn't you go to Jantzi's funeral? You have been ranching neighbors with the Sabblontis for decades. I am not criticizing you. I just want to know. If you don't feel like telling me, that's okay."

"Actually, I think it's important for you to know as it's a vital piece of the cattle ranch puzzle in these parts. Some of the new comers don't know about it, but it happened, nonetheless. Just a minute while I put another juniper log into the stove."

"I can tend the fire for you, Merna."

"Thanks, Wyn. I will take our dishes and put them into the sink. Let me take a peek to see if my beloved is sleeping. Then we can chat for awhile."

"If you need to take care of Tom, I can come for a visit some other time. I realize I sort of showed up uninvited."

"Yes, Tom seems to be resting soundly. Let me see, where do I start?"

"The beginning is usually a good place."

"Agreed, Wyn. History and background are vital in most anything pertaining to life. Tom and I grew up in Ignee County. He is four years older than me, so was a senior in high school when I was a freshman. My parents lived in town. My father was an elementary school teacher, and mother stayed home with the children. Tom grew up in the country, and his father had a very small acreage. The family struggled to make ends meet, and his mother took in laundry, sewing, and other odd jobs to help put beans into the pot. My in-laws were very loving and accepting people. When they were alive, they treated Tom and me with the utmost respect and kindness. They may not have had a lot of material things, but they had what was most important in life, which is a good value system, honesty, and unconditional love.

"When Tom started junior high, he raised Hereford

cattle and showed them in the Ignee County Fair. I am so pleased to tell you that he won the Grand Champion ribbon for the next six years and sold his cattle for top dollar. That helped him to start a little nest egg. My father-in-law used to say, 'Son, you are as tight as bark on a tree.' Tom would reply, 'If you take care of the quarters, dimes, nickels, and pennies, the dollars will take care of themselves.' It isn't that Tom is stingy; he just knows the value of a dollar. He would like to be able to say that he has a dime of the first dollar he ever earned.

"There was an outstanding FFA instructor at the high school. He taught the interested students that there is more to ranching and farming than planting a few crops and hoping you reap a harvest. There's a definite science to it; however, there's also a business aspect along with many other things. When Tom wasn't helping his parents, he would spend time at the public library reading about cattle breeds, developing a ranch, and the like. He was not interested in sports, so that did not consume much of his time.

"When I was in high school, I had heard of the Toppens family, but did not really pay much attention to them. I took a lot of home economics classes and enjoyed domesticated sort of things. I sewed my own clothing to help with the family budget. At the start of each summer, I would order a couple of new clothing patterns from a mail order company. After they arrived, I would figure out how much fabric it would take to make each outfit and purchase it from the local mercantile. There was a family that lived next to us in town that had two sets of twins. I earned enough money from babysitting them during the summer to help buy my patterns, fabric, and notions. My high school years flew by!

During that time, I determined that I wanted to be a homemaker and a mother. My handsome country boy would appear soon enough.

"The summer after I turned eighteen, I started to work part time at the mercantile in the dry goods department. One day Tom came into the store, and we struck up a conversation. When he left, I heard this grating noise outside. I looked out the store window and saw the muffler of his old pickup scraping the street as he drove away. I laughed out loud and commented, 'Tom had better buy some more baling wire and get that thing tied up!' He started to frequent the store a little more often, which just happened to be during the hours that I worked. Long story short is that we started courting late that summer and were married the next year. We have been very happily married now for fifty-two years.

"Oh, I got a little bit ahead of myself there for a minute. Right after we were married, we lived with Tom's parents for the first year. We would drive around Ignee County to see if there was a little chunk of land that we could make a down payment on, but it seemed that prices were much higher in Ignee County than Shadow Butte County. One day Tom got the bright idea to drive to this area and check things out. Our first little purchase was a bit of land in the southwest corner of the county. It had a modest little house sitting in the middle of it surrounded by some nice trees. We were both very content and God blessed us with our first child. I had no clue at the time that we would only have our little bundle from heaven for such a short period of time.

"Then a most fortunate thing happened. Because of the natural slope of the area where our land was located there was a company that was looking to build a large feed lot.

The small portion of land that Tom and I had just made our first down payment on sat at the tail end of the area that the future owners of the feed lot needed for their operation. They made us a cash offer we could not refuse. We used that money to make a down payment on this ranch. The previous owners carried the papers on this place until we could pay it off, so we did not need to get involved with Cattlemen's Central or anyone else. It was one of the finest days of our lives when we held that title deed in our hands. Days like that help to make up for the ones when life isn't so good. You have got to be able to take the ups with the downs and the sadness along with the joy. There are many double-edged swords everywhere.

"So now you have the basic history of how we got here. Let's move onto the Sabblontis. I discovered in later years that Jantzi and I were the same age. Tom was two years older than Ace, whose family had homesteaded their ranch in the 1800's. It's a large ranch including the prime grazing areas that buttress up against the northern and eastern boundaries of our neighboring state.

"There were just Ace and his younger sister, Shirley. Ace graduated from Ridgemonte High School in 1943 and worked on the ranch until he died in 1993. His parents were of the opinion that the first-born son got the double inheritance. Well, since Ace was the first-born son, and the only son, he did in fact get the double inheritance. I was never told the inside story if Ace bought his sister's share of the land, if in fact Shirley had any share after their parents died. Upon graduating from high school, Shirley married a local rodeo announcer, and the two of them virtually lived on the road for years, staying in hotels and horse trailers with sleeping quarters. One of our other neighbors, who has since passed away, said that Shirley was as wild as a March hair when she was in high school.

"Ace put his whole heart into continuing to develop the Sabblonti Ranch, especially the upper grazing areas. Since there are portions where there's not much water, he also had to plan where to put in some reservoirs to catch the spring run-off. He was quite reserved and was a bachelor for fifteen years. I never did hear the straight of how he met Jantzi Belle Siddonz. She graduated from the high school in Blunte County. Knowing her, she probably proposed to Ace and asked him to marry her.

"The Siddonz family had three girls, Jonsey, Jillian, and Jantzi. Sounds like their mother had the whole 'J' thing going as far as names were concerned. I met the two older girls when Chet and Stormy got married. Jillian had one of those high and mighty sorts of attitudes. Jonsey was pleasant to be around. Jantzi's mother, Mabel, had a sweet disposition, and I got to know her a little bit during the times when she visited while Stormy and Sarita were growing up. If I heard that Mabel was in the area, I would drive over to the Sabblontis, and Mabel would sit in the front yard with me so we could get to know one another. None of the other neighbors, including myself, were ever invited inside the Sabblonti ranch house.

"Ace could be neighborly if he decided he wanted to be. He visited us more often than our other ranching neighbor, Nelson Merrill. Ace would stop by and have a cup of coffee every now and then. I always felt sorry for him because he seemed so lonely. When I would bake a chokecherry or wild currant pie, I would save a piece for him to enjoy with his coffee.

"Jantzi spent a lot of time fixing up the big ranch house.

She totally snubbed the merchants in Shadow Butte County and drove clear over to Blunte County to select her furnishings. Periodically, someone would spot her riding her horse in the high country. She would turn her little girls loose during the day with instructions to be home by supper time. She didn't really seem to make time for them. Sarita liked to spend more time in the house and front yard, but Jantzi would shoo her out of there like a fly. Of course, kids grow up in the blink of an eye.

"After the girls graduated from high school, Stormy worked for various businesses in town, but always seemed to be discontented. She would work one place for several months and then quit. This went on for a few years. Finally, Jantzi ordered her to move back home until such time as her perfect cowboy rode into Shadow Butte County.

"Sarita, on the other hand, moved in with her Aunt Jonsey after graduation. Simon Siddonz, Sarita's maternal grandfather, was a blacksmith and wheelwright by trade. According to Mabel, of her three girls, Jonsey seemed to be the one that inherited the craftsman traits. After she married, Jonsey opened up a little store in Blunte County called Jonsey's *Novelties.* She taught Sarita how to make jewelry and other craft items. They took their little enterprise on the road to county fairs, art shows in the city parks, and the like. Sarita was gone for almost a decade and moved back shortly before Ace died.

"Chet Castins seemed to blow in during one of the winter storms. He was looking for work of any kind and did odd jobs around town. How he and Stormy connected is yet another mystery. Initially, Jantzi was not keen on Stormy marrying Chet. If she's half as strong willed as her mother was, she probably told her to ride off because she was going to marry Chet, come heaven or high water or both. Before Chet and Stormy were married, Jantzi had the house built for them down on the lower portion of the ranch, along with the barn and other outbuildings. I imagine that turned out to be a wise decision so Chet could help manage everything, especially after Ace died.

"Jantzi donned her best duds for Stormy's country wedding in the beautiful meadow of the Sabblonti Ranch. Ace was fairly well thought of so everyone who was invited was in attendance. It was a very enjoyable celebration even if some of the cast of characters was challenging. Ace killed the fatted calf and his ranch hands helped to cook it on a spit. There was enough food there that day to feed Coxey's Army. Jantzi ordered it from some catering company. The wedding was done in a horseshoe theme. Even Stormy's wedding rings form the horseshoe shape. The wedding cake was baked in half chocolate and half carrot cake flavors and formed a horseshoe as well. I don't think there was one crumb left.

"Truth be known, people in these parts preferred Ace and Sarita over Jantzi and Stormy. That's probably quite ugly to say, but the truth isn't always pretty.

"Sarita started to work for Dr. Diller after her dad died. In many ways, there's a lot of mystique surrounding the Sabblonti family. In saying that, I am not trying to be hyper critical, especially since you just got engaged to Sarita."

"Merna, can you tell me how Ace died? It sounds like he was an okay guy. I sure do wish I could have known him. I agree that Sarita might be a lot like him. After I met her at the Shadow Butte annual county fair picnic, and whenever I would ask her anything about her father, she would just start to cry. So, I quit asking as I do not like to see her shed tears."

"Yes, I can. It was the spring of the year in 1993. We had quite a bit of snow in the high country during the previous winter. According to Jantzi, Ace rode out early one morning on his horse, Snipper, to check his herd after placing them on the range. Unbeknownst to anyone else at the time, he did not return for three days. I still find it odd that she did not dispatch one of their ranch hands to try to find him when he did not return the first night.

"Eventually, Jantzi must have become concerned as she rounded up Chet along with two of their hired helpers, and the four of them rode until they found Ace. Reconstructing events after they occurred, what Jantzi floated out to the ranching community was that Snipper had stopped at a small stream to get a drink. There was a coiled rattlesnake behind one of the rocks that struck Snipper. This caused him to rear straight in the air and throw Ace to the ground, and he hit his head on a large rock nearby. Ace died of a subdural hematoma. When Jantzi and her helpers finally found Ace and Snipper, both of them were bloated up like twin toads. How much of the aforementioned is fact or fiction, I would have no way of knowing. The Shadow Butte County Coroner supposedly completed a thorough investigation and signed it for the official records. So now you know as much as I know regarding the death of Ace Sabblonti."

Wyn opined, "It seems so strange that Jantzi wouldn't be the least bit concerned about Ace not returning for three days, unless he had the habit of being gone for a few days at a time. Part of that story is a head scratcher, for sure. Thanks for telling me though. It does help to fill in some of the background material that I needed to know."

Merna continued, "Now for the most important piece of history that I need to tell you. In the fall of 1994, roughly a year after Ace had passed away, Jantzi Belle Sabblonti stepped foot onto the Toppens Ranch for the one and only time. I invited her to come into our house, but she refused. Tom was tending to some horses on the walker that morning. Standing flat footed in our front yard, Jantzi offered to buy our ranch from us. Tom informed her that we were not interested in selling. She stated, 'Name your price, and I will pay it. No questions asked.' My husband informed her a second time that we had no intentions of selling our land. Jantzi squinted those evil eyes of hers, and said, 'You will be sorry you refused my offer.'

"A year later, 1995, Tom had one of the largest and healthiest cattle herds in all of his combined years of ranching put together. He had trained himself from his earliest days in 4-H and FFA to keep exact records. In fact, I have records going as far back as 1937. I've never thrown any of them away because Tom likes to compare present years to prior ones.

"So, in late August of '95, Tom rode out to our summer range along with some of our ranch hands and counted his herd. He came home that evening and entered the various numbers in the correct columns in his record book. He was bursting at the flat-felled seams of his shirt when he told me how many cows and calves he had. It was the happiest I had seen him in a very long time. I rejoiced with him and told him that I was immensely proud of him. I thanked him for being such a good husband and provider.

"One week later, Tom had a dream that something had happened to his cattle. He shared the dream with me. I encouraged him to ride to the range and count them again.

When he and our ranch hands completed a recount, which they conducted twice that day, we were short seventy-three head.

"Tom was very upset at the disappearance of our cattle, and rounded up some nearby ranchers to help him ride to look for them, along with the volunteers from the Shadow Butte County Sheriff's Posse. Interestingly enough, when he asked Chet to help out, he offered the lame excuse to Tom that he was too busy after Ace died to help out with anything other than running the Sabblonti Ranch.

"The men rode for the next three weeks, off and on, to try to locate our missing cattle, to no avail. There had been some cattle rustling in the area during the 1980's, but due to a great combined effort of local law enforcement along with county officials, they had almost ground it to a complete halt.

"What we did hear quite a while later on was that one of Sabblonti's hired hands, Lashe Lemmons, was singing like a bird one night after getting tanked at the local watering hole. According to him, he participated in a midnight cattle carving off routine wherein a most interesting thing occurred with cattle brands. Lashe had participated in some shady deals in the Midwest before coming to our part of the country, but he had never seen a maneuver done quite like this one. Just a minute, Wyn, I need to get a piece of paper and a black pen so I can illustrate this for you.

"From the account reported by Lashe, which was ultimately reported to a couple of our hired hands long after the dirty deed, the following is what happened, in words or substance.

"Chet, acting upon direct orders from his new boss, i.e., his mother-in-law, rounded up a half dozen of their cow pokes. While our cows and calves were on the upper portion of our summer range, Chet and his band of thieves carved off the seventy-three cows and calves and herded them to the highest point on the Sabblonti Ranch, which meant they would be completely out of sight.

"The Toppens cattle brand is a triangle with a dot at the top of it.

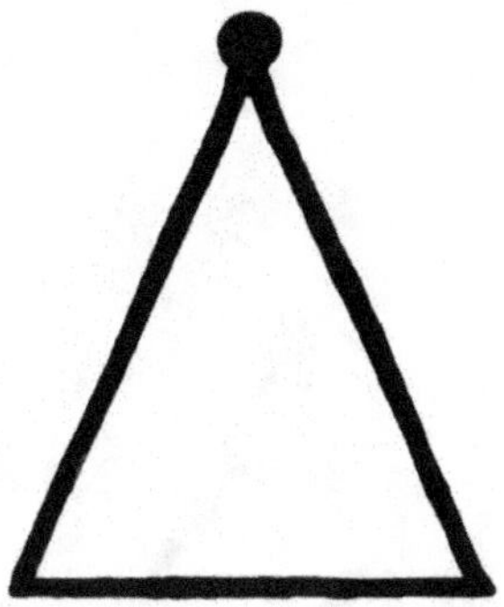

"The Sabblonti cattle brand is an S with a dot on the tail end of the S.

"So, what those rustlers did was place the Sabblonti brand inside our brand so it would look like this:

"The new brand inspector, Blake Benson, participated in the deal as well. He helped to escort the stolen cattle across our state line and loaded them onto trucks to be shipped to a slaughter house in the southwest. Even though cattle prices were not that high during 1995, we still ended up losing quite a bit of money.

"Granted, we can't actually prove any of this as it's all based upon hearsay from a cow hand who would be like trying to find last year's snow. Lashe Lemmons skipped the country right after this happened and has not been heard from since. Blake Benson is still here, but he is as shifty as the evening shadows and will never look us straight in the eye when he talks to us. He looks down at the ground and moves the dirt around with his cowboy boot when he tries to converse. There was a period of time when Blake spent a lot of time at the Sabblonti Ranch under the guise of introducing himself to all of the ranchers in these parts, since he was the new inspector.

"Wyn, you asked why a lot of people did not attend Jantzi's funeral. I stopped by to see her a few days before Christmas and asked if I could visit with her for awhile. I had this foreboding feeling about her. She was very rude and did not invite me inside. I believe in being neighborly, but have enough self-respect to know when it's time to quit trying to get other people to like you. As a child and throughout my adulthood, I have never really been one that has liked to play games of any sort, including people games. In my heart of hearts, I still believe that it was Jantzi who was responsible for the theft of our cattle. I would be a hypocrite if I told you that I had not forgiven Jantzi for the whole cattle rustling business, because I have spoken to you tonight about the importance of forgiveness. There's also the chapter concerning the Merrill's Ranch. That just might have to wait for another time. Land sakes, child, it's two in the morning! You had better get down to the bunkhouse."

Standing up, Wyn approached Merna, "Thank you so much for taking the time this evening to bring me up to speed on the history of this area. It means a lot to me. You and Tom are so important to me. Would you mind if I called you, Momma Merna?"

Merna placed her right cupped hand over her mouth as she laughed with joy. Suddenly, she bent over at her waist as tears gushed from her eyes.

"What's happening, Merna? Are you okay? I don't know how to perform first aid or anything so you better be alright."

Merna sobbed uncontrollably for the next few minutes as Wyn stood helpless by her side.

"Toby died before he uttered the word *Momma*. He was just learning to talk and said, *dah-dah* but never *ma-ma.* No one has ever called me Momma before, and I did not realize how my heart ached all these years just to hear that one simple word. By all means Wyn, I would be honored if you wanted to refer to me as *Momma Merna*."

"Sarita would like to come out tomorrow night for supper. Is that okay with you and Tom? She and I would also like to have a few quiet moments to ourselves as we sit in your den, if permissible."

"That's just fine, son. We would love to have Sarita join us anytime. Since you are becoming like a son to me, she will be like a daughter-in-law. A healing of the heart can come along when we least expect it."

Wyn was in no hurry to return to the bunkhouse despite the late hour. Walking outside, he searched the night sky to see if he could spot the constellation, *Bootes, The Herdsman*. Craning his neck in all directions, he could not find it. "No wonder it's not up there! It's visible only during the summer," Wyn chided himself. "I will have my own herd someday. Where there's a will, there's a way."

CHAPTER THIRTY-FIVE

"I thought you told me I could have New Year's Day off," protested Brent Dawson.

"Son, the sun is shining today, and we are really making hay!" Delbert Dawson said gleefully. "This is a red-letter day to start our new year. One of the neighbors swung by the house because he was bored. He decided he wanted to spend some money. I wasn't about to discourage him. We drove to the dealership where he ended up buying two new pickups, one for himself and the other for his wife. I guess it does pay to stay home part of the day. At any rate, he drove his home. I told him that we would deliver the other one, so I need a driver."

"Well, your daughter-in-law isn't going to be any too happy. She's making my favorite supper right now. How long before you will be here to pick me up?"

"Tell her to keep it on *warm* and remind my daughter-in-law how great she is. I will be there in fifteen minutes."

Brent grabbed a piece of jerky from the pantry, located his wallet with his driver's license, and stepped onto the sidewalk where his dad was waiting for him.

"Let's get this delivery taken care of right away. There's also another little project I need your help with that shouldn't take more than an hour or so."

"I get it, Dad. It's the whole failure to give me all of the details routine. Pry me out of the house on a national holiday. I'm just joshing you. I am happy to help you. I couldn't ask for a better father. I appreciate you so much."

"Now don't go getting all sentimental on me. You must think I am going to die soon or something."

"I don't think that at all! I just felt like expressing what's inside my heart. Maybe I take after Mom more in that regard. She's a real encourager. She raised us with a lot of affirmation. I am so blessed to have great parents."

"Speaking of death, Brent, did you hear about that Sabblonti funeral? I guess there were only a handful of people that showed up. Your mother and I attended Ace's funeral a few years back. I felt zero obligation to attend Mrs. Sabblonti's."

"Why is that, Dad? You are the one who is always preaching 'customer satisfaction', and all that hooplah. I don't think I have ever seen you miss a community funeral since I started working at the dealership."

"Son, I believe in supporting people within the community; however, I am keenly aware of what has transpired over the decades in this valley. I do not endorse evil or wicked behavior."

"Dad, how can you know everything that happens around here to be able to separate the evil from the good?"

"I don't pretend to know everything that transpires, but I do know certain accounts of people's intentional actions that have harmed others. Obviously, others do as well. Otherwise, that school auditorium would have been packed out the other day. When Ace Sabblonti died, it was standing room only in that big open meadow on the ranch. What a contrast. Story to be continued. Let's get these new pickups delivered post haste."

Delbert followed his son to deliver the pickup to Delbert's neighbor.

Getting out of the pickups, Delbert and Brent walked to the neighbor's front porch and rang the doorbell. Jim, Delbert's neighbor, opened the door and invited them inside.

After introducing Brent to Jim, Delbert said, "We are running short on time, so here are two sets of keys to your wife's new rig. I sure hope she enjoys it. Don't forget to tell her that you purchased the extended warranty. It's wise to do that in mountain country. Let us know what else we can peddle you. Don't be a stranger!"

"Oh, Delbert, you know me. I'll drop by sometime in the next couple of days for a cup of coffee."

Walking back to the pickup, Brent asked, "Now what, Dad?"

"Back to the dealership for a quick minute. We have another delivery to make. Then we will be done for the day."

"Good thing," said Brent. "I am in the middle of a little woodworking project that I need to finish. It should have been ready for Christmas, but I didn't quite make it in time."

Arriving in the parking lot, Delbert gestured to one of the new pickups in the first row. "See that dark green one over there? I'll grab the keys so you can follow me."

Climbing inside the cab, Brent glided his right hand across the steering wheel, console, and front seat. Wow, this is a beauty! Who bought this one?"

"You ask too many questions, son."

Delbert headed out of the city limits onto the county road.

Brent pressed the scan button on the dashboard until it registered upon his favorite country western station. "Might as well listen to some tunes while I head on down the highway. I wonder if Dad knows where he's going. We've been driving for over forty minutes already. It's not like he doesn't know where everyone lives in this part of the country. I hope he isn't daydreaming and forgot to turn down the correct side road."

A few minutes later, Delbert turned from the main road onto a well-traveled road and drove for another fifteen minutes or so. He parked his pickup in the front yard. Brent parked the new pickup beside him.

"I didn't know they were looking for a new pickup," commented Brent.

"Well, there's really no way you would have known they were. It was a fast and furious few days toward the end of last year to say the least."

Delbert and Brent stepped onto the front porch simultaneously. Delbert rapped the front door six times, hesitating after four raps, and before the last two. It almost sounded like he was sending a message in door knocker code.

"Hello there, you must be looking for Tom. Just a minute. Let me get him for you," offered Wyn.

"Oh, that's okay," Delbert said reassuringly. "Why don't all of you come out here in the front yard for a minute? I think there's still enough daylight so you can see what's going on."

Wyn scratched his forehead as he walked into the kitchen to inform Tom, Merna, and Sarita there were visitors waiting outside.

"Goodness sakes alive, who could be stopping by on

New Year's?" asked Merna.

"Delbert, what brings you out here?" asked Tom. "I told Brent the other day when he called that I didn't need a new truck yet, unless of course you just wanted to give me one to test drive for a year or so."

"You can test drive it for more than a year if you like, Tom", kidded Delbert. "Actually, it's not for you. It's for Wyn Moreland. His name was on the piece of paper that was drawn for the winner of the new pickup in the annual promotional we have titled *Rigs 4 Ridgemonte.*"

"So that's what you called for the other day, Brent! Why didn't you say something then? I delivered the message to Wyn to have him call you back. Honest I did."

"I believe you, Tom. It's not a problem."

Wyn was quick to offer his apology. "Brent, I apologize that I did not get your call returned. The day got away from me. That's real poor manners on my part."

"Brent, have you got those two sets of keys? Please hand them over to Wyn."

"Wait just a second," demanded Wyn. "I didn't enter that contest. I was never inside the dealership to fill out the form or whatever it was. Don't take that wrongly. I didn't stop in there because I don't appreciate you folks. I just don't get into town that often. Who filled out that piece of paper for me? Was your drawing rigged, per chance?"

Delbert smiled, "All of our drawings are conducted properly. I would have to say it's probably someone who thinks the world of you!"

Wyn turned to Sarita, "Did you enter the contest on my behalf?"

"Not me. December was very hectic for me."

"Please excuse my lack of professionalism," Delbert

continued, "Sarita, please accept my deepest condolences on the recent loss of your mother. I should have said something earlier. I just got caught up in all of the excitement. We try to stay in stealth mode as much as we can each year to surprise the winner of the new pickup. We have managed to pull of some real first-rate acts over the years!"

"Thank you, Delbert. I appreciate you thinking of my family during this time."

"Say, Sarita, is that a diamond ring I see sparkling in the porch light?" Brent asked.

"Yes, it is. Wyn has asked me to marry him and I have accepted with joy."

"Congratulations to both of you!" exclaimed Brent.

"Wyn, please give me back one of those sets of keys," directed Delbert. "Sarita, here's your set so now each of you has one. Will that work for you, Wyn?"

"For sure!" exclaimed Wyn. "We still have not solved the mystery of how my name got on that entry paper, unless, of course, Santa Claus filled it out for me."

"Well, you could say **Mrs.** Santa Claus had something to do with it," explained Delbert. "She must have left the North Pole just long enough to come down here in her borrowed sleigh and take care of the last-minute details."

Sarita jumped when the word *sleigh* was mentioned.

"Did something startle you, Sarita?" asked Merna.

"No, not really. A sudden sleigh image flashed through my mind. It's nothing."

Wyn reached out his hand while Sarita placed hers inside his.

"Do you want to tell them or shall I?" asked Delbert.

"I will tell them," said Merna. "I almost completely forgot about the annual drawing that is so popular. I had to go into town to get some groceries at The Shadowy Merc for our Christmas Dinner along with taking care of a few other items of business. As I was leaving town, I saw the *Rigs for Ridgemonte* advertised on your big marquee, so I turned around and went inside the dealership. I filled out a piece of paper with Wyn's name on it, hoping all the while that he would be the winner."

"I had our bookkeeper draw the winning name like I do every year," Delbert explained. "She's worked in that capacity for over thirty years. She's as honest as they come. We complete the drawing with about seven people present so we have lots of sets of eyes on the project. We had over 8,000 entries this year, so it's really gaining in popularity. Wyn, I can't think of a more deserving winner. Enjoy your new rig. It looks like the road ahead is full of lots of promise for you. All the best to you and Sarita."

"Thanks, Delbert and Brent. I am overcome by all of this generosity. I feel tongue tied and don't really know what to say. Maybe life really is starting to break in my favor."

There were lots of handshakes all the way around the circle complete with "Happy New Year's", too.

"Momma Merna, how can I ever thank you enough for following that prompt to enter my name in that contest? I am a most fortunate man. 2000, here we come!"

CHAPTER THIRTY-SIX

Stormy determined that this day would need to be calculated and executed with precision as she placed her first important telephone call. "Happy New Year, sister! I hope you have been able to get some rest following Mother's funeral. Since it's Sunday, I was wondering if you would have time to drive out to the ranch this afternoon as there are a few things we need to discuss."

"How much time will it require?" asked Sarita.

"Oh, it should not take too awfully long," assured Stormy. "Why, do you have other pressing matters? I would not think there's much happening in your life right now. Sure, you just got engaged, but with Wyn's meager earnings, it's going to take a couple of years for you to scrape together enough money to even get a marriage license. Once you can do that, I am sure your wedding will be nothing like the royal country doings that Jantzi Belle and Ace shelled out for Chetter and me."

"Since when have you started referring to our parents as Jantzi Belle and Ace? Whatever happened to Mother and Daddy?"

"Quit being so childish, Sarita. It's high time you grew up. You are such a whiney, contrary juvenile. It's only the offspring who have failed to progress in life who still refer to their parents with such adolescent terms of endearment. Answer my question. I have a lot of ground to cover today and a very pressing schedule. You need to plan to work around my priorities because I am certainly not going to adapt to yours."

"I will be at the ranch house at 4:00 this afternoon," assured Sarita.

"Fine, and be sure to leave that marginal boyfriend of yours behind. I don't want him hanging around here. We have enough flies to contend with as it is."

"Wyn is my fiancé. He is not my marginal boyfriend, and most certainly not a fly."

"Say what you want. It's too bad you don't have two normal eyes so that you can see things for what they really are. 4:00 o'clock it is."

Now to the second call. "Chetter had better be in the house so he can answer on the first ring. I don't have time to babysit him either. "Oh, hello, darling, I was so in hopes that you would be inside the house. It looks like everything is going my way today. Life is just blissful!"

"If the grease would not have splattered all over the wall when I was cooking my late breakfast, I would not still be in the kitchen," Chet explained. "I did not expect to hear from you today."

"You didn't? How's that? Let's not get our new year off to a bad start. I have great plans for 2000. Why wouldn't I call the love of my life so I could talk to him?"

Chet continued, "Well, you sure could have fooled me with all of this love of your life business. You have been as cold as ice lately. It's like a switch flipped inside you the day your mother died. You are not the same woman I married."

"I would watch your words very carefully if I were you.

Think before you speak. You have a lot to lose if you don't play your cards just right."

"I was never much of a card player, so I really don't think it matters much."

"Speaking of playing cards, it's only the Jokers in the deck that matter in the long run."

"I am nobody's joker, Stormy."

"Really? We shall see about that. I need you at the main ranch house at 4:00 o'clock on the dot. Not a minute after that. I have summoned Sarita out here, and we have some important business to discuss."

"I doubt any of the business involves me, so why do I need to be present?"

"I feel like I am dealing with a bunch of two-year olds. First, Sarita gives me grief about calling our parents by their first names, and now I get push back from you about being where I tell you to be when I tell you to be there. You move so slowly you could be a sundial. Get the lead out and get your work done so you can be here on time. I want you showered, clean shaven, and dressed in some decent clothes as well."

"I have not had time to wash my clothes the past few days. Hopefully there are some clean ones in the dresser and closet. I used to have a loving, caring wife who took care of those kinds of things."

"Do not try to take me down Guilt Trip Lane because I am not walking there."

"I have never heard of Guilt Trip Lane. Would you like to walk down Loving Husband & Wife Road with me?"

Slamming the phone receiver down, Stormy busied herself with unwrapping all of the unopened Christmas gifts stacked by the fireplace in the family room. She was perplexed as to why so many of the boxes were empty. Why would her mother have bothered to waste her time elegantly wrapping empty boxes?

Stormy collected the cash that was inside the boxes intended for her and Chet and took it upstairs to her office. All of the remaining gifts, boxes, wrapping paper and bows were stuffed into large garbage sacks. Stormy planned to dispatch Chet to the ranch garbage pit so he could burn the bags and their contents. He could do this when he completed the remainder of the cleaning inside and outside the house.

Drama required just the right setting along with the correct cast of characters. Stormy concentrated on setting up the family room to where she would be the focal point. She had entertained the thought of making some warm winter tea with special spices ahead of time and placing it in a decanter. She reconsidered as she did not want Sarita staying one minute longer than necessary. Stormy was unsure of what Sarita's reaction would be following their discussion. "No need to start a fire in the fireplace, either. If everyone's teeth start to chatter, too bad. That will ensure that I can do all of the talking."

∞∞∞∞∞∞∞∞∞∞∞∞∞∞

Sarita placed a call to Wyn at the Toppens' bunkhouse. Fortunately, he answered on the first ring.

"Bunkhouse, Wyn speaking."

"Oh, Wyn, I am so thankful you were inside to answer my phone call. Stormy has called for a meeting at the ranch this afternoon. I told her that I would be there at four o'clock. She does not want you present, but I need you to be there with me. My sister cannot control my life, and the sooner she gets that message, the better for both of us."

"Sarita, wild horses could not keep me from going with you to that family meeting. There's no way in this world I would even dream of wanting you to be alone in that rattlesnake den."

"Wyn, my hero on the white horse, I knew I could count on you!"

Wyn suggested, "After I make myself presentable, I will drive into town and pick you up so we can ride together to the ranch. That will give us the chance to see how we like our new rig."

"Yes, it will be a great ride," agreed Sarita.

Traveling from Ridgemonte to the main ranch house afforded Wyn and Sarita the opportunity to continue to process the events of the past few days. Wyn encouraged Sarita to hold her ground in any matters pertaining to her sister.

With no dogs in the front yard to announce anyone's arrival, Stormy jumped when Sarita knocked on the front door.

Stormy opened the door and saw Sarita and Wyn standing there. After scowling at Wyn, she said, "You didn't need to knock, you know. Sarita, you grew up inside this house. You act like a stranger. What is your problem?"

"I don't have any problems, Stormy. Since you are living alone now, I thought I would be courteous and not startle you by opening the door."

"What do you mean by living alone?"

"Just what I said. You are kidding yourself if you think that no one is wise to the game you are playing. Relegating Chet down to the lower ranch house and requiring him to live there alone is the same as you living by yourself in the big house. News like that travels like wildfire across the range."

"Things have been so hectic, and with our lack of sleep, we just thought it better to function like this for a short while until we got a few things figured out."

"We shall see if a short while turns into a long while."

"Well, don't just stand there like two statues while you continue with your challenges. Come in."

As Sarita and Wyn walked into the large entryway, Stormy directed, "Take a take a seat in the family room. Don't expect anything to eat or drink because there's nothing prepared."

"I wasn't expecting anything to eat or drink," countered Sarita. "Hostessing was never your long suit anyway."

"Like hostessing is your long suit? That's laughable! But, then again, how much can you really be *The Hostess with the Mostess* in that drab apartment of yours? And you sure as the world couldn't get any practice in that blown out bunkhouse where Wyn is living!"

Chet walked up the hallway, stopped behind Stormy, placed his hands on her shoulders, and asked, "My, my, my, is that the way two loving sisters are supposed to be talking to one another?"

"Take your hands off me and remove your boots. I don't have time to clean the floor after you leave. How did you get in here without me hearing you, anyway?"

"Done, and done," laughed Chet. "I already took my boots off. I came in the back door and through the mud room. Wyn and Sarita, Happy New Year."

"Thanks, Chet, Happy New Year to you, too!" replied Sarita. "You look like you could use a hug. Do you mind if I give you one?"

"Not at all. Hugs are always welcome from my favorite sister-in-law. Can I hang your coat up for you?"

"Oh, don't give me that favorite sister-in-law line," Sarita laughed. "May I remind you that I am your one and only sister-in-law on the Sabblonti side?"

As Stormy turned and strode into the family room, she commanded all of them to follow her. Chet excused himself to go into the kitchen to make some coffee. As he walked past the window, he stopped and let out a double whistle. "Now that's an impressive set of wheels if I say so myself! Wyn, did you just win the lottery or what?"

"No, I don't buy lottery tickets," replied Wyn. "Happy New Year, Chet! How's everything going for you?"

"Oh, it's going!"

"That's all you can say?"

"Pretty much. Looks like your new year started off with a bang! Cattlemen's Central float you the loan for that rig? The only thing you need to make it complete is a cow dog riding in the front seat."

"Not exactly. You could say the Bank of Providence smiled upon me. It will be complete when my beautiful bride and man's best friend are riding with me."

"Bank of Providence? Never heard of it. Is there a new bank in this part of the country? Would you like a cup of coffee? I am getting ready to fix myself some."

Having already taken a seat in the family room, Stormy

yelled, "Chet, get in here right now! I don't want you making a mess by trying to prepare yourself a cup of coffee in my kitchen. Cleaning up messes is far beneath me now. That will be one of your new chores."

Wyn and Sarita entered the family room and walked over to the love seat to the right of where Stormy was sitting. Sarita gave Wyn a big hug before the two of them sat down. Chet followed them and plopped into the overstuffed brown leather chair to the left of Stormy.

Stormy refused to look at Wyn and continued to ignore him. Perched in her high-backed chair, she opened the drawer of the end table and selected a sheet of white paper. "The purpose of our little meeting here today is for the official reading of Mother's Last Will and Testament. It is short and sweet, so I won't need to take much of your valuable time. Like the rest of you have anything important to do with your lives in the first place. I don't want any questions or interruptions until after I have finished. So here goes:

"Last Will and Testament

Of

Jantzi Belle Siddonz Sabblonti

I, Jantzi Belle Siddonz Sabblonti, being of sound mind, do hereby make my last will and testament.

I appoint my beloved daughter, Stormy Suzanne Sabblonti Castins, as my personal representative. If she does not survive me or is unable to perform such duties,

then I appoint my beloved son-in-law, Chet Carleton Castins as my personal representative.

I leave my entire estate to my beloved daughter, Stormy Suzanne Sabblonti Castins.

If my beloved daughter, Stormy Suzanne Sabblonti Castins predeceases me, I leave the remainder of my entire estate to my beloved son-in-law, Chet Carleton Castins.

Signed: *Jantzi Belle Siddonz Sabblonti*
Dated: A.D. December 4, 1999

That concludes the reading of the will."

Stormy continued to look down at the piece of paper. Sensing and hearing nothing, she raised her head, tilted it to the left, and cradled her left cheek in her left hand. Jutting her chin forward, crossing her legs while holding the will in her right hand, she did not move or speak.

Sarita broke the silence. "Wyn, are you ready?"

"Yes, quite ready, My Sweet."

Standing to their feet, Wyn and Sarita held hands as they walked from the family room to the front entryway. Chet followed them.

Wyn helped Sarita into her coat. Chet opened the front door as the three of them walked into the front yard.

Stormy ran after them. "Sarita, you must believe me when I tell you that I had nothing to do with the penning of Mother's will. I did not even know it existed. I just happened to find it here in the ranch house after she died. I thought it was important for you to know what you could expect in the future. Mother chose to leave everything to

Chet and me. I promise you that I had nothing to do with any of her choices. How was I supposed to know that it would turn out like this? Maybe you and Wyn can plan to buy a part of the Sabblonti Ranch in the future. I realize it would be decades down the line, but that might give you some hope."

Sarita turned around slowly. "Stormy, there's no truer test of character than when money enters the picture or walks into the room. Money cannot corrupt someone by itself. Managed and administered properly, it can bring life, healing, and hope. Mismanaged and administered improperly, it brings death, disease, and despair. I have unhitched myself from your drama wagon. I have unwrapped myself from the Sabblonti Ranch axles. I have never felt freer in my entire life. I am ready to soar with the eagles. Everyone has a value system, belief system, and choices to make. I choose life and hope for the next generation. I am no longer a joker in your game."

Wyn opened the passenger door of his brand-new pickup. After assisting Sarita inside, he graced her right cheek with a little peck of a kiss. Sporting a smile as big as all outdoors, he walked around to the driver's side. Turning the key inside the ignition and the steering wheel to his left, he looked at Sarita, "Shall we cut your losses and move on?"

"Yes, my love, we shall."

As he drove down the lane to the main road, Wyn happened to look in the rear-view mirror and catch a glimpse of Chet standing in the front yard, head hung low.

Running back inside the house, up three flights of stairs, Stormy fell on her knees in front of her mother's closet. Sitting cross legged on the floor, she slipped on Jantzi's boots. Jumping to her feet, she danced around the room until her head was spinning like a top. Winding down, she walked down the hall and entered her office. Gingerly approaching the roll top desk, she steadied herself on the edge of it. After opening the window, she sat down in the black office chair and rolled it backwards to just the right length.

Propping both feet on the desk, Stormy looked out the window and screamed at the top of her lungs,

"SABBLONTI RANCH, YOU'RE ALL MINE NOW!"

Leaning her head back, Stormy unleashed a wickedly intense laugh that echoed down the canyon for miles.

"Mommie's red boots will guide my every step of the way."

ABOUT THE AUTHOR

Sheila Eismann, author and publisher of twelve books, is third in her lineage of five female writers and poets. She endeavors to enhance the lives of others through education and encouragement via penning her inspirational and fictional books. Eismann, co-founder of Idaho Creative Authors' Network (ICAN), speaks at Womens' and Writers' Conferences.

Please peruse Sheila's website www.sheilaeismann.com and sign up to receive her blog posts and newsletters. Send her an email at sheila@sheilaeismann.com to let her know which character was your most favorite in this novel along with the best part of the story. Happy Reading!

Where to find Sheila Eismann online:

Email: sheila@sheilaeismann.com

Website: www.sheilaeismann.com

Facebook: www.facebook.com/sheila.eismann

Blog: www.sheilaeismann.com

LinkedIn: Sheila Eismann

Etsy Store: www.etsy.com/shop/BooksbySheilaEismann

OTHER BOOKS AVAILABLE FROM AUTHOR SHEILA EISMANN & DESERT SAGE PRESS WHICH CAN BE PURCHASED FROM: WWW.SHEILAEISMANN.COM OR WWW.AMAZON.COM.

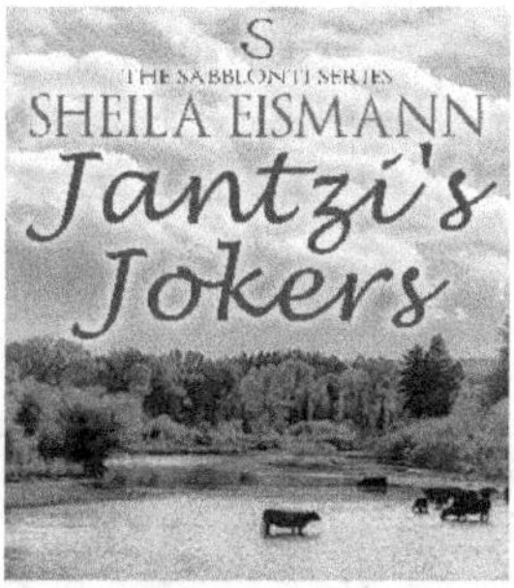

Western Fiction Book One of The Sabblonti Series, ***Jantzi's Jokers***, features Jantzi Belle, matriarch of the Sabblonti family, who has worked for decades to keep her cattle empire intact. Life takes a drastic turn when she receives a late-night visitor. The brief disappearance of her Last Will and Testament could complicate matters between her daughters, Stormy and Sarita. Stormy and her husband, Chet Castins, are struggling to work through the loss of their three children. Against all odds, drifter Wyn Moreland makes a bold move when he decides that Sarita is his beauty to rescue. The county veterinarian, Dr. Ben Shaw, is also vying for her affections. Will Wyn emerge as the winner? Just prior to the dawn of the New Year, revelations come forth regarding forgery, cattle rustling, and land exploitation. Will the Sabblonti Empire survive, and more importantly, who will control its reins?

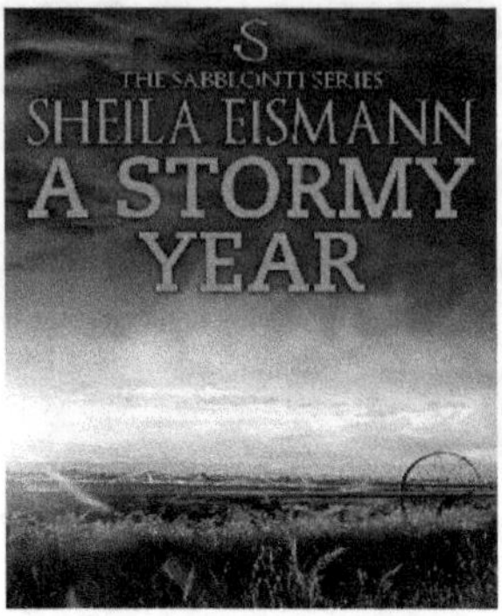

The Sabblonti Saga accelerates in Book Two of the Series, ***A Stormy Year***. Riding her high horse after inheriting the family fortune, Stormy Castins is determined to reinvent herself following her husband's accident. Blinded by jealousy, ambition, and naivety, she hires Less and Meg Alotto to oversee her vast high desert mountain domain. While Stormy is away, the cattle herd ends up in disarray.

Amidst the hot dry season, romance is blooming on several fronts despite a major showdown during a mid-summer celebration. The pesky Black Raven continues to wreak havoc at the most inopportune times.

Unable to overcome the vengeance which strikes by way of a mysterious range fire combined with the dire deeds of a cagey couple, the Sabblonti Ranch is in shambles just as Stormy starts to regain her senses. Humility is the prescription needed to open her eyes in order to realize what's truly important in life. The sparks from a belated holiday rendevous set Chet and Stormy on their path to recovery.

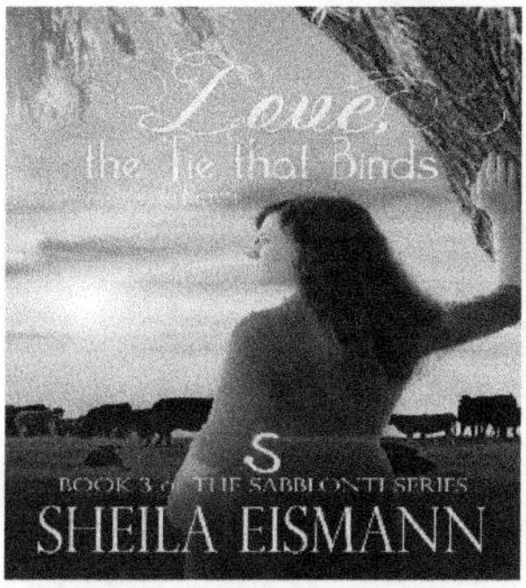

Desperation explodes when heiress Stormy Sabblonti Castins calculates her dwindling fortune in Book 3 of the Sabblonti Series, ***Love the Tie that Binds.*** Is she capable of learning the painful lessons of having to rely upon someone and something other than inherited wealth? As her husband, Chet, continues to heal from his near fatal accident, tormenting shadows of The Black Raven lurk in the background.

These high desert hills are alive with blessed babies, enchanting engagements, skillful scavengers, sophisticated scoundrels, rich revelations, timeless treasures, and western weddings.

The Main Sabblonti Ranch house abounds with an unexpected marriage, childrens' voices, and Sir Shelton sporting his silver bell.

In a captivating story of courage, trust, and faithfulness, will Stormy still be tied in knots or find lasting love by year's end?

Share the joys and sorrows of a mountain community in this swirling saga.

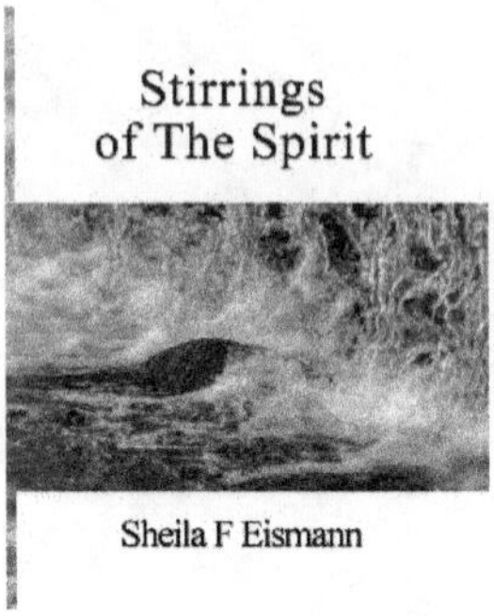

In this collection of true stories titled ***Stirrings of The Spirit***, author Sheila F. Eismann invites you to walk through several valleys en route to some mountain tops with her family as they learned to rely on God in the most harrowing of circumstances.

Have you ever wondered why you were the last one to hear of THE big social event of the year? Well, wonder no longer after reading this e-book titled ***Recognize Your Circles***! When volunteering for an organization years ago, author Sheila F. Eismann was introduced to the concept of "the circles of your life." Since the idea was so beneficial to her, she decided to share it with all of you.

Straight from the Horse's Trough is a humorous read to render assistance to the suburbanite or urbanite who desires to live a healthier lifestyle by growing his or her own food but is faced with the challenge of a small space in which to do so. This e-book is chock full of how-to steps and includes pictures to remove guesswork from the project.

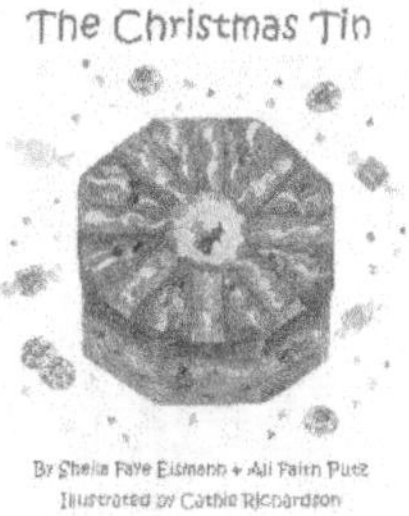

The Christmas Tin is a most delightful read for the young at heart anytime during the year. This endearing book is based upon a true story featuring the older of the two authors when she was a young girl and conveys the timeless message that "love truly is the greatest gift of all." Children will especially enjoy all of the colorful illustrations contained within this treasure!

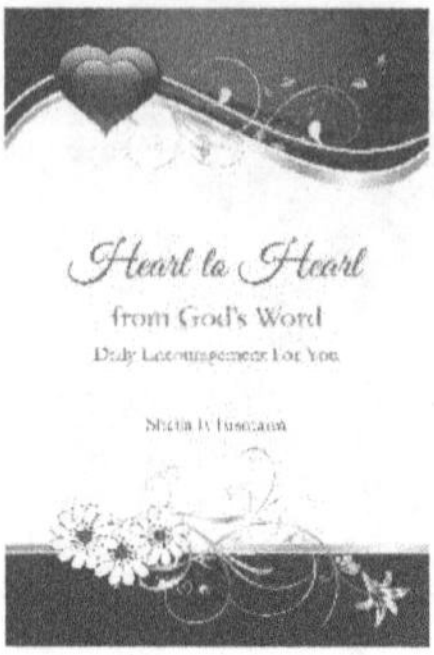

Everyone can use a little encouragement ~~ a dose of what is beneficial, ethical, and honorable. ***Heart to Heart From God's Word*** provides this for you. Penned with humor and wisdom, the daily tidbits are paired with Bible verses that convey life-changing principles which are designed for readers of all ages transcending cultures and continents. This devotional also doubles as a prayer journal.

A Woman of Substance is a practical, interactive, and entertaining 12-week Bible study penned to help equip you to fulfill your God-given destiny and impact the culture for Jesus Christ as the same time. It can be used as a stand alone study or devotional and works well in a group setting too. It is designed for women ages Junior High through adult.

Freedom is Your Destiny! Vietnam Veteran, Dan Eismann, using combat experiences to illustrate spiritual truths, invites you to take a journey with him as he presents a rock-solid strategy for not only fighting your spiritual battles, but winning the all-important war. In the midst thereof, the most vital aspect is realizing you can experience freedom and become all that God has destined you to be!

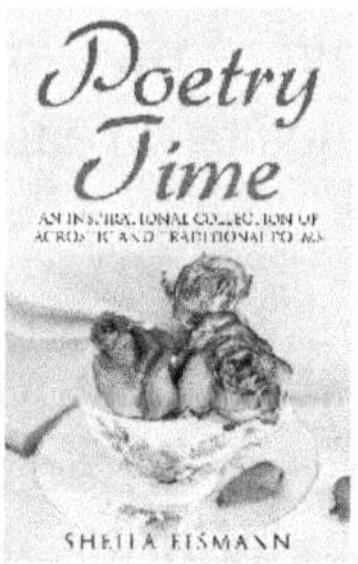

Settle into your special reading spot, grab a cup of tea or your favorite meal, and plan to enjoy **Poetry Time, Volume One,** which is a wonderful collection of traditional and acrostic poetry.

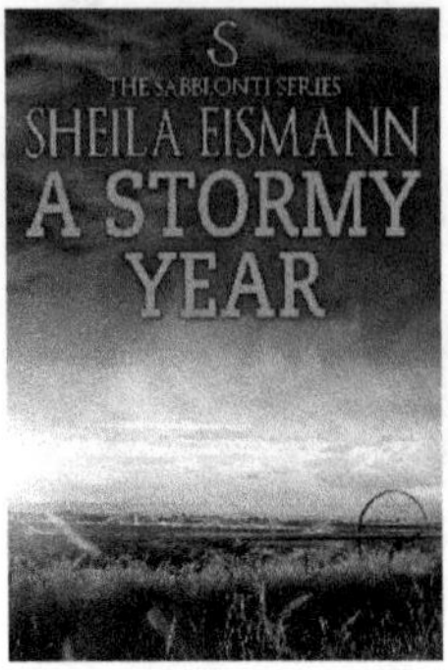

The Sabblonti Saga accelerates in Book Two of the Series, ***A Stormy Year***. Riding her high horse after inheriting the family fortune, Stormy Castins is determined to reinvent herself following her husband's accident. Blinded by jealousy, ambition, and naivety, she hires Less and Meg Alotto to oversee her vast high desert mountain domain. While Stormy is away, the cattle herd ends up in disarray.

Amidst the hot dry season, romance is blooming on several fronts despite a major showdown during a mid-summer celebration. The pesky Black Raven continues to wreak havoc at the most inopportune times.

Unable to overcome the vengeance which strikes by way of a mysterious range fire combined with the dire deeds of a cagey couple, the Sabblonti Ranch is in shambles just as Stormy starts to regain her senses. Humility is the prescription needed to open her eyes in order to realize what's truly important in life. The sparks from a belated holiday rendevous set Chet and Stormy on their path to recovery.

CAST OF CHARACTERS

A

Ace Sabblonti, Stormy's and Sarita's deceased father
Al Gibson, member, Ignee County Rodeo Board, in charge of rodeo grounds and maintenance
Anne-Marie – Dr. Diller's wife
Aprilily – young homeless mother with two children; clerk, Jodell's Jeweler's, Cinder Valley
Aunt Jonsey Kiddle – Stormy and Sarita Sabblonti's maternal aunt

B

Beau Cheval, Dr. Ben Shaw's Appaloosa gelding
Betty Lou Bradford, elected Clerk and Recorder, Shadow Butte County
Bolo & Browny – Tom Toppens' matched pair of draft horses
Brent Dawson, employee, Dawson's Dealership, Ridgemonte; Delbert Dawson's son
Blake Benson, Southwest District Brand Inspector

C

Caper Sadler – rodeo clown
Carl's Car Corral – auto dealership, Cinder Valley
Caroline Crutchens – Mintner Medical Center Nurse
Carson Tayer – Chairman, Ignee County Rodeo Board
Catherine Harrison – free-lance artist, greeting card designer, flower shop supplier, and Daisy's childhood friend
Chara Tankton, bank teller, Cattlemen's Central
Chet Castins, Stormy Sabblonti's husband
Cinder Valley Scoop – Cinder Valley newspaper
Clark, salesman, Carl's Car Corral, Cinder Valley
Cord Calhoun – Rodeo Announcer
Coye's Stringers – Country Western Band

D
Daisy Freemille – owner, Daisy's Floral Shop, Ridgemonte
Dawn Rowann – Mintner Medical Center Nurse
Dean Kendall – member, Ignee County Rodeo Board, in charge of rodeo announcer, clown, and musical group
Delbert Dawson, owner, Dawson's Dealership, Ridgemonte
Dr. Ben Shaw – Veterinarian, Ridgemonte
Dr. Den Merenspinn, medical doctor, owner of Evergreene Medical Clinic, Ridgemonte
Dr. Diller – Dentist, Ridgemonte
Dr. Linke – Mintner Medical Center Physician

E
Earl's Saddle Shop – Cinder Valley
Ed Tilmore – manager, Bank of Blunte
Evan Briarley, Chet Castins' Physical Therapist
Evergreene Medical Clinic, Ridgemonte

F
Fenn Bridgemore – ranch hand, Toppens' Ranch
Francie Fletcher, Priscilla Fletcher's mother

G
Gib's Gas – gas station in Ridgemonte
Gwen Hybrenth – retiree, Ignee County Rodeo Board

I

Ignee Grange Hall, Cinder Valley
It's Sew Time – fabric store, Ridgemonte

J

Jacobe Davone – employee, Shaw Veterinarian Clinic, Ridgemonte
James Harrison, Catherine Harrison's husband
Jantzi Belle Siddonz Sabblonti, Stormy's and Sarita's deceased mother
Jed Brennon – owner, Jed's Appliance Center, Ridgemonte
Jodell's Jewelers – jewelry store, Cinder Valley
Joyce Stone – Mintner Medical Center Charge Nurse

L

Lane – cowboy drifter, Ridgemonte
Leo Jeelon – Shadow Butte Deputy County Sheriff
Less Alotto – Sabblonti Ranch Foreman
Lilac Novis – Aunt Jonsey Kiddle's great-granddaughter
Lindi – bank teller, Bank of Blunte, Blademere
Logan Novis – Aunt Jonsey Kiddle's great-grandson
Lonnie Browne, Assistant Manager, Cattlemen's Central, Ridgemonte
Lorena, head clerk, DMV, Shadow Butte County Courthouse
Luger – ranch hand, Toppens Ranch
Luetta Londers – Parade Chairwoman, 75th Annual Ignee County Rodeo & Roundup, Cinder Valley

M

Macey Meadows – Mintner Medical Center Nurse
Marita Merrill – Nelson Merrill's wife, Shadow Butte County
Meg Alotto, bookkeeper, Sabblonti Ranch
Merna Toppens – Tom Toppens' wife, Toppens' Ranch
Mintner Medical Center – Ridgemonte hospital
Mitch Bentz – member, Ignee County Rodeo Board, in charge of rodeo stock

N

Neil Rolan, member, Ignee County Rodeo Board, in charge of rodeo grounds and maintenance
Nelson Weston Merrill – rancher, Shadow Butte County

P

Priscilla Fletcher – employee, Shadow Butte County Recorder's Office

R

Res Broomfield – cattle rancher, Shadow Butte County
Ridgemonte Rider – Ridgemonte newspaper
Rory, motel clerk, Silver Jack Motel, Cinder Valley
Ruston – younger cowhand who works for Sabblonti Ranch

S

Sagebrush Sorority Sisters – in charge of annual parade for Ignee County Rodeo & Roundup, Cinder Valley
Sage Hen Café – restaurant, Ridgemonte
Salina Bevvins – store clerk, The Shadowy Merc, Ridgemonte
Samuel Stixon – owner, broodmare farm, Ridgemonte
Sarita Sabblonti – Stormy Castins' sister; Wyn Mooreland's wife
Shade Stock Company – rodeo stock supplier
Shane – cowboy, ranch hand employed by Toppens' Ranch
Shasta – sales clerk, County Cate's Western Wear, Cinder Valley
Sheriff Jeff Jensen – Shadow Butte County Sheriff
Silver Jack Motel – Cinder Valley
Slim Shade – owner, Shade Stock Company
Spence Woodson – Assistant Ranch Foreman, Toppens' Ranch
Stanley Elson, Treasurer, Ignee County Rodeo Board
Stewart Sanders, manager, Cattlemen's Central, Ridgemonte
Stormy Sabblonti Castins, heiress to the Sabblonti cattle ranch and family fortune; Sarita Sabblonti Moreland's sister

T

The Mane Place, hair styling salon, Cinder Valley
The Second Time Around – thrift shop, Ridgemonte
The Shadowy Merc – grocery store and mercantile, Ridgemonte
The Tall Blues – country western singing group
Tom Toppens – owner, Toppens' Ranch
Tonette – Sarita Sabblonti's co-worker, Dr. Diller's office, Ridgemonte
Travis Fisen – employee, Lambent's Funeral Home
Trent Davies – Assistant Chairman, Ignee County Rodeo Board

U
Uncle Kent Kiddle – Stormy and Sarita Sabblonti's maternal uncle

V
Verntoola – thrift shop owner, The Second Time Around, Ridgemonte
Vonnetta, hairstylist, The Mane Place, Cinder Valley

W
Wilbur Drebner – cattle rancher, Shadow Butte County
Wyn Moreland -Toppens Ranch Foreman, Sarita Sabblonti's husband

Y
Yatey – older cowhand that works for Sabblonti Ranch

Z
Zib's Towing – Ridgemonte Tow Truck Business

Jantzi's Jokers